The Silencer

About the author

Paul Alkazraji worked as a freelance journalist in the UK from the mid-nineties. His articles were published in *Christianity Magazine, The Christian Herald, The Church Times, The Baptist Times* and other publications. His travel articles were also published in *The Independent*. His first book *Love Changes Everything,* a collection of seven testimonies, was published by Scripture Union in 2001. His second book *Heart of a Hooligan,* a biography of ex-football hooligan Dave Jeal, was published by Highland Books in 2000. His third book *Christ and the Kalashnikov,* a biography of missionaries Ian and Caralee Loring, was published by Zondervan in 2001. From 2004 to 2010 he was editor and publisher of *Ujëvarë* magazine in Albania. He is currently planning the follow up to 'The Silencer'.

The Silencer

In the Balkans, publishing can be deadly

By Paul Alkazraji

First published in 2012 by Highland Books Ltd,
2 High Pines, Knoll Road, Godalming, GU7 2EP.

This is a work of fiction. References to political events,
places or brands are intended to create an atmosphere while
any resemblance to real people, living or dead, is entirely
coincidental.

Cover design by Peter Wilson

ISBN-13: 978-1897913-89-5
ISBN-10 1-897913-89-3

Printed in the UK by CPI Cox and Wyman

Dedication

To my Albanian friends...
and the 'Sydney Cartons' of His service.

Albania

One summer in the late 2000s

Chapter 1

Jude Kilburn looked back over his shoulder. The narrow road behind was empty. He sat at the rear of a taxi van gripping the seat in front to steady himself as they bounced and climbed. A man-sized dummy like a Guy Fawkes doll flashed by hung by its neck from the roof of a half-built house. He knew it was a common practice thought to ward off evil in Albania, but it was as if on the edge of his own spirit he felt the passing of a shadow with it.

An old man with a hawkish nose and a dark blue cloth cap sat on his right with a package wrapped in newspaper on his lap. Jude nodded him an acknowledgement then unbuckled the front pocket of his bag and took out his mobile phone. It had a clip-over Union Jack cover that he'd bought on Portobello Road in London; it was kitsch but he liked it, more so for living abroad. He checked it for text messages. There was just one with a heart shape of asterisks and 'Alexandria' written in the centre. He ran his thumb softly over the glass. He lifted out his copy of *A Tale of Two Cities* by Charles Dickens, which he was re-reading, and then a packet of mints. He offered one to the old man.

"Where are you from?" the man said keenly.

"The North of England," said Jude.

"*Anglia. Shumë mirë.* Good," he replied, his eyes brightening. He unfolded the newspaper and took out half a cucumber and a piece of white cheese. He then offered Jude a twig of dried meat.

"*Faleminderit.* Thank you," said Jude.

"What are you doing here?" he said leaning closer.

"Work," replied Jude not wanting to open that discussion more, and looked again through the window. Vine groves in tidy stone-walled enclosures passed by, and a huge, rusty tank on the forecourt of a petrol station with the word '*Lavazh*' sprayed roughly on it in red. Jude smiled with a touch of lament that it did not signify his favourite brand of Italian coffee but a car wash.

He pushed his glasses up the ridge of his nose and his mind turned briefly to work that morning in Tirana. He remembered the director of Speedy-Print, Jetmira, with her tailored Italian clothes and marble-topped desk, evading giving an exact price for printing the book he was going to publish. Later, drinking coffee with Edona, a student of Political Science with long, fragrant hair, he'd asked her how she was progressing writing the story from the tapes the subject had recorded. She seemed concerned and hesitated to say something as he'd watched her. She'd then moved the subject along.

He shuffled to the left of the seat and peered through a small, glassless window frame towards a ridge of mountains stretching back to the east of

Tirana. The warm, early-August air ruffled his fringe and he pushed it back off his forehead. It was beyond that range that members of the British Special Operations Executive, Amery, Smiley and Maclean, had hidden in a forest from the Partisans sent to capture them one summer late in WWII. A smile rose in the corner of his mouth at recognising the place.

The old man slapped his hand down on Jude's thigh and laughed. Jude turned to him and smiled fully. He looked forward to the rear-view mirror and caught a glimpse of a dark-coloured car way back before it passed out of sight. The van's front window had a knot of cracks in it like a spider's web, and more cracks striding out to the edges like the creature's legs. A bolt was loose on the seat in front of him between a leg and the van floor. He wondered if it might shake free. Everything was rattling and creaking. Look at the state of this, he thought: the driver's probably not had the brakes serviced since the fall of the Berlin Wall reverberated down here. He was not standing on formality either, just a white vest and a golden chain around his neck. He was in his mid-fifties and Jude could see the white stubble on his cheeks, the glistening bald patch and the greying curls hanging below it. He was singing along to the radio: a gritty smooth rock ballad by, the announcer said, the singer *Aleksandër Gjoka*. Next came some Euro-pop track with a heavy beat that he seemed to like more and turned the volume up. They were climbing steeply now and Jude lurched sharply as they cornered a hairpin bend. Across a ravine he watched the massive rock ledges fall away like the ends of a giant's collapsed bookshelves.

Behind the driver a youth was jerking his mobile phone as he played with it. His legs were stretched out on the seat showing his trainers in the aisle: dirty white and split. A row back on the right a woman with strong, careworn features held her daughter as she lay sleeping on her lap. The girl had white ribbons in her hair and shiny, black sandals with buckles. She began to stir.

"*O, shoferi.* Could you turn the music down a little?" Jude called to the driver.

"*Pa problem!*" he said obligingly. The girl sat up.

"*Mami,* I'm sick," she said. The driver tossed back some blue plastic bags and the girl snatched one and vomited in it. She lay back down on her mother's lap. The welcome scent of pine came in through the window from trees by the roadside that looked battered and broken. The youth's phone suddenly exploded in a high-intensity Techno ring tone and he shouted into it: "*Po, po.* I'm on the *Krrabë* road. Well what can I do about it? Okay. Okay."

"*Budalla.* Stupid…" the mother shouted at him. "Can't you see my daughter is sick! Now you wake her up again?"

"Keep it down boy, will you?" shouted the driver turning around.

"Yes," said the old man, "she needs to rest! When my niece was sick…" The 'paaarrrp' of an oncoming car horn jolted the driver's head back towards the road and he swung the van to the right on a corner.

Away to the west the view opened out before him. The ridgelines of mountains, light brown and then deep brown into shadow, rose beyond each other for over fifty kilometres fading into the blue haze. The sun was falling lower over them tingeing the dust with an orange-pink. Jude leant forwards to see and felt pleasure well up. There was an eruption of birdsong from beneath the old man's jacket. He reached inside it methodically and Jude watched half-expecting him to draw out a canary in a protective caress. He lifted a mobile phone to his ear.

"*Alo*. I'm on the *Krrabë* road! What? Wait, I said. I'm coming!" he shouted. All eyes turned to glower at him. He sniffed and seemed oblivious to it.

Jude turned around to drink in the view through the rear window. A dark blue '90s Mercedes with a broken headlight was drawing up behind them. The van driver now began to accelerate as the road levelled out along the top of the ridge. He tapped out a cigarette from a pack on the dashboard and slipped it into the corner of his mouth, glanced in his side mirror, and squared himself at the wheel. The Mercedes pulled out to the left and began to draw alongside. A sign with white arrows on black indicating a sharp turn left was coming closer. An old, Chinese truck came rasping around the bend with its horn on. Jude tightened his grip a little on the seat in front. The Mercedes braked and swung back sharply in behind them. He could see a faint grin of pleasure on the van driver's face in the rear-view mirror as he touched the lighter to his cigarette. He manoeuvred the gears upwards.

A line of pylons marched up the mountain's flank and across the road ahead of them. In seconds, the wires flew over their heads. A white stony riverbed snaked away on the valley floor, perhaps five kilometres away, the water catching the sun and flashing its message. The driver's mobile phone rang with the *Nokia* tone and with one hand on the wheel he put it to his ear.

"*E, mo!*" he shouted. "What's up?" As they took the bend the van tires began to sing on the road surface. He dropped the phone and the cigarette into his lap and gripped the wheel. Jude ran his hand through his hair and felt his heart beat quicken. The driver began beating the burning tobacco off his lap.

"*O, zoti Schumacher*? Take it easy there!" Jude called to him. The youth turned around and grinned. The Mercedes pulled out to the left for another attempt to pass and began to pull up level. Jude looked down at the two men sitting in the front. Both wore clean, blue shirts and sunglasses. The passenger looked up at Jude, and then seemed to nod to his driver. The road swung to the left over a narrow bridge and the Mercedes was forced back again in behind the van, beating on its horn.

Whitewashed, stone walls, holding back the mountain dirt behind them, streamed past stencilled with logos and sprayed with graffiti: 'Albanian Exhausts', 'Geri', 'LSI'… Then came a café plastered with *Nescafe* posters, a man selling ice cream from a scratched refrigerator, and an old man bobbing side-saddle on a mule laden with white sacks, flicking its rump with a stick. The old man in the cloth cap called something to the driver who didn't respond. Jude could feel touches of cold sweat on his palms. He took his glasses off and cleaned the condensation with his T-shirt.

"Lord, keep us on the road!" he prayed under his breath. He glanced backwards. The Mercedes was right up to the van's bumper. It swung back to the left and pulled parallel, the driver hammering his horn. Then it touched the side with a metallic grate.

"*Zot i madh!* God!" shouted the driver, jerking his head to the left and back to the road ahead. The youth pressed his face to the glass angrily waving the car to pass. The road forced the Mercedes back.

Old concrete telegraph poles flashed past, tilted, fallen and then gaps, some with scraps of wire hanging down. Below them were short white posts topped with a red tip that looked to Jude like cigarette sweets. A policeman standing in a dirt lay-by vainly lifted his traffic lollipop and then stood back, hands on his hips and cap pushed back. Jude leant forward to see if he could catch the driver's eye in the rear-view mirror. The speedometer was past 120 km/h.

"O, *shoferi*. Slow down... you have five lives as well as your own in your hands!" he called out.

"Yes. The foreigner is right," the youth chipped in. A petrol station painted like a racing flag of yellow and green squares flew past, and the driver braked into the bend. The road then twisted from left to right down through pine trees. The barrier here was made of low, white, concrete arches that looked fitting for the perimeter of a garden feature, not to restrain a vehicle careening off course. It had telling gaps in it: a car lay undercarriage up a little way down the mountainside. The road straightened out and they passed a yellow mosque with a minaret topped with a metal cone, and huts built from wood scraps where villagers were selling olive oil in old *Sprite* bottles and holding out bowls of blackberries.

The Mercedes made its move. It swung out to the left and accelerated then swung in sharply clipping the van's front. The driver pulled the steering wheel sharply to the left to correct the push of the collision. He over-compensated and the rear of the van began to screech around. Jude was thrown against the old man. The youth tumbled into the aisle. The mother screamed. The van struck something hard and seemed to lift up into the air. It then came to a jolting halt and Jude bit his tongue as his head was thrown forwards. Seconds like minutes of silence followed.

The mother and daughter began to sob. The old man was holding the side of his head. The youth crawled up from the floor and began a torrent of cursing then pulled the handle and slid open the side door. Jude could taste blood in his mouth and his heart was pounding. Slowly, he moved through the seats and jumped down stiffly onto the road. He could smell the hot tarmac and the dust. The youth sat down on the road's edge and put his head in his hands. Jude helped the mother and her daughter down. They seemed shaken but fine, tears in their eyes. The old man followed holding his head; blood was running through his rough, withered fingers.

"I called to get out at the top, but he didn't stop," he said. Jude opened the driver's side door. He lay over the wheel and sat up slowly when Jude touched his arm. His face was greyish yellow and his hands were shaking. He looked blankly at Jude as he helped him down and led him to a rock to sit. He fumbled for his matches and dropped them.

"You are crazy, *i çmendur!*" the youth shouted at him. "My uncle is in the police... he's going to burn your licence! Do you understand me?" The other passengers then began rounding on him. Jude took some bottles of water from the front of the van and brought one to the old man with a tissue. He gave the other to the driver and put his hand on his shoulder pressing it gently. The man was still shaking. He did not need a lecture, Jude thought. He would be taking it easier on the roads for some time.

Jude walked back to the van. It was resting, gashed, against a low stone wall. Behind it the mountainside sloped steeply downwards into the valley. A white metal cross stood up against the sky near by. He breathed deeply several times. Over a thousand feet below by the city of Elbasan a great industrial complex lay flat on the blackened ground, wheezing out brown smoke. By the edge of the wall he noticed a white geranium had bloomed. He picked it, and opening his wallet placed it carefully inside a folded photograph of his mother. A grey metal nail fell out and he picked it up and put it back.

The Mercedes had not stopped. Why? Surely they had heard and seen what happened, Jude thought. Were they just reckless drivers? There were plenty of those on the roads here. Had they cut the van up out of vindictiveness for their driver? He whispered a prayer of thanks for their preservation. Then another thought occurred. Could it have been premeditated… against him?

Chapter 2

A finger of sunlight fell across Alex Kilburn's eyes and woke her. She looked around. Squares of light lay on the bed sheet as it streamed in through gaps in the curtains, but Jude's head was inclined in shadow. She beamed at him and felt a flutter of joy in her stomach for the bright morning. She kissed him on the back of his head and he rolled over and muttered unintelligibly, still immersed in sleep. She smoothed back his caramel coloured hair and smiled again at those eyes, almost almond shaped, that she had looked at so frequently. His sideburns had a few early flecks of grey she noted. She had missed her husband during his overnight stay in Tirana. A quick glance at the face of his mobile phone told her it was 7.05am. She slipped her legs out of bed, pulled over a light dressing gown, and stepped quietly into the living room of their apartment.

She picked up her Bible and turned to the reading-plan. It was the second chapter of Ruth today and she read again how Boaz allowed the poor to gather free grain in his fields, and how Ruth had laboured there under protection. She felt its strengthening influence immediately. She dressed and opened the door to their small balcony stepping outside. From the fourth floor she could see over the dirt ground below. A man wobbled across it on his bicycle over-loaded behind the saddle with a crate of full plastic milk bottles. The honking of horns from the taxi van drivers had begun. She could smell fresh bread. At the foot of an identical apartment block on the opposite side of May 5TH Street was a café with a blue *Don* espresso sign, where three tables would shortly be placed on the pavement. There was a general store too with crates of peaches and green peppers already set out, and Bestar's Bakery by it. Their street led down to a main road into the centre of the town of *Shënomadh*. She unfolded a small wooden table and put a plastic chair either side of it. She trod quietly back through the living room into the tiny attached kitchen and began to prepare breakfast.

She heard Jude's slippers on the carpet behind her shortly.

"You've not opened the 'English Breakfast in a Tin', have you Alex?" he said, sniffing as he came closer. She felt him wrap his arms around her waist. She leant her head back; it fitted under his chin.

"No, I found some bacon… and *Lavazza*… at the Greek supermarket," she said. "Just go sit outside you!" Ten minutes later, she brought out the cooked rashers and the cafetiere on a tray and placed them on the table next to the bread rolls and saucer of fig jam. Jude was wearing a baggy white shirt, unfas-tened at the neck and cuffs. It gave him the aura of a romantic literary figure, she thought, like those he'd studied, which was offset by his heavy, black framed glasses. They made him look more like a comedian her dad had liked, Eric Morecambe. Jude pushed his glasses up the ridge of his nose with his finger and grinned.

"Mr Rochester, sir. Is your breakfast to your liking?" she said, imitating the heroine of Charlotte Brontë's novel *Jane Eyre*, which she knew he liked.

"It is so my Jane... come hither. You are not vexed of spirit this morning?" he said frowning.

"No, sir, it is not proper... for I am but yet governess at Thornfield Hall." Jude began to laugh. He had a full, heartfelt laugh that sometimes built to such a pitch it was infectious and set others laughing with him. He sipped his cup of coffee and spilt it down his shirt. Alex smirked.

"Ooh," he said. "That stung!"

"From yesterday? When the taxi van spun?" she said. She watched him nod, and put a finger to the edge of his tongue, feeling a little guilty now. Then concern came over her. She'd sensed last night that he'd had something unresolved in his mind. It's connected with this book; there are dangers with it, she thought. She knew the story, and had a good grasp of the region's recent history, an interest that had deepened during her European Studies degree in London.

"When is Mehmed coming here?" she asked, thinking back momentarily to TV news footage she had seen during the Kosovo conflict.

"In a day or so... It wasn't connected to him! Alexandria Kilburn you've been watching too many episodes of that *Hercule Poirot* DVD I gave you," said Jude in an affected tone of chiding.

"So, what else happened in Tirana?" she asked, cutting through a bread roll and dabbing on a little butter with a knife.

"Well, there was a man making money off a public phone booth… by letting people use *his* card only, and charging a good rate for the units they used," he said. "He wouldn't let me use mine!"

"Some people don't have a lot of options Jude," she said softly, a little disappointed with his attitude. "Can I show you something?" Jude nodded as he chewed on a bacon roll. She stepped back inside the living room and unfolded a cardboard box that she'd left next to the fold-down sofa bed. She took out a basket she'd made from pine cones sprayed with silver paint and fastened together with wire and tacks. She carried it carefully outside and set it down on the balcony floor.

"Hey," said Jude, flicking some breadcrumbs off his shirtfront. "That's not bad at all!" She smiled.

"Pine cones are free and plentiful… we can gather more sacks of them in the mountains. The paint and wire are not expensive," she said eagerly. She wanted to organise some craft-making activities with her women's group. Then they could sell the best items to market traders with the money going to the women to help them supplement their family incomes. She knew many of them needed it badly.

"Sure Alex, we can do it," Jude smiled.

"I'm going to show it around a few places today," she said, looking the basket over and glancing at him. "Do you need anything whilst I'm in the centre?"

"If you pass the County Police Directorate… that officer Llazo has had my passport for over two weeks with the residence permit application.

I've been twice and he says he hasn't finished. Is he waiting for a tip?"

"I'll go," she said. She reached over the breakfast table and held his hand.

* * *

Jude walked cautiously with an occasional skip to the Planet Internet café two blocks from his apartment that evening. It was dark outside and he kept the beam of his torch ahead on the pavement watching for open manholes. The café's basement entrance was badly lit. Inside too the lighting was low and it took his eyes several seconds to adjust. That rotating globe on the outside wall is draining all the electricity, he thought. Heads turned to look at him as he entered: a group of boys gathered around one cubicle, and a young woman whose face was visible partially by the light of her computer screen arched an eyebrow defined boldly with pencil.

He sat in a corner for privacy, pulled the chair into the cubicle, and slipped the earphones over his head. He typed in his password, *Alexandria777*, and waited to see which of his contacts was on-line for a link up via webcam. Jack was there and he smiled in anticipation. He pressed the green dial button. It rang twice and a black window sprang up in the centre of his screen. Seconds later, the head of his old friend, peroxide hair cut in a 'flat top' and dark stubble, formed and peered at him grinning back.

"Jude Kilburn… the literary missionary," he said laughing. "You look dark and horribly pixelated!"

"I actually look like this now, Jack. It's something in the local water," said Jude, enjoying the banter already. "Has the sun shone yet this summer through the carpet of cloud that hovers… stubbornly… over your postal-zone of Leeds?"

"There was a morning in May when that happened," said Jack.

"Have you done any hiking then recently?" said Jude.

"I walked from Bolton Abbey to Simon's Seat just last weekend, in fact."

"You used to do that on half a *Curly Wurly*!"

"We can't all be Byronic adventurers like you Jude. Have you been wrestling with any brigands in the mountains there?"

"No, but you've got to watch the drivers! Funny you should mention the poetic lord. He used to take his holidays down here, you know?"

"What… picking up last-minute bargains with EasyFrigate?" There was an outburst of raucous laughter from the group of boys behind. Jude turned around to look. They were downloading ring-tones and had discovered a cockerel's crow and a donkey's bray, which they were replaying again to much hilarity. He turned back to the screen shaking his head and smiling.

"So how's your book coming along? What's it about again?" said Jack putting his eye up close to the web-cam in playful scrutiny.

"Well, it's in the works," said Jude. "It's the story of an Albanian guy who fought against the Serbs in Kosovo with the UÇK… the Kosovo Liberation Army… a Muslim… by culture not observance. Before then, in the Nineties, he was involved with some criminal gangs, trafficking, smuggling… but he's served his time for that."

"Sounds like the sort of guy you'd keep your niece well away from!"

"He was a real Slav-hater, Jack, for the siege of Sarajevo up in Bosnia, for the massacre at Srebrenica... Then he came upon scenes in Kosovo with his own eyes, terror done in the name of the cross as it was sprayed on walls and doors to intimidate. In his mind, these people represented Christ."

"So what happened to him?" said Jack looking a little more serious.

"Well, back home in Albania, he hears a foreign missionary and his team has been doing door to door visits in a village in the next valley. He's enraged! He sets out with his rifle and a hunting knife... For his people's honour... he's going to do something really nasty to them." Jude shuffled in his chair and looked around the dark café behind him. He saw the young woman turn her head away quickly. He turned back. "When he comes face to face with them, though, he can't do it. He is restrained by this overwhelming sensation of divine love... like Paul on the road to Damascus, without the light and sound show, but he feels it! This is a man who has killed and who is not afraid to kill. Instead of hate, he feels humanity for them." Jude watched Jack raise his eyebrows and nod as he listened intently. "He takes a copy of the Scriptures they give him, and turns around for his village... bewildered and in emotional turmoil. There, he buries it in a hole in the garden. A month later, he digs it up and begins to read it." Jude leant in closer and lowered his voice. "He emerges a year later in a church in Puka... in the north here. He tells them that when he was in the refugee camps he has met believers serving his people... medically and psychologically. When he needed food and a temporary wooden shelter, it was these believers who provided him with it… He's changed. He's talking about the need for forgiveness. He knows he needs it from others."

"So… has he gone on with the Lord?"

"He's been in that fellowship for the last seven years, growing in faith… a fine example to all. Now he's ready to tell his story publicly. His pastor and other Christian leaders who've known him here are positive about it…"

"Is everyone happy he's telling his story Jude?" He felt a hand on his shoulder. He turned around startled. The young woman from the nearby cubicle was standing behind him.

"I heard you speaking English," she said. "When you've finished, will you help me with something in my on-line visa application?"

"Oh, erm. Sure. Just give me ten minutes," said Jude a little ruffled.

"Keep your skin on!" said Jack.

"We are not aiming to spill the beans on all his past associates," he said. "It's a story about Jesus' transforming work in the life of a man. Payback is big here Jack… honour rests on it. Mehmed has torn up his mental checklist of targets for vengeance. He's showing there is another way… and he's an Albanian showing it, not a foreigner like me telling them about it."

"It sounds quite something. I'll tell the home-group and we'll pray."

"Mehmed could be a leading light. In fact, I can introduce him to your niece if you like?"

"You're a real pal," said Jack grinning.

He talked with Jack for ten more minutes until a power cut sent the screen tumbling into a blank of crackling static. He felt the loss of connection. A generator whirred into action and the monitors shone a half-light again on those hunched over them. He thought about redialling Jack but decided to save it for another time. He walked over to help the young woman briefly with her visa application.

"It's not the Promised Land, you know?" said Jude.

"It's better than here!" she said.

"Things can be better wherever you are."

Chapter 3

The pavement of May 5ᵀᴴ Street glared in the afternoon sun as Jude walked briskly along it towards the church building. He passed a group of men squatting around a game with pebbles that had been scratched onto the flagstones in a grid. One man flicked a little dust at another and protested noisily. Jude smiled to himself about it, and about Alex: she had walked into the office of the police chief and told him that one of his men had had her husband's passport for two weeks. "It was hardly a fitting service for a country aspiring to EU membership," she'd said. He'd picked up his phone and she'd walked out with it in her pocket.

As he turned a corner the meeting place his fellowship rented came into view. It was an oblong, two-storey building with crumbling, dirty-red roof tiles and mauve plasterwork on the outside walls that had fallen off in chunks. Across it the faded slogan 'Long Live the Albanian Communist Party' was flaking off. It now had a wooden plaque on the door reading '*Shënomadh* Church': an epitaph for the ideology that had claimed Albania as 'the world's first atheist state', thought Jude. Before it on a patch of dusty ground was an old gun bunker like the helmet of some massive stone soldier sunk deep below it into the earth. It was sprayed with graffiti and used by many as a public convenience. He covered his nose with his forearm as he passed it.

He was ten minutes early for his English class, but two of his students were already waiting on the steps. Kristo was a clever young English teacher in a local school who kept his black attaché case spotless, and often flicked it under his arm in closure of situations. He greeted Jude with a cordial nod. Mira was holding new books she'd bought for her only child Lule, keen to pass on all she learnt to her, and was one of the few students in Jude's group from the church. She smiled.

He unlocked the door to one of the downstairs rooms and arranged twelve chairs in a semi-circle. He set up a white-board and placed his photocopies neatly beside him. He chatted a little with Mira as more students arrived and then passed out the first task.

"Good afternoon everyone," he began. "Let's begin with this British life and culture quiz. The answers are multiple choice… and later you can work in pairs to create an Albanian version." Three more students arrived late including Liridon, whom he felt in equal measure surprised and pleased to see continuing to come. A teenager with buckteeth and bulging eyes, he smelt of animals and rough sleeping. He spent much of his time caring for a distant male relative's goats in the nearby mountains. According to Mira, this relative, Shpat, owned him, which Jude was struggling to understand. He gestured to

Liridon to sit on a chair near to him and he shuffled quickly into place nodding gratefully. Jude noticed Kristo's nose screw up as he inched away discretely.

"So," said Jude shortly. "Let's check your answers! What can we find in London's Trafalgar Square? Big Ben... Buckingham Palace or Nelson's Column?"

"Nelson's Column," said Mira softly and everyone agreed.

"Is that for Nelson Mandela?" someone asked.

"No," said Kristo a little pompously. "Lord Nelson of the Admiralty!"

"Who lives at 10 Downing Street?" said Jude.

Liridon put his hand up, "Sherlock Holmes?"

"Well, no Liridon, good try," said Jude trying not to discourage him. "It's the home of the British Prime Minister and not, therefore, option C, Prince Charles."

"Why doesn't the Prince tell his mother to get off the throne?" said Bledi, a heavy-set taxi driver. "What kind of a man is he? *Qullac.*" Jude observed Fredi, a lithe, young waiter with perfectly-creased, black trousers, struggling to stifle his giggling at this.

"Why do English people drink so much tea, Jude?" said Fredi a few seconds later. "We drink tea when we are sick... are they sick more than Albanians?"

"I don't think so," said Jude. "It was brought from our former colonies. Now... when you are driving in Britain, what must you carry? A driving licence... an identity card... or neither."

"A little something for the policeman's wallet!" said Fredi grinning and looking at Bledi, who was nodding vigorously.

Jude left the students to form their own questions about Albania and checked the time on his mobile phone. He wanted to keep to the timing of his activities and get away promptly. He was meeting Mehmed Krasnichi at the Blue Café in the town centre at 5pm. He passed around an activity about English proverbs, and as he sat back down he noticed that Kristo was eyeing him for something.

"Mr Kilburn," he said. "Would you mind explaining to us the difference between countable and uncountable nouns?" Jude sighed inside. He guessed that Kristo, knowing the answer, was trying to elevate himself over the teacher before the other students.

"I'll do that," he said. "But as we are studying proverbs, would you mind to tell us what you understand 'A stitch in time saves nine' to mean?" He figured he probably wouldn't know it, and that it would stitch his attitude for a while.

"Well…" Kristo began, and after stumbling Jude jumped in to help him. As the students worked quietly, Jude took out nine copies of an Easy Reader version of Charles Dickens' *A Tale of Two Cities* and handed them around.

"Try to get into the book before next week, please. Then we can talk about it together," said Jude. He watched Bledi receive his with an ambivalent face, but Liridon flicked quickly to chapter one and began running his finger steadily under the words.

Jude gave out a speaking activity with boards and counters for use in groups.

"Throw the dice… and wherever your counter lands, talk about that subject for thirty seconds," he said. There were laughs of excitement. A dice flew at Liridon. Jude walked around forming groups and listening to the students. Mira's counter landed upon the topic, 'Something you'd like to find'.

"It is not something, but someone," she began. "The only son of my neighbours is missing. They wait and hope, but he has not come. It is very bad for them…" The other students turned to listen as she exceeded the game's time limit and spoke on with touching clarity. "… I would like to find him for them."

"Go to visit them Jude," said Fredi. "They'd like that!" Jude glanced at Mira. She nodded.

"I'll do that," said Jude.

"Jude is a good man," said Fredi, leading most of the others in approval. "You can do your religious bit now if you like!"

"Thank you for that… Fredi," smiled Jude. "I have a Bible verse for you all to take away and read." He handed out slips of paper with *Luke 15*, verses 1-7, typed in English.

> *"When he finds the lost sheep, he is so happy, he puts it on his shoulders and he carries it back home…"*

…he said, and he dismissed them. Kristo was waiting outside the door of the building for Jude.

"You should not let Liridon attend these classes. His smell is off-putting to the other students," he said flicking his attaché case under his arm. "This *çobani*… This goat boy… is also a thief."

* * *

The lighting was low inside the Blue Café: tubes of white glass lit with blue bulbs mounted on the clean stone walls, and spotlights concealed behind panelling along the front of the bar. Behind it, rows of bottles filled glass shelves that had been set before a wall-length mirror. A waiter polishing glasses nodded as Jude passed him, glancing around. The tables were of clean-lined, dark wood and had a single flower placed in a glass of blue liquid on them. Groups of men were seated talking in hushed tones. He noticed two men sitting on a low sofa by the window, and as he stepped tentatively towards them they rose looking at him.

"Mehmed?" said Jude offering his hand.

"Jude," said Mehmed. "I thought it must be you."

"It's very nice to meet you… after all the phone calls," said Jude glancing at his companion.

"This is Marko. He is from our church in Puka. He is my driver… and body-guard for this trip, aren't you?" said Mehmed with a look that made Marko smile. Jude's first impression of Mehmed in the flesh was that he did not look like a man who needed one. He was several inches taller than Jude and wearing a clean, white shirt over his broad frame. It had stretched tightly over his muscular arm as he bent it to shake his hand. Marko was even taller than Mehmed, but wiry and with hair lighter than Jude's. He wore a crumpled, black T-shirt and blonde stubble. Jude noticed that his eyes were a little red. Marko asked to be excused briefly.

"He looks more like an Englishman than an Albanian, doesn't he?" said Mehmed as they sat down. "He's from *Mirditë*. His family is 'in blood'." He paused to check Jude understood and Jude nodded. "They are pushing him to act... he has come to our fellowship for a month now, but he is not strong," said Mehmed looking concerned. A waiter walked over and it was Fredi.

"I thought you worked at the Elita Café?" said Jude.

"Thursdays to Sundays. They are short-staffed here. Make grass while the sun shines... that's an English proverb," he said grinning and glancing at Mehmed.

"A macchiato for me Fredi... not tea. Make *hay!*" said Jude punching him on the arm in fun.

"Two cappuccinos. Plenty of cream," said Mehmed. Jude made small talk with Mehmed about his journey to *Shënomadh* and took a closer look at him. His dark hair was tied neatly behind his head in a ponytail. He was clean-shaven with thick lips that had a small scar above the top one, and his eyes held Jude with a natural bearing of authority. He looked like he could still snatch a pistol tucked in another man's trousers, and put it to his nose before he could raise a hand to protect himself.

Fredi returned quickly with three blue glasses, ice and a bottle of still mineral water. He then brought over the coffees. The cups were set off-centre in the saucers by design, and had blue serviettes on which two small biscuits dusted in icing sugar had been placed. As Marko returned he caught a coffee spoon with his leg as he passed, and flipped it over the edge of the table. Mehmed's hand was down and caught it before it touched the floor. He placed it discretely back on the edge of Marko's saucer. He put his hand on Marko's shoulder and squeezed the muscles at the base of his neck.

"Are you strong today?" said Mehmed.

"*Po, po,*" Marko grinned and sat forward eagerly. He wanted to be, thought Jude. On the right side of Marko's T-shirt Jude noticed '*Phil. 4:13*' had been printed in small golden letters. The words ran through his mind:

I can do all things in Christ who strengthens me.

Mehmed too now sat forward resting his elbows on his knees. His eyes seemed to scan around the café quickly as if he was assessing all exit points.

"It is better if we keep our voices low as we discuss these things… as a precaution," said Mehmed. "How is the book coming along?"

"Well, Edona has been writing the account from the tapes that you recorded for us," said Jude and sipped at his glass of cool water. "There is a man, Spiro… a teacher in our church, who is going to help me check and edit her work. And then, I'm hopeful that we can print it by the end of the month." Mehmed smiled and sat back in the sofa looking pleased at Marko. He leant forward again and stirred the sugar slowly in his coffee.

Jude asked Mehmed questions about his life for his own clarification: about his activities in the Nineties, his role inside the UÇK, the day God's power arrested him, and his faith journey since. Marko leant in intently, and Jude felt his respect grow for Mehmed. He sensed no residual pride in him for his criminal accomplishments, no bragging about what he had been or done. If anything there was discomfort, a shame even, as he recounted incidents, some horrific, that he'd seen. Jude topped up his glass with mineral water and took several gulps. They moved from the years of the life he'd had to those of the new man, and Jude perceived an awakened conscience and gentleness in him. He saw above those qualities love. He has taken this Marko under his wing, he thought. It is those who have been forgiven the most that so often love the most. He has let Christ in to the deepest places, and come from a long way back right up to the front ranks.

"Mehmed… there are some things I want to say to you," said Jude feeling that they had covered the necessary ground. "There may be reactions to your story… Your past associates… criminal, military… could fear what you'll reveal about them. Others might identify you from painful memories. Some will see you as… a religious defector. They may feel threatened by you… hate you. In their eyes you will deserve punishment. They will not want you to lead others to do the same. They may wish to silence your witness… Are you sure you want to go on with this?" "You mean reactions from people like me?" he smiled.

"As you were… maybe," said Jude. He watched him look at his hands and turn things over in deep places. A fighting spirit seemed to rise up in him.

"I gave my brother here his T-shirt," he said, bringing his hand down on Marko's thigh. "It is the right thing to do." Jude took a sip of his coffee, which he had hardly touched. It had now turned cold. "I have a cousin who lives with us," said Mehmed, lines forming briefly on his brow. "Her name is Selime.

She has been talking to her women friends about this. They have been talking to their husbands... they too have been talking. I had a phone call..." He did not elaborate. Jude searched his face and began to fill in the gaps.

* * *

Jude did not feel like cooking that evening. "Are you hungry Alex?" he called over his shoulder from the kitchen. She was watching *Hercule Poirot* intently in the living room.

"I'm okay... I ate a slice of pizza on my way home," she said. "Jude... will you take a look at the hot water pipe in the bathroom. It's coming undone!" He opened the fridge door and took out a block of white cheese from the F.R. of Macedonia and a jar of pickled green chilli peppers. He quickly put the ingredients into a bread roll and took a huge bite. It seemed to ease him. A car alarm flared up in the street below, and he made his way through the living room and onto the balcony. Alex followed and rested her arm on his shoulder as they peered down. The tail lights of a car parked on the road by Bestar's Bakery were flashing. It did not seem that anyone was concerned about it. After five minutes, he followed Alex back inside and returned to the kitchen. His mobile phone, left by the cooker, had one missed call from Edona. It also had a text-message from her: 'Jude, can we meet? Something has happened.'

Chapter 4

The window glass was cold as Jude touched his nose to its surface. He looked north over the centre of Tirana and drank in the thrill of the panorama. From a restaurant in the Sky Tower he could see down over the lush, green square of land criss-crossed with paths that was Rinia Park. He had arranged to meet Edona there at 3pm. To his left the apartment blocks clustered densely away to the horizon in colours of mustard, olive and denim blue. Ahead he could make out the rouge and yellow government ministry buildings on the edge of Skanderbeu Square, and the white needle of the Et'hem Bey Mosque. His eyes turned to the east past the black glass panelled Twin Towers and concrete Pyramid to the traffic flowing up the Gjergj Fishta Boulevard, where the harsh mid-day sunlight was glinting off car roofs and windscreens. Beyond that, through a haze of heat and light smog, Mount Dajti rose up to the blue, utterly cloudless sky.

He ambled back to his chair and picked up a menu from the white linen tablecloth. He checked the time on his mobile phone: 1.10pm, August 5th.

Shpetim Gurbardhi was not yet annoyingly late, but he was approaching it. On the taxi van from *Shënomadh* that morning his friend had called him; realising they would both be in the capital that day they had arranged an impromptu lunch. A couple of minutes later, Jude watched Shpetim saunter in through the restaurant entrance checking his mobile phone. He caught Jude's eye and then spun around to take a call. The light grey jacket of his suit was slung over his shoulder. He was wearing a pair of black trainers with three white stripes like a sergeant on them, and they made Jude wonder just what his rank was in SHISH, the state intelligence agency of Albania.

Minutes later, he smiled apologetically. "Jude," he began, pulling up a chair, "*Ç' kemi? Mirë?* Are you well? Alex? Your family in England?" Jude returned all the polite greetings beloved of Albanians before Shpetim's phone rang again: its ring tone was Lionel Richie singing, *'Hello… is it me you're looking for?'*

When he'd finished, Jude said, "Why don't you set it to espionage tone, or better still turn it off?" grinning with mild reproof.

"What can I do?" he said lifting his shoulders and opening his palms out in appeal. "I'm tied to my work!"

"What are you doing here?" said Jude. "Not that I expect you to say much as usual."

"Listen," he said leaning forward conspiratorially. "I was on protection duty here with a senior politician. The man spent his lunch hour drawing a pencil sketch of a grilled chicken on his plate… and showing it to the foreign diplomats. I tell you he is crazy!" He lifted a finger up and touched the side of his head. A waiter approached and stood expectantly. Shpetim grabbed a menu and scanned it quickly. "Soup with *fasule*. Pizza with *bejkon dhe kërpudhë*," he said.

"Biftek me garniturë," said Jude. The waiter nodded and snapped the menus closed as he took them.

"Look," said Shpetim, reaching inside the folds of his jacket where Jude noticed he'd concealed his shoulder holster and pistol. He took out his wallet and produced a playing card that Jude had torn diagonally in steps into two halves that spring, giving one to him. Jude unfolded his wallet and slid out his half. The two pieces made a photo of Ouse Bridge from the Kings Arms in York.

"A promise," said Jude. "When we go there together, we will make the match." It was a play on a piece of spy tradecraft that he had seen in a film, and which appealed to Shpetim's inclinations instantly. He knew that promises should not be lightly made, and then most definitely kept, for an Albanian could put himself to ruin even to honour his promise. Jude took out another pack of cards still wrapped tightly in fresh cellophane and gave it to him. "You should find these interesting. Smuggler's Cornwall," he said stifling a mischievous grin. He knew how much Shpetim delighted in collecting postcards, beer mats, picture playing cards and keyrings to add to his little Anglophile shoe box at his family home in *Shënomadh*. Jude watched the eyes light up in this man with a dour expression and serious duties.

The waiter returned and placed Shpetim's soup before him with aplomb. Shpetim looked at him with a moment of incredulity. "Where is the bread?" he snapped.

"It is coming *zotëri*," replied the waiter.

"Do you eat beans soup like this in England?" said Shpetim glancing at Jude as he squeezed a lemon slice over it.

"Not quite. You do it well here... Do start," said Jude.

"What's new at the church?" said Shpetim. "How is Jaap doing? He's seemed so dispirited recently, walking around with that bandage on his head."

"I've not seen that much of him since we got back from Istanbul at the end of July," said Jude edging back a little as the waiter lowered his plate past his nose. He took in the aromas with anticipation: tsatsiki, potato fries and slices of cucumber and picked green tomatoes, neatly presented around a thin beaten slice of grilled beef sprinkled with fresh parsley.

"What exactly happened over there?" said Shpetim.

"Well, you know we took some of the youth group there for a week of outreach."

"Why did *you* go Jude?" Jude pushed his glasses up the ridge of his nose. "Turkey is Jaap's field... he's the missions pastor. He's been working up to initiatives like this for years, but he's been labouring short-handed. I just went along to help him out with some practicalities... make travel arrangements, plan the sight-seeing for the youth." Jude noticed that Shpetim had filled his mouth with so much bread that his left cheek was bulging like a squirrel's as he chewed. "We set up on the first day, down among the crowds by the ferry piers near the Galata

Bridge. They performed a little dramatic sketch... Fadil played his clarinet; Milena made a speed painting on an easel. The others talked to those who gathered around and passed out some tracts and pocket Bibles. It all went smoothly without any incident... Good beans?"

"*Shumë mirë*! How's the *biftek*?" said Shpetim gesturing with his spoon.

"Excellent," said Jude chewing. "On the second day, it was the same routine. I was talking with people who'd stopped to watch and listen... Two young men pushed through the crowd. They started to raise their voices, and pushed Milena and another girl. One of them pulled out something... like a black truncheon... from his trouser waist. He lunged at Jaap striking him on the forehead and kicked over the easel. It just happened so suddenly... Red and blue paints splattered over several people. Jaap hit the ground with a slap. The other young man picked up the box of literature and threw it... fluttering down into the waters of the Golden Horn. They then ran off shouting that they were going to get the police on us!" Shpetim was looking, saying nothing. Jude lowered his knife and fork to his plate. "Some others in the crowd helped me get Jaap to his feet... He was reeling and had a nasty red gash. The youth were in tears. We packed up quickly and made our way back to the hotel on the tram."

"And then?" said Shpetim.

"We really just laid low... We got Jaap's head looked at by a doctor the hotel had on call. He was physically fine... We did a little tourism, the Hagia Sophia and the Spice Bazaar, but we didn't return to the ferry piers. Jaap and I discussed calling the police, but he didn't want to get involved with them, or risk some protracted embroilment."

"Did anything else happen after that?"

"I… don't think so," said Jude.

"What?" said Shpetim, his thick eyebrows rising a fraction.

"It was just that evening… I thought I saw someone standing on the opposite side of the street from the hotel… watching," said Jude.

"Had you seen him before?" said Shpetim looking levelly at Jude.

"There was someone at the waterside, maybe, he reminded me of."

"What did he look like?"

"Short. Sort of hunched… He seemed to shift his weight from leg to leg." Shpetim sat back and took a white linen serviette folded like a fan from inside a large wineglass and cleaned his lips with it.

"Was this trip… wise?" he said. Jude thought to himself. Wisdom according to whose counsel? He did not answer Shpetim.

"When are you back in *Shënomadh*?" said Jude.

"Soon," said Shpetim. Jude smiled at his friend. He keeps much to himself, he thought… professional obligations. Shortly, they both made to leave. Jude reached for the bill but Shpetim snatched it. "I invited you! *Ik, tani*. Get out of here," he said. Jude complied and as Shpetim offered his hand in a 'high five' he grasped it.

* * *

At the park corner by the *Rruga Myslim Shyri* Edona Mollasi was waiting as Jude approached just before

3pm. She was a palm tree of a girl with long hair dyed blonde and brown roots showing. A second year student of Political Science in Tirana, and with a desire to write, she was already volunteering at the national newspaper *Shekulli* during her spare time. She would likely go far, he thought. He had met her through a student in *Shënomadh*, though she attended a church in Tirana. She took off her sunglasses, white-framed with heart-shaped lenses, as she saw Jude approaching and blushed a little. She looked both awkward and anxious.

"Hello Edona. Shall we get an ice-cream… then we can walk and talk a little?" he said as he stepped up to her. She nodded. "How are you doing?"

"I'm good. But the lecturers just give us books to read," she said with a shrug. "They don't put much heart into their talks."

"I remember some like that," said Jude. "We had a lecturer in Old Norse literature who could talk himself to sleep. We put a 'do not disturb' sign on him once… and tiptoed out."

She smiled as Jude ordered a chocolate cone for her and a blackberry one for himself. They threaded their way back through the stationary cars and ran the last three metres as the traffic lights changed. Jude jumped over a low wall onto the park grass and splattered his glasses with ice cream. Edona covered her mouth to suppress the laughter, spinning around and bending double before recomposing herself.

"You are so funny!" she said.

"Well, I do try to please," said Jude smiling and cleaning his lenses with a corner of his T-shirt. "So what has happened?" He noticed her amusement wipe away so quickly that he regretted not lingering a while for her sake before coming to the point.

"My grandma told me she had seen someone below our apartment block watching... twice," she said joining him on the footpath as they walked in the direction of the Sky Tower. "I'd thought to tell you when you were here last week, but it was nothing sure. This is Tirana... strangers come and go... seventy people live in our block alone, but grandma still thinks like a villager. If people are not with someone she knows, what are they up to?"

"I have a friend who could use a woman like her as a 'watcher'," said Jude licking the melted purple liquid off his finger.

"Yesterday, she called me when I was in lectures," she said. "She'd left to buy some fish and a watermelon along Bajram Curri Boulevard... below the Hotel Diplomat. She'd been gone around an hour. She said we'd been robbed." She held her cone still by her cheek and looked at Jude. "When I got home from the university, I could see that the wood was splintered around the lock... the apartment door had been forced open. Grandma was inside with a neighbour... They could not have been thieves because they took nothing. There was 5000 *lekë* left untouched in a folded electricity bill in the kitchen. They didn't damage anything... but things were lying out of position, or open, more so in my room." A small boy with dark skin and large brown eyes walked up to them offering salted almonds wrapped in little paper cones. Jude gave him 100 *lekë* for one and asked him where he was from. He did not know the place. He thought about the break-in as they walked. They came to the edge of a pool, turquoise and brilliant from the sun's rays, with three fountains springing from the middle. Café tables were laid out along its edge and waiters were attending to a brisk trade. Jude saw an empty park bench and walked across to it. They sat down together. "Do you think they were looking for these?" she said. She reached into her white, boutique shoulder bag, and drew out a pack of eight ninety-minute audio cassettes in their cases bound together with paper tape. Each one was written with 'Mehmed Krasnichi Interviews' and a number. "I've been carrying them with me recently." She sought Jude's face for approval.

"It might be someone was... you did well. Shall I hold them?" said Jude. He put a hand on her shoulder. "I'm sorry this has happened."

"I've finished with them now. I'll email you the manuscript when I've done a little more work on it," she said holding Jude's eyes with a look. A flicker of fear passed there. A strand of hair blew across her cheek and she brushed it off. Her hair smelt of sweet apples.

"Did your grandma tell you anything about the man she saw?" said Jude thinking déjà vu of his conversation earlier with Shpetim.

"Only that he was tall and 'must have money, because he was wearing a nice shirt like those people who work in offices... not on the land with animals'," she said, a giggle escaping her mouth at her grandma's words. Jude noticed she had a smudge of chocolate ice cream above her top lip. He felt an impulse to wipe it off. A cool spray from the fountain came down on them in the waft of the breeze. He stood up and stepped a pace away. He turned around.

"Better let the police know about this. Put your grandma on guard... and call them again if she spots any more 'office workers'," he said trying to reassure her with a smile. He began to form prayers amongst the clamour of his thoughts. It eased a mounting disquiet.

Chapter 5

The dust stirred up in little clouds around Jude's feet as he walked over the dry ground by his apartment block. He was swinging bread rolls from Bestar's Bakery, morning fresh and steaming up their blue plastic bag. He looked up to the fourth floor. Alex had drawn the curtains and he saw her pass the living room window. In the building's entrance youths had boot-marked the wall and burnt ugly soot crosses with cigarette lighters under the stone lintel. Someone had urinated there. He felt a tinge of regret at how the people were degrading their own living environment. He reached into a small wooden cupboard mounted on the wall for post and drew out their electricity bill and a package from England. It had been opened. There was a gift card inside it and an extra-large *Fry's Peppermint Cream* bar, which had one bite taken out of it. Little natural light reached the block's stairwell as he climbed, and today those bulbs that were there smouldered like dying candles from the low power supply.

He turned the key and pushed open their door. He could hear Alex singing an old gospel song as she clattered breakfast items in the kitchen.

"*Go down Moses… way down in Egypt land, and tell old Pharaoh, to let my people go,*" she voiced striving for a depth beyond her range. It gave her the slightly comic earnestness of a child in a talent show, he thought. He closed the door carefully with a click, tiptoed through to the living room and peeped at her. She was poised with a wagging finger, moving from heel to toe in time. His own singing voice was comic enough, he knew. He had no pitch and warbled from bass to squeaks, but he jumped in with the line: "*Oh who's that wo-man all dressed in white?*" She turned, a little flushed, and threw a tea towel at him.

"Don't think of entering '*Shënomadh's* Got Talent'," she said pulling a face. He threw a bread roll back at her. It glanced off her head and skewered itself perfectly on a toasting fork.

He now watched her for the pleasure of it as she poured two glasses of fizzy apple juice with an easy gracefulness. Her dark-brown hair was boyish and still ruffled from sleep. A pinched nose and height of 5ft 2" gave her a pixie-ish quality. She was wearing one of her many items of fairly-traded, ethnic clothing from around the world.

"Is that waistcoat from Bulgaria? It's nice," he said.

"It is… and these are from Peru," she said tilting her head towards him and smiling as she handed him a glass. Her earrings looked to him like several minute *Liquorice Allsorts* threaded on fishing wire. He remembered her riding in the cabin of the Volvo truck emptied of its aid boxes in Tirana, back in the summer of 1999, just months before they were married. She was wearing a white Fez that some old man had given her, and the Albanian women had pointed and giggled, and the men had jested that she should drink coffee with them now.

"You're dressed to wow at the UN then… We've got mail," he said handing her the electricity bill. "And… something to watch a Norman Wisdom film with." He held up the chocolate bar. "No doubt the postman will swear it was the handlers in Tirana!" He gave her a knowing smile.

"Naturally," said Alex with a little roll of her eyes. "Oh, just cut the good bit off!" She pulled out the flap of the envelope and glanced at the amount, "Are we really using so much electricity?"

"Maybe the neighbours are using some of it for us," he said. A loud and insistent banging erupted on their apartment door. He walked back to the entrance hall and unlocked it. The woman who lived opposite them, Julieta, was standing there, her huge hips almost splitting her pink tracksuit bottoms and feet similarly straining her blue plastic sandals. She handed him the instruction manual for a satellite TV receiver box.

"Alex said that she would translate it for me. Is she here?" she said imploringly. "Only my brother is coming to stay with us tomorrow… and we need it by tonight."

"I'll pass it to her," said Jude doubtfully and closed the door. He handed Alex the tome. "Here you are! You weren't planning on doing anything else today were you?"

"I'll only do the highlights," she laughed. She set down her juice, her eyes becoming suddenly intent.

She stepped lightly onto the tops of his shoes and ran her hands down his arms from shoulders to elbows. "Jude... I'm worried about what happened at Edona's house, but don't stop doing it... for that or any other reason. I'm with you in it. You know that?"

* * *

Mira's apartment block was ten minutes walk away from Jude's. She was standing outside it just before 4pm as they had arranged at English class. It was a building just like his yet as they entered he noticed a different smell of fresh whitewash and pickling vinegar. The wooden banister in the stairwell had been buffed to a lacquered finish by the residents' hands.

"They are waiting inside," said Mira. "They are so happy to have a visitor coming. I'll stay for a little time... but I need to help Lule with her school work this afternoon." Jude nodded and smiled.

A door on the second floor was opened quickly after Mira knocked, and an old woman not much above Jude's waist in height beckoned them enter. She was wearing a tightly-buttoned, black cardigan and headscarf. Her husband, no taller, hovered behind her in an oversized, brown suit jacket and a thick woollen vest.

"*Mirëdita*. I'm pleased to meet you," said Jude.

"Oh, you speak Albanian very well!" said the woman.

"My wife has it much better," he said. "What a nice house you have!" The woman smiled with pride. Their living room was scrubbed and tidy with thick, red-checked blankets covering the sofas. White plates were displayed in a glass-fronted wooden cabinet; a ceramic dolphin there leapt in its own space; a white tablecloth rimmed with intricate crochet-work was laid on a low table. There was a faint smell of mothballs.

She offered Jude and Mira a sugared fruit jelly from a small, stemmed glass bowl. She then left for the kitchen and returned shortly with a Turkish coffee and a glass of raki on a silver-like tray. There was a glass of juice on it too for Mira.

"Your family is in England?" she said.

"My father is there. I have no brothers or sisters," said Jude.

"How old are you?" she said.

"I'm in my early thirties."

"You are the same age as Roland," she said pointing at a photo of a young man with tight brown curls cut in an Eighties style.

"Their son," said Mira. The photo was set in a wooden, gilt-edged frame. The woman picked it up and cleaned the glass with her sleeve. It was already spotless. She kissed it three times.

Jude sipped the raki for politeness and set it down. He lifted the miniature cup and saucer and tasted the Turkish coffee. It was bitter and powdery but had enough sugar in to make it palatable.

"Did he leave here recently?" said Jude sensing they wanted to talk about him.

"*Ç'thua, more!*" said the man. "It was in '97, after the troubles!"

"He got on a boat to Italy," said the woman sucking in her breath as she spoke. "He telephoned and wrote to us. He was in the city of Bologna. He was a good son; he sent us money... He sent us this photo." She took down a faded print from a cabinet shelf. It looked to Jude like he was working in a pizzeria. "After six months, he stopped calling. We received no more letters. Maybe the post office lost them!" she said looking at her husband. "We don't know what has happened to him..."

"They sought help from the Italian Embassy in Tirana," said Mira. "They've had his details broadcast on a TV programme here... 'Lost People'... it tries to reconnect people with their missing relatives. Nothing." The woman brought her hands over her face and began rock and sob.

"*Ku je, tani?* Oh my Roland! When will you come back to us?" she said. The old man took a handkerchief from his pocket and wiped his eyes.

Jude felt his own sadness rising for them and for the obvious conclusion: too much time had passed. It touched him too for his own mother and her death when he was young. A little water rose into the corners of his eyes. He felt the pricking there and a hungry feeling - a vacancy of the heart left by the absence of a close family member - opened in him. He brushed a tear from his cheek with his fingers. He thought of things he could say to them, about He who gave his only son, who grieved as they did for so many absent children, who knew where Roland was, and who knew the end of all things. If it seemed right on another occasion, he thought, he would do it. He stood up and put his hands on the woman's shoulders. She fell around his waist and shook. Mira whispered behind him she was leaving.

Jude let them fuss and dote on him for the next hour. They brought him apple slices and slabs of baklava. They put their hands on his knee and pinched his cheek. To have a young man in the house again he could see brought out the love they still had to give and it brought them alive.

"Roland likes apples and quinces… and hens," she said. "He liked to walk in the hills behind *Shëno-madh*. What do you like?"

"Walking there too," he said nodding, "…and apples."

"You'll come again?" she said giving him a large crimson and yellow one as big as a small turnip when he rose to leave.

"I'll try to," he said.

* * *

On the evening of the next day, Jude felt in the mood to cook. He stepped into their kitchen, rubbed his hands and clapped them. He set a pan of pasta boiling. He grated a bowl full of Gouda and cut open a carton of cooking cream. He sliced a red pepper and some mushrooms thinly and put them in a steamer. He cut some slivers of cured ham, slipped one in his mouth, and simmered the rest in a frying pan with drops of olive oil. The ham was sweet and tender on his tongue.

"I'm cooking you some of that delicatessen food you like," he teased Alex, looking back over his shoulder into the living room. "There's no little transparent plastic tub to put it in… but you are safe tonight from my 'grockle food'… as you call it."

"Oh," she said feigning disappointment as she sat reading a book on the sofa, "it's just not the same without the tub!" He pulled open a drawer and drew out a steak mallet. As he closed it, the drawer handle came off in his hand. He held it for a few seconds indecisively and then dropped it inside and closed it with his thigh. He began to crush some whole, black pepper corns with whacks that jangled the cutlery drawer below.

"So how is your pine cone basket project coming along?" he said.

"Two market traders have said they'll take a look at them when we've finished a batch," she said closing her book. "There's a woman in my group, Mirela, who sews clothes seven days a week for ten hours a day... and takes home about £75 a month for it! Can you believe that Jude? The talk is that the owner trucks the clothes over the border to Greece... where a 'Made in the EU label' is stitched on."

"There's only so much you can do for them Alex... Just fight the battles God gives you, won't you?"

"I know that," she said a little testily. "Did you look at the hot water pipe yet?"

"I'll do that now," he said checking the pans before he slipped out. He glanced around their cramped little bathroom and toilet. The plasterwork on the ceiling was wet and beginning to sag down. He pulled at a plastic pipe and it came away from the wall. It just needs some sort of bracket thing to secure it, he thought. I must get one.

When the pasta was ready he drained it and mixed in all the ingredients before sprinkling black pepper and salt on top. He smelt it and his appetite rose. He spooned out two bowls full and sat on the sofa next to Alex. They ate their dinner, and second portions, as they chatted and an hour passed. Alex took the bowls to the kitchen sink, and Jude leant across to their pile of DVDs and began to rifle through them.

"Shall we watch a Norman Wisdom film?" he said.

"Go on then," she said a little lacking in enthusiasm Jude noted. He chose a film called 'The Early Bird' and slotted the disc into the player ready. He walked over to the living room window and looked outside. It was dark and he could see directly into the facing apartment where a large TV screen flickered before a family of five lined up neatly on their sofa. Below in the street it was still busy with people: a group at the Don Café was laughing loudly. He opened a window for the cool evening air and closed the curtains. He turned a side lamp on and the main light off as he waited for Alex to finish the washing up.

"Where's that chocolate bar? There are no more bites in it are there?" he called to her. She brought it through and held it out to him before grinning impishly, withdrawing it, and snapping off a piece for herself. As they settled in front of the screen, she nestled up to his shoulder.

They watched the black and white film as Norman the milkman was drawn into a battle with 'Consolidated Dairies', who were trying to take over the little patch he worked with his horse and cart. A milkman from 'Consolidated' made Norman's horse Nelly sick with some doped apples, so he took her up to his bed to rest. As he lay down beside Nelly, a big, stuffed horse's leg came up to hug him. Jude broke out laughing, slapped his knee, and looked at Alex who began giggling partly with him and at the story. Jude wiped a tear from his eye.

"You know, I've just got it... why the dictator Enver Hoxha let the Albanians watch these films!" he said. "He would see this one as being about how the little proletarian worker stood up to the evil capitalist!" The side lamp flickered. The TV screen cut, and as it came back on the DVD had stopped playing.

"Maybe someone is flicking the master switch in the entrance hall again!" she said. The side lamp flickered again and went out. The room was now in complete darkness.

"I'll get a candle," he said. He trod cautiously to the window and peered through the curtains. The facing block was also without lights. "It looks city-wide."

Jude's mobile phone rang. He moved back to the sofa where he'd left it and glanced at the face.

"The number is withheld," he said to Alex. He pressed to receive the call.

"Hello?" he said. There was no answer, but he could hear small noises. He waited.

"You are Jude Kilburn... publishing the book about Mehmed Krasnichi," the voice said in statement, but with a note that sought confirmation.

"Who is this?" said Jude.

"You will desist, or there will be... repercussions," said the voice. He heard a metallic click, and the crack of a gunshot that seemed to echo in a long chamber. He dropped the phone to the floor and drew his hand up to his ear to try quell the ringing in it. His heart accelerated until it hammered at his ribs. He moved towards the kitchen and caught his knee on the coffee table edge. He could not find the handle to the drawer with the candles. He sat down on the kitchen floor. The darkness seemed to swirl around him and press his head towards his feet.

Chapter 6

At the handrail of the Galata Bridge Sheref Dushman looked out onto the waters of Istanbul's Golden Horn. His black fishing rod was balanced on his right with the line running down into the calm blue waters. He regularly returned a precise eye to its point of entry. He watched the white ferryboats with their green interiors ease up to the Eminonu piers from across the Bosphorus Straits. He noticed a distant cruise ship, like some piece of opulent wedding cake, which seemed improbably buoyant. A horn reverberated rudely across the water from it. The traffic rumbled past behind him. A seagull cawed and ducked at him out of the sky. To his right the roof of the grand, pink-fronted terminus of Sirkeci Railway Station poked above the tourists and commuters swarming along the waterfront. To his left the Galata Tower squatted on the hill with its conical top. The sun was high above him to the right and the light on the buildings below the tower seemed to intensify to white-out. He took it all in with little movement along the flat-line of his emotions. He had seen it all too often since he was a boy.

The fishing line twitched and he snatched his rod shifting his weight from leg to leg. He drew it upwards and wound at the reel rapidly. The rod's end was bent and shimmying. He brought a writhing grey mullet over the handrail and it thudded down onto the walkway. Passers by gathered around to watch, laughing excitedly. Sheref deftly pressed the fish to the ground with one hand and removed the hook from its mouth with the other. He took out a thin knife from his back pocket and flicked out the blade. He placed it behind the fish's head and inserted it with a vicious thrust. For several seconds, he watched it, his eye fixed on the eye of the dying creature. He stepped up to the handrail and dropped it off the bridge into the water. It floated there on its side. He turned around and saw a Japanese girl with a half-eaten bread ring in her hand staring him. He held her gaze until she averted her eyes quickly and moved on.

He checked his mobile phone: 2pm, August 8th. He decided he would call in at his place of work to see if there was anything for him to do. He packed his tackle and walked along the bridge to Eminonu tram station. He waited as the blue-topped carriages glided to a halt on the platform and the tone of four notes and the station name came over the PA system. He stepped inside. As it climbed up Hudavendigar Avenue, he stood just inside the automatic door swaying on a hand strap. It was hotter out of the sea breeze and the sun began to burn his back through the glass. He watched a young man trying to embrace and kiss his girlfriend on a nearby seat. If she were his, he would show her a care and respect that would leave this man looking pitiful by comparison, he thought. As it reached the top of the hill, the pale orange walls and high dome of the Hagia Sofia came into view. The gardens before it with their palm trees and fountains were jammed up with tour buses and groups in matching T-shirts. One tour guide held up a rainbow-coloured parasol as she led her hordes towards the six minarets of the Blue Mosque. When the tram stopped at Sultanahmet, the crowds poured on. A man with white, hairy legs and an oversized rucksack pressed against his fishing rod, and Sheref jabbed at his leg irritatedly.

"Verzeihen Sie mir! Pardon," said the man. Sheref did not acknowledge him.

As the tram drew closer to Beyazit, he lowered his head and hunched himself into a hidden space. His father would be working there now in the Grand Bazaar at his carpet store. He wanted to be welcomed there with pride by him, but he could not bear another lecture, another pronouncement of his worthlessness and his shame at him, which is what he would receive.

"Aptal oglu! Stupid!*"* he heard him shout. "I came up from the soil of Anatolia and made something of myself... and you? You wasted the gains of my hard work!"

The tram drew in to Aksaray five minutes later. He pushed his way through the carriage and stepped down. He barged through the rotating steel barrier and set off walking towards Aksaray Avenue, past the expensive clothing stores lined with rows of maniquins and four story high photos of models in fashionable outfits. The *Laleli Teknik Servis* had a window full of mobile phones for sale in rows along white shelves. Above the door an electronic display board ran adverts and other information across its red bulbs news ticker style. It was 28°C. Sheref stepped inside and nodded to Osman the owner before entering the service room in the shop's rear. He set his fishing rod down under the workbench and sat on a high wooden stool. A range of small pincers and screwdrivers, a soldering iron, circuit board pieces and small components were carefully arranged before him by a spotlight and an ashtray. Three jobs were bagged up in little transparent folders and labeled neatly. Osman came through and tossed him a new folder with an LG phone in it.

"An English tourist just brought this in," he said gruffly. "She'll be back in an hour for it." Sheref said nothing. He neither liked nor disliked Osman. He paid him okay. He could do this kind of work in his sleep.

He slipped the LG from the folder, slid a thin screwdriver in the side, and eased the back off. He remembered sitting in a lecture theatre at university in England looking down over the students' heads to the white board during the first term and frantically taking notes. He was thrilled by the knowledge and by this particular presentation of system-on-chip design. He was full of excitement about where his B.Eng. in Electronic and Communications Engineering could take him. How could he have come to this? He rammed the screwdriver down onto the workbench snapping the shaft and cutting his hand. He tore off a piece of paper towel from a roll by a sink and pressed it into his palm. He ran his other hand slowly over his face. He lifted out the keypad from inside the LG's casing and examined the phone. The display unit had a single disconnected wire: it could be repaired with a minute's work. He pushed it all back inside, clipped on the back, and put it in the folder. He set to work on the three other phones and had completed their repair in forty-five minutes. A small television was mounted on a bracket in the room's top corner and he turned it on with the remote. It was set on NTV and he watched the national news for a while. A reporter had been filming people in a church with a hidden camera. Osman came through and he passed him the three repaired phones.

"What about the English girl's?" said Osman. Sheref lifted the folder towards him.

"Tell her it's dead," he said and turned back to the television.

It was dark when he left *Laleli Teknik Servis*. The flow of passing car headlights was bright in his eyes. Groups of men stood around on corners biting at kebabs and dropping onions onto the pavement. Street vendors were hustling the passing tourists to buy boxes of fake perfume. He did not want to eat at home again, so he walked in the crowds along the Ataturk Boulevard to a restaurant where rows of chickens were spit-roasting outside. He took a corner table and glanced at the photographs on the menu. He chose an aubergine salad and stuffed peppers with a serving of mash. As he waited he glanced around the red plastic tables set ready with cutlery at the other clientele. There were some Greeks and Somalis in tonight pointing at the trays of food behind the glass counter. He watched Omer the waiter ease an armful of plates before some diners. He had one continuous eyebrow across his forehead and eyes that seemed to effortlessly take in all details around him.

"So… you are here again?" said Omer stepping up to his table with an electronic order pad in hand.

"The tea is drinkable," said Sheref, denying him the satisfaction, and placed his order. Omer gave a wry grin and returned with a basket of pita bread quickly followed by the salad. He dipped a bread piece in the sauce and placed it in his mouth. The tomato and garlic rolled sweetly over his taste buds. Omer arrived with the peppers.

"Can you look at my Motorola for me?" he said and left it on the table. Sheref nodded. He finished off his meal quickly and wiped the oil from his lips with his fingers like he was smoothing down an imaginary moustache. He checked the phone. Omer returned with two small glasses of tea and sat down with him.

"Get yourself a new battery," said Sheref and handed it back.

A flat-screen television was mounted on a wall and set on CNN Turk. He listened as an official commented again on the presence of foreign missionaries in the country.

"Political motives… that's what they have," said Omer sipping at his tea, and watching him. "They are damaging the peace… the social unity here… spreading *their* culture. They are undermining our values… don't you think?" Sheref nodded reservedly, but he was alert to hear him voice such views. It stirred up feelings and thoughts that had been burning hotter, white hot even to the point of shorting on some deep circuit in his head, and sending an acrid smell in his nostrils. "Have you seen the footage TV channels have been showing from that church?" said Omer still watching him. "They are bribing our young people... with inducements!" Sheref watched him take out a little white box of oval cigarettes and hand one to him. He examined it... *Sobranie of London.* Expensive, he thought. He took out his lighter with an acorn leaf emblem in the centre and lit both tips. "Oh, you are with Fenerbahçe for football! I'm Galatasaray," said Omer.

"Don't talk to me about Galatasaray," spat Sheref. He saw that Omer was a little startled. He drew on the cigarette deeply and exhaled away into the aisle. The taste was very smooth. He would tell him. "Listen," said Sheref in a low, almost whispering voice. "About two weeks ago, I was down on the Galata Bridge. I saw this crowd gathered by the water's edge near the ferries. I went over out of curiosity. There were some *Arnavutlar*, Albanians... and a few more foreigners giving out literature and Bibles. I got talking to an English guy with them. I knew his accent right away, believe me... Leeds. I studied there. Some other boys broke through and pushed them around. They scattered like chickens..."

He took a sip of his tea and flicked the ash off his cigarette. He could see Omer's eyes were piercingly alive. "But I followed them... They got on the tram and rode right here to Aksaray, and scuttled off down to the Hotel Emperor Constantine. After they left, I got the name of the English guy from the receptionist... I Googled him. His mission agency web site had all his details there... even his favourite dinner." They both snickered with contempt. "He lives in central Albania. *Shënomadh* is the name of the town."

"So?" said Omer.

Sheref waited a few seconds before answering. "I've been thinking through a plan."

Chapter 7

With his Bible open before him on the coffee table, Jude sat back on the living room sofa. He had been seeking the verses he needed for their precious inner strength. He had slept intermittently last night; a tightening in his stomach had come on; a cold perspiration had passed over his back. He'd thought again about the dark blue Mercedes on the *Qafë Krrabë* ridge road, but inconclusively. It could equally still have been reckless driving. Now, in the mid-morning peace of the apartment, he was recovering his equilibrium. Sparrows were chirruping and fluttering up the face of the apartment block. A breeze was ruffling the curtains of an open window. The faint fragrance of pine trees was coming in from the mountains. He had been resting in the stillness of prayer for around thirty minutes, imagining he was sitting near to where the Lord was reclining by Lake Galilee. He had taken the verse from *John 14:27*,

> '*My peace I give you... do not let your hearts be troubled...*'

and meditated upon it. He had decided that he would

not double back on himself at the first instance of someone trying to make him with a phone call. Dogs bark, he thought, but it is much rarer they actually bite.

He had mounted a black and white Ansel Adams poster of Yosemite on the facing wall when they'd moved in. The sheer terrain had areas of deep shadow and rocky highlights with a single dark cloud approaching the penetrating rays of the sun. It was a dramatic and inspiring scene and he looked at it again. Alex had filled his pint mug with hot water and two teabags before leaving that morning. It had a picture of a rugged looking nobleman in a fine morning coat, and on it was written 'Mr Rochester's Mug'. She had bought it for him in a souvenir shop in Yorkshire. He had drunk the tea down in deep draughts and felt additionally fortified. She had also given him a red, hard-backed notebook and a silver pen, each with the double-headed black eagle of Albania on them. "It's for sketching an action plan for the book in," she'd said brightly. Now he was really ready for work.

Edona had emailed the manuscript. He now had it sitting on the desktop of his laptop ready for Spiro, who he'd arranged to come at 11am to begin the editing work. He was not entirely certain about his choice of the man to help with the project. A tall schoolteacher in his fifties, there was still a whiff of old communist officialdom about him, he reflected. The depth of his faith was questionable, though he'd been hovering around the edge of the congregation for some time, profiting financially from foreigners' need of the Albanian language. He was an entry-level character, known to be present in the church for what he could get out of it. That was overlooked, though, with the view that as he was exposed to the Word and Spirit, they would eventually elevate his participation in the life of the Body a level.

There was an officious knock on the door at 11.45am.

"Jude," said Spiro shaking his hand stiffly as he entered. "I hope that I have not upset you by being late?"

"It's alright," said Jude doing his best to mask his annoyance at this on his first showing. Spiro was wearing a slightly crumpled brown suit with the faint smell of grilled meat and cigarette smoke that attached itself in local cafés. His bald head had a frond of greying hair combed over the top from above his right ear.

"Come through to the living room. Would you like a coffee?" said Jude.

"That is most civil of you. Black… three sugars," said Spiro. 'It really is a privilege to serve our Lord in this modest manner. Is that a Turner print you have on the wall over there?"

"Well, I'm glad you see it in that light. Yes it's of Bolton Abbey," said Jude as he brought the coffee to him.

"Oh. Your wife is out?" he said. Jude nodded.

"You teach English still?" said Jude.

"I was head of department. But I do *many* things now," he said with a grandness that had the touch of an amateur thespian performing Shakespeare, Jude thought.

"What we have to do with the manuscript of Mehmed's book is check it for grammar, spelling,

clarity of expression, double-check any questionable facts with external sources… and watch for
repetitions or dull sections," said Jude. Spiro's eyes
flicked around the room, and Jude wondered if he
was really taking in the briefing. "We also have the
interview tapes to refer to."

"*Mos ki merak.* Don't worry about a thing," said
Spiro. Jude opened the document on his laptop
and set a chair at a small side desk ready for him to
work. Spiro placed his coffee beside the computer
and checked his mobile phone.

Jude picked up Alex's new notebook and pen,
sat in an armchair and began to jot. He brainstormed
some titles for the book: *The Shame of Honour Killing*,
Revenge: A Passion Never Quenched, *Forgiveness:
Weapon of Choice*… I like that last one, he thought.
He wondered about the cover design. Should he
use a photo of Mehmed, or buy an agency image
from reportage taken in the Kosovo war? Or maybe
he could find an Albanian illustrator? It must be
ready and printed by early September, ready for the
biennial conference of Albanian church leaders and
missionaries. If it is not, the best chance of distribut-
ing it far and wide on a single weekend is lost for the
next two years! He caught himself chewing the ends
of the arms of his glasses and stopped.

Spiro's mobile phone rang. He took it from a
brown leather pouch attached to his belt.

"*Alo… Alo. Jam i lirë. Jo,* it is no problem for me!
I can come now for a coffee," he said and closed it,
slipping it back in the pouch. "Jude. I have a meeting
with a very important associate… I need to leave."
Well, this is important too, thought Jude. We've
agreed terms. You've just had a coffee. You've only

just got started. We've made no progress with this and there is a huge distance to go with it! I just don't believe this. "Don't worry about a thing," Spiro said for the second time as he stood up and smoothed his frond of hair. "I'll call you." Jude pushed his fringe back over the top of his head. He was hardly reassured. In fact, he was very worried.

* * *

The sun was red on the whitewashed walls of the old stone houses in Shpetim Gurbardhi's neighbourhood. His friend was back from Tirana and Jude was strolling through *Shënomadh* to meet him. Families sat outside on their stone steps watching him curiously as he walked along the shiny cobbled street. It doesn't matter how I try to dress, he reflected with amusement, they can always tell I'm a foreigner. Three boys rolled an old tractor tyre out from a side street in front of him and down a dusty brown road. They shouted at each other as it plunged into a pile of household rubbish bags splitting them open. Shpetim was leaning over his wooden gate.

"Ku je mor, burrë? Where have you been?" he shouted.

"Well, I might ask you the same if it weren't a state secret," said Jude grinning back.

Shpetim drew the gate inwards and Jude stepped through a small doorway in the stone wall into an enclosed yard where the flagstones had been cleanly swept. He greeted Jude with a hug, touching his cheek to the left and right with his own. The yard was cool and shaded under a vine canopy thick with bright green leaves and hung with bunches of purpling grapes. A table and chairs were arranged at the foot of a flight of steps that led up past two stone columns to the house's front door. Shpetim's father Skender and younger brother Luan rose to greet Jude as Shpetim led him forward. They each had the family nose, prominent and masculine, like the actor Liam Neeson, he thought, and warm, clever eyes. Skender's eyes, though, were dissipated with concern, raki and *Karelia Slims* cigarettes, all of which he imbibed too heavily. He exuded a quiet despair, which burdened Jude for this former army officer each time he met him. Luan was almost a facsimile of Shpetim. He shared his taste for stylish clothes and high-end mobile phones, but was stockier with less reflective analysis and more bravado than his older brother. He too was in line to join SHISH, making security seem like a family business. Jude shook hands with them both and sat down.

"*Ç' kemi?* How are you?" said Shpetim resting his elbow on Jude's shoulder.

"I'm okay. Something… last night. I'll tell you later," he said.

"O, Alma! Shpetim's friend Jude is here. Bring the *raki kumbulle*… and some *mezet*. Go wake up my father," Skender shouted up to the open window.

"*Mirë*! Does he like *piperka me gjizë?*" came a faint female voice from the interior.

"I don't know woman… just bring some!" Skender shouted back impatiently.

Shpetim's mother, Alma, came down the steps shortly carrying a large, round, metal tray filled with saucers of *mezet*. She was a handsome woman in her late-fifties, who cared attentively for her hair and makeup and wore a pink, household pinafore over a smart, dark dress.

"Good evening," she said in English smiling.

"Piperka me gjizë, Mrs Gurbardhi, is a dish I like," said Jude. She shook out a tablecloth and placed the saucers down one by one. There was a tomato and onion salad dressed in olive oil and oregano, a yoghurt sauce with bread sticks, olives, a slab of white cheese, and the pickled peppers filled with curd. She returned with a bottle of raki and eggcup-sized glasses, and a bowl of cubed watermelon. Jude cut off a fork-full of pepper as the others began to pick at the *mezet* and put it in his mouth. It was the perfect sour counterpoint to a sip of sweet, plum raki.

"Do you have yoghurt sauce like this in England?" said Shpetim.

"Nope," said Jude.

"Then what do you dip your bread sticks in?" said Luan looking concerned. The stars were glinting brighter in the falling dark and Jude leant back and looked at them. The warm evening air on his arms felt liberating. He noticed the crickets' chorus, a higher note then a lower one, rising all around them.

Shpetim's grandfather shuffled slowly down the steps and indicated with his stick that he wanted a cushion for the chair.

"How do you like Albania?" said Skender refilling his own glass with raki.

"I like it," said Jude. "Great weather… great dust! Expensive Mercedes cars with roads to break their suspensions on. Warm, hospitable people living in cold apartment blocks… You are a family-loving people… providing you don't get into a disagreement with another family." There was an outburst of hearty laughter from all at the table.

Shpetim raised his glass. "*Gëzuar!*" he said.

"*Gëzuar!*" everyone toasted, chinking the tips of glasses together.

"Luan here broke the suspension on uncle Burim's Mercedes," said Shpetim gesturing to his side with his thumb.

"I did not. It was the axle… and it was already defective!" protested Luan and jumped up to grab his brother in a neck-lock. The two brothers play-wrestled with each other from the table across the yard until Shpetim took hold of Luan's leg and up-ended him. They both tumbled together into a bush cracking the branches and rolling out together covered in twigs and leaves. Everyone roared with laughter. Shpetim's immaculate, white shirt was now soiled and the front pocket torn.

"What about England? Don't you miss it? Great Britain! It is a high culture Jude… and we will see it together, won't we?" said Shpetim frowning at his brother as he brushed himself down.

"We will," said Jude. "I miss it… and I worry about it. People call light darkness there now. I don't know… it's as if it's lost its compass."

"Old Petrit here… he loved the British officers when he was a boy," said Shpetim.

"He was a child Partisan!" said Luan standing up and saluting with a clenched fist. "*Vdekje fashizmit!* Death to fascism! Freedom for the people!"

"Who did you meet, *xhaxhi* Petrit?" said Jude, his interest pricking up.

"Dëgjo…" said Petrit putting his stick against the table edge and lifting a piece of tomato to his mouth before sucking it noisily. He was not going to be rushed; he'd been given the spotlight.

"My family is from Dukat near Vlora… not here," he said. "The war was terrible. I remember the Italian soldiers starving… they fell down at the roadsides together with their mules and died. There were some British officers who had a base in the mountains near us… some Italians would come and buy food for them from the villagers. One time, a big plane, a *Halifaks* they said, came in with supplies and more British soldiers and crashed into the mountain killing everyone on it. Some of the Partisans looted it… I was angry with them. It was not right. They had come to help us fight the Nazis!" He sat upright now and a boyish pride shone through his eyes. "But I went with my father… We took some bread, cheese and dried meat, and packed it in a bag on our mule. We travelled for most of the day through the mountains and down to the sea. The sun was setting across the Adriatic… all the way to Italy. The British had a base in a cave there… we knew. There was a man I remember… who came out to meet us. He had a fat face and small eyes. He looked sick and yellow… Major *Toni Kueill* he was called. He gave us a gold sovereign for the food. He gave me a photo of a film star and he said, "I'm sorry it is torn." My father gave the sovereign to me and I still have it. Later, I joined the Partisans… that is another story."

"If it was Major Anthony Quayle, *xhaxhi*, you met a special man. After the war, he became a famous film actor. Did none of you ever see him on the television?" Jude looked around at the blank faces. Luan shrugged his shoulders.

"*Ice Cold in Alex... The Guns of Navarone... Lawrence of Arabia*? I'll get copies!" said Jude. "Enver Hoxha sent Partisans after the British officers who'd helped him as the war was drawing to a close. They were just a small band of men trying to fight off an evil tyranny... as another home-grown one moved in to take its place."

"Enver Hoxha was a killer of the Albanian people!" shouted Luan and thumped the table.

"They were almost caught, but they escaped with their lives," said Jude. "Those that died during those special operations, we know, are buried in Tirana Park."

"It was a fight they lost," said Skender. "It was obscure and far from the front lines. The war was won on the beaches of Normandy."

"It's sometimes said... that the victory over all evil was won at Calvary," said Jude glancing at Shpetim. "That was our D Day. But we are in the days before VE Day... when He will come again. Until then... that battle is still on."

Chapter 8

Jude tapped his fingers buoyantly on his lesson plan. He was keen to see how the Dickens discussion in this afternoon's English class would go. He checked his mobile phone as the students entered and sat in their chairs in ones and twos. It read 3.15pm and several were late. He craned his neck to look out through the classroom window. A woman by the gun bunker seemed to be arguing with a neighbour on a balcony above her. As Fredi the waiter and Bledi the taxi driver strode past, she threw a bowl of wastewater down at her and it caught them too as it fell.

He tutted and turned quickly to jot down an idea for Mehmed's book with his silver pen. Liridon sat on a chair next to him reading his Dickens 'Easy Reader'. He noticed a purple and yellow bruise above his cheekbone. Liridon saw him looking at it and indicated that one of his goats had done it as he slept. Jude was not so sure. Flutura had sat as far away as possible from Liridon. She worked in a beauty salon, she said, and had a stack of tinted hair woven improbably skywards above her head.

Today, she was pouting like a fourth-former as she spoke into her mobile phone, her voice raised in an indignant huff as she mouthed some long grievance. He had seen her force someone into answering their phone by ringing them repeatedly into submission. He needed to have words with her and others about their phone use in class. Fredi entered brushing his shoulder and sat down next to her. She gave him a dismissive look. Bledi sat next to Liridon, rubbed his hair, and then thought twice about it. He slipped his hand onto his trousers to wipe it, and then slapped Liridon's back in a gesture of friendliness.

Jude decided to begin. He drew a diagram of a guillotine on the whiteboard. "This is a version of a game called 'hangman'," he said. "You call out letters to discover which are in this missing word. For each letter not here... the blade falls six inches towards the aristocrat's head. Who shall we make the aristocrat?"

"Fredi's family has a cat. He's bourgeois!" shouted Bledi. There was a round of laughter.

"It's not a problem for me. You can put my name there," said Fredi looking a little grazed. As the letters were called out and the blade drew nearer to Fredi's neck, the laughter built until Fredi saved himself by shouting out, "The word is JUSTICE!" much to his own gleeful satisfaction.

Jude then asked them to get their copies of *A Tale of Two Cities* ready for a time of discussion. "'It was the best of times, it was the worst of times...' It was the time of the French Revolution," he said theatrically. "The French aristocrat, Charles Darnay, has returned from London to Paris to help his servant... who has been denounced by the new citizen's committees for helping Darnay the emigrant. What does Darnay deserve? Are you ready?"

"He did not deserve to be arrested... What had he done to the French people?" said Kristo. Bravo, thought Jude, we're off!

"He was still a French aristocrat... they had lived in luxury and thought nothing for the needs of others around them," said Blerta, a girl with dark ringlets fixed rigidly with hairspray. Jude knew she was active in student politics.

"He was an enemy of the people! His class was guilty," shouted Fredi then burst out laughing at his own joke statement.

"He went to help his servant," said Liridon looking around anxiously for agreement. "He was a good man!"

"If Darnay had lived here," said Kristo pointing a finger at Blerta, "your family would have denounced him to the citizen's committees!"

"Don't you talk about my family like that!" said Blerta, who was bristling ready for a counter-strike.

"If a person had emigrant links here under Hoxha, Jude, the *Sigurimi*... the secret police... would soon be coming to their door," said Fredi.

"Under Hoxha, I'd have been with you Fredi... below the blade," said Jude.

"I think for all those who went to the guillotine... the justice was very rough," said Mira with a quiet seriousness. "Maybe some of them were guilty of crimes, but the innocent too were swept away by those zealots... who did not have the eyes to differentiate. They could not reckon all things in person's life, and see through to the heart... like God can."

"It was done for ideology, resentment, revenge… those women… *tricoteuses*… sitting doing their knitting as the heads were cut off," said Kristo with a thinning of his lips as he looked at Blerta.

"Who were those *trico…*?" said Flutura flicking through her pages.

"It was done to remedy a grave social injustice," said Blerta sternly. "People sometimes deserve what they have coming to them." Her eyes narrowed a touch as she looked at Kristo.

Jude picked out words used in the discussion and wrote them on the whiteboard. He wound up the activity and asked the students to copy them down.

"I have another Bible verse for you all to take away and read," he said. He handed out slips of paper with *Isaiah 42:1* typed in English.

'Here is my servant… in whom I delight. I will put my Spirit on him and he will bring justice to the nations.'

"We are going to finish with a game that has been popular with Britain's working people… so your forebears would have approved ideologically," Jude said smiling. "It's called *Bingo*, but we are going to play it with verbs!" He gave out the black and white paper grids, but as they played and the majority cheated it descended into a ruckus of accusation and counter-accusation. He terminated the activity quickly without giving out the chocolate bar prizes he'd brought. He rummaged through his papers and looked under the desk as he packed up. He could not find Alex's silver pen.

Kristo was waiting outside the door of the building again for him.

"I hope you have no more denouncements to make about Liridon, Kristo. He is staying," said Jude.

"It is your choice, Mr Kilburn. I've told you about him… In fact, I wanted to talk to you about something in my family… if I could," he said with a new note of humility. "My auntie's husband has been getting into difficulties with a neighbour over a strip of land. We are fearful about the situation. Would you… come with me one time to meet him?"

"Yes Kristo, I will," said Jude. Kristo flicked his attaché case under his arm. This time it was accompanied with a smile. As Jude walked back down May 5ᵀᴴ Street he sent a text message to Edona: 'Seen any more 'office workers'?' Her reply came back in less than a minute with the Morse code SOS tone, but it read, 'None'.

* * *

Sheref shuffled from leg to leg as he stood in the darkness on a corner of Ataturk Boulevard with Omer. The waiter's eyes scanned around them, seemingly taking in details on all sides. The traffic was flowing past them heavily, and after Omer checked his watch Sheref noticed he concentrated on the oncoming cars more closely. A silver Ford Focus drew up with a minute screech of tyres. Omer opened the rear door and they both jumped inside. The car smelt of clean leather seats. The driver pulled away in seconds.

They drove next to the tramlines along Ordu Avenue towards Beyazit. Sheref looked at the driver from behind and in the rear-view mirror. He was wearing a black suit and thin tie. His dark hair was swept back thickly over his head. A triangular tuft of hair pointed from his chin. He listened to the tick of the indicator. The fluorescent red hand of the speedometer set in the low light of the dashboard fell as they turned towards Buyuk Reshit Pasha Avenue and then rose again. No one spoke. Who were these friends that Omer had said wanted to meet him, he thought? Was this man one of them? What did they want from him? He felt a cold sweat on his palms as he fiddled with his mobile phone. Its backlight was not coming on consistently. He held it up to the streetlights as they passed behind Istanbul University. It read 9.20pm. Was he being trapped, he'd wondered? He'd still agreed to come. He wanted to know who was interested in him. It gave him a curious feeling of importance as the smooth car wove down through the streets towards the Golden Horn.

As they passed Sirkeci Station the traffic lights were green and they accelerated through them and swung left. He watched the taxicabs lined up in front of the piers flash past in a streak of yellow. The distant lights of Uskudar twinkled across the water as they crossed the Galata Bridge and then drove along the shore of the Bosphorus Straits. The Dolmabahçe clock tower, lit with a bright, sandy hue, slid past on his right. He noticed that the driver was watching him. Soon they were driving along the edge of Yildiz Park, and the thought passed through his mind that they were heading for the O1 highway and the Bosphorus Bridge.

The driver's mobile phone vibrated in a tray by the gear stick. He lifted it up to his ear and listened. Sheref thought he heard the voice say: "Gazi is ready." He said nothing and lowered the phone. Sheref eased himself back into the seat as the driver manoeuvred into the left-hand lane as they joined the O1. He thought about his sister Hanife. She would be at home now, probably studying by the bedside lamp in her room: away from their parents. He had not seen much of her recently with coming home late. It was her birthday soon; he would get something special for her.

Thousands of violet lights covering the span of the suspension bridge came into view ahead of them. The land fell away on the right as the highway ramped onto it, and below a road lit with the contra-flowing lines of red and white car lights stretched away into the silhouettes of buildings. Two minarets of the illuminated Ortakoy Mosque were mirrored in the black water's edge. The thick steel suspension cable rose up to the first tower of the bridge, the base of which flashed by the car window seconds later. The water below was speckled with an occasional cluster of lights from a passenger ferry or freighter away down the Straits to the distant Sea of Marmara where the near full moon hung low.

Soon they were over the Asian shore and they quickly drew off to the right and passed back underneath the highway. Sheref had not been into this district of Istanbul before, but he could see they were heading towards Çengelkoy. After several turns along side streets, they drew up outside a café with a dimly-lit interior visible through the front window. Omer opened the car door and gestured that Sheref should follow.

The plain, wooden tables and chairs inside were worn and scratched. Chipped little saucers were laid out as ashtrays. A carpet was hung on the wall with a scene of some vizier whispering intrigues into a sultan's ear under the starry night sky. Behind the counter a fat-faced old man with thick, white stubble was drying tea glasses. It was the kind of place old men frequented, thought Sheref. One man sat with his head drooped over a half-full glass of tea. Another sat with his back to them facing the café's front window.

Omer drew out three chairs from a table and they sat down. The driver entered and his chair grated on the floor as he moved it in to join them.

"Tea?" he said. Sheref nodded. The driver indicated to the man behind the counter.

"You may call me Kadir," he said, his finger rising to touch an itch by his tuft. "Omer here speaks of you... frequently. He has told us about your feelings. Your... plan."

"You are state security," said Sheref. "You will detain me now?"

"No."

"Who are you?"

"We are patriots. That is all you need to know."

"What kind of patriots?" Kadir did not answer. The man behind the counter brought three teas to the table. Sheref took his and stirred the sugar around with a tinkling of the tiny spoon. He sipped it. So Kadir is not just the driver, he thought. Why bring me here then when we could have talked in Aksaray? He glanced around the café and fixed his eyes on the man with his back to him. He was tall, even sitting down, and looked dignified. He had a verge of closely-cut greying brown hair around the back of his bald head, and wore a pressed, white shirt. Sheref's eyes moved to the café window. He could see the reflection of the front of his *Sabah* newspaper. The man lowered it and Sheref thought he caught his eyes watching him in the glass. He had a high forehead and a thick, well-trimmed moustache. He looked like some kind of officer. He lit a cigarette and the tobacco's aroma swirled across. It was a *Sobranie,* like Omer had given him. Was this man Gazi?

Kadir nodded to the waiter who stopped his glass-washing and left through a door.

"Your studies were in electronic engineering?" said Kadir.

"And communications engineering," said Sheref.

"And now you replace batteries in mobile phones?"

"I am capable of much more."

"You failed your course!"

"Others took the same... short-cuts, but I was singled out."

"Now... you hate them." It was as if this man had kicked him on a gangrenous leg. He jumped up and knocked his tea with the back of his hand at Kadir. He grabbed his shirt at the neck and pushed him back against the wall, snorting the air heavily through his nose. Kadir did not resist him. He felt Omer pull him away slowly and sit him back down. His breathing slowed. Kadir grinned at him and wiped the tea leaves from his cheek and collar.

"So now, state your business with me... Mr 'patriot'," said Sheref, "or take me back to Aksaray."

"We will *drink* our tea... and then take you back Sheref," said Kadir calmly.

Chapter 9

On the sofa in his apartment Jude sat reading through ideas about Mehmed that he'd written in Alex's notebook. His pint mug of tea was now half drunk and sat on the coffee table in front of him. He checked the time on his mobile phone: it was 10.15am, August 12th. Spiro should be here shortly, he thought, or at least shortly after that. In his favour, the man had kept his word and called, and had a copy of the manuscript to work with. Alex sat in a nearby armchair, her Bible open on her lap and her eyes closed. The room was silent save for the heels of someone's shoes tapping lightly across the ceiling from the apartment above.

He pressed the top of his biro and leant forwards. He'd decided he would title the book, *The Shame of Honour Killing. The True Story of Mehmed Krasnichi.* He had found a stock photo of a line of militia emerging with their heads low from a dug out in a forest near Prishtina, and he began to write the blurb. *'Amid the horrors of war in former Yugoslavia, another man emerged with vengeance in mind. He set out with a rifle on the road to make someone pay... But the love of the Saviour was waiting to arrest him.'* He took another gulp of tea.

A firm 'rat-tat-tat' came on the door around 11am. Alex looked up from her studies.

"That'll be Spiro," said Jude.

"I'll go through to the bedroom," said Alex. Jude walked into their entrance hall and turned the latch. Spiro stepped inside with a single stiff stride, and smoothed his frond of hair over the top of his head.

"My apologies Jude. My cousin came from Tirana for a visit," he said. Jude knew the culture of unannounced visits, and the hospitality necessary for those who made them, but how did one make a timetable of work with these people, he thought?

"Well, it's good you are here now," said Jude. "Come on through." He gestured to Spiro to take a seat and sat down on the sofa. He thought momentarily to offer him a coffee, but was dissuaded by the idea that he'd probably had several already this morning.

"So," said Jude. "You've been able to look at the manuscript on your computer?"

"Yes, it was no problem," said Spiro with a wave of his hand to indicate it had been effortless.

"How does the story seem to you?" Jude asked keenly.

"*Pa diskutim.* For sure, it is very good," he said with little enthusiasm.

"How far would you say you've got?"

"Maybe... soon... twenty percent," he said edging backwards a little in the armchair. "I have had work... The development agencies pay well for translation. It is difficult. What can I do? I have a family to take care of!" His eyes were now flicking around the prints on the walls. Jude felt a slump of disappointment followed by a spike of frustration. It shouldn't really be any more than three days of concentrated work for anyone who put his back into it, he thought.

"I see," said Jude neutrally. "Were there many repetitions or dull sections? Is there enough dialogue do you think?"

"*Mos ki merak.* I know how to put in enough," he said rising up a little as he sat. Jude was a little surprised. Suggestions as to how to do this seem an affront to him, he thought. If he didn't know, though, would he actually admit it?

"Well, the tapes are ready for you... there... if you want to check anything," said Jude pointing. "But I need to keep them here." He had placed his laptop on the small side desk with a tape recorder and the numbered interview tapes next to it ready. Spiro seemed to move sluggishly towards it.

Spiro spent around forty-five minutes listening to sections of the recordings through the earphones, and then checked something in the open manuscript on the laptop. Jude looked at his notebook and made more mental preparations.

"May I smoke here?" said Spiro suddenly holding up his pack of cigarettes.

"On the balcony is fine," said Jude. Spiro turned the door handle and stumbled on the ridge along the floor as he stepped out. Jude watched him through the window. He tapped one out, lit it and then tossed the match down into the yard. His eye seemed to catch something or someone below and remain there. His mobile phone rang and he took it from his belt pouch. "*Po, po*. How much?" Jude heard him say. He flicked the cigarette down after the match.

"Jude. I need to leave," he said as he re-entered. Jude looked at him. He did not know what to say. He was lost for words. "I'll call you," said Spiro as he brushed invisible dust off the shoulders of his brown suit jacket. He followed him to the door. The lock clicked after him. Jude turned around and ran his hand over the top of his head through his hair. He stepped back into the living room and sat down heavily on the sofa. Alex entered from the bedroom.

"He's gone?" she said with a tone of surprise.

"And he's not made much progress with the manuscript either," said Jude. "I... I just don't get him!" Alex went into the kitchen and poured a glass of fizzy apple juice. She sipped it and looked over the rim at him.

"You know how there can be two levels of co-operation here," she said. "The 'go slow'... until you make a proposition more attractive. Then the 'fast track' after you've oiled the wheels a little." She lifted her hand and rubbed her fingers and thumb together.

* * *

The setting sun inflamed the low clouds with red and orange hues as Jude stood on the balcony watching it. On the roof of the facing apartment block a man squatted on his haunches adjusting the position of a satellite dish towards the skyline. Another man tipped food from an old paint tin into a trough for his pigeons, which swung around him in fluid formations. Below them an old woman in black clothes hung out her washing on two lines beneath her window ledge and peered into the road below. Bunches of onions flaking off their brown skins hung behind her and firewood was stacked up high against her balcony wall.

Alex had laid their balcony table ready for dinner. There were small plates of black olives, pickled red peppers, a cucumber and tomato salad, chipped potatoes and some grilled pork chops placed on a white paper tablecloth that fluttered at the edges. He could hear her singing along to, *'Why does it always rain on me?'* on the kitchen CD player. He remembered her at a party near Clapham Common in the late-nineties, effortlessly parodying the dance movements to the 'Macarena' song and being drawn to her then, so at ease with things he was clumsy at. Then he heard a crash of cutlery. She came through shortly carrying a plate of bread rings dusted with sesame seeds. She was sucking her finger.

"Jude... can you *please* look at that drawer," she said. She was wearing a red T-shirt with 'Travis' printed on it and a pair of tatty, sky blue *All Star* baseball boots.

"I will," he said. "You're a bit *Brit Pop* tonight, aren't you?"

"*Travis* are post *Brit Pop*," she said with mild correction. "I don't know. I just wanted to wear what I wanted." Jude saw that she set the cutlery down listlessly. "I wore a floral print cotton dress over my jeans today... and the women at the group asked me why I was dressed like a gypsy? It's not the comparison... it's the way they seem to challenge and grumble about things. Why is my hair so? Why do I wear earrings from Peru? And how much did they cost? One of the pine cone baskets sold in the market,

Mirela's, but none of them were happy for her. Why was it hers and not theirs? Mirela was my favourite, they said, so I'd given her an advantage with the traders… I have no influence over whose work sells, Jude!" He watched her fork an olive aimlessly around her plate. "And another thing… when Julieta came in here and I gave her the Sat TV manual translation, you know what she said? When are we going to get some new furniture?" He could see that her eyes were glistening with water. "I sometimes feel like… a chicken in a dirty yard… being pecked at by the others." She let her fork drop to the plate.

"You're trying to help them… that's a good thing. But you can't always count on seeing their gratitude," he said wanting to comfort her before he added a grain of salt. "You know what Tolstoy said… if you are unhappy with your life, you can change it in two ways… either improve the conditions you live in or improve your inner spiritual state. The first isn't always possible but the second is… In the end, Alex, people need to go directly to the source of Grace for themselves."

"Jude, just *listen* to me! I don't want Tolstoy quotes," she said with increasing emotion in her voice. "And anyway aren't *we* His hands and feet?" A loud knocking on their front door intruded and continued insistently. Jude flashed her a knowing look. He got up and walked to the door. Julieta stood in the low light of the stairwell.

"My brother needs some help… with his American visa lottery application. Tell Alex to come over Jude," she said pointing a finger as if challenging him for her entitlement.

"Now is maybe not a good time, Julieta, I'm sorry. But I'll tell her about your brother's need," he said. She turned away and Jude closed the door. There was a loud knocking again. Jude reopened it.

"What about tomorrow morning?" said Julieta.

"I'll ask her to call you," he said. He closed the door and stepped into the bathroom. He set his glasses down on the sink's edge and splashed some water on his face. He noticed the plasterwork was sagging lower above the bath. He walked back through the living room to the balcony. "You heard that?" Alex nodded. "On second thoughts, maybe it is better not to delay. Let the tired people of New York… or Chicago have Julieta's family knocking on their doors!" He saw Alex look at him and then avert her eyes. "I'm sorry. I… should not have said that," he said running his hand back through his hair. The telephone began to ring. "Alex please… would you get that?" She brushed past him and into the living room. She lifted the receiver with her back to him.

"Yes… it is. Hello Bernard," she said glancing back at Jude. "Erm… could I get him to call you back! Fine. Yes, we are doing very well… I will." She put the receiver down. She stood without moving.

"I do know how you feel Alex… and thanks… dad would have been hard to deal with right now," he said. He walked over and put a hand on her shoulder. She turned around and he led her back to the balcony. He put some olives and a red pepper on her plate and handed it to her. "I fought with him once. Did I tell you?" he said. "He hit me… I have forgiven him for that now. It was really hard for him after mum was killed. He just could never find any solid ground to stand on... let alone the Rock of Ages."

"You said that he had a faith of a kind once," she said.

"He had, for a time, wanted to be a Methodist Minister... but they'd had the sense to show him the chapel door," he said. "That's when he became an RE teacher at a local comprehensive school... providing his rational, scientific explanations for every miracle and supernatural occurrence he came across in the Bible. He spent his professional career teaching young teenagers all the wrong things about someone he had never personally met." He chose an olive with his thumb and forefinger and lifted it up. "A single experience of the Holy Spirit would have dispersed all his arguments like a shotgun blast scattering rooks... Why does that not happen for so many people Alex?" He put it in his mouth.

"You've got to want it... more than ground you've staked out," she said with empathy now brightening her eyes. Jude lifted up his glasses and took out a little water from the corner of his eye.

"He gave me my middle name, you know?"

"Bartholomew!' she said stifling a smile.

"Don't laugh. A name like that gets you a lot of teasing in a Yorkshire playground!"

"He was a fine disciple. He went to Turkey... and later was skinned alive by brigands at the southern end of the Caspian Sea."

"Oh, thanks for that nice thought," he said laughing. "Jude ended his days in Northern Persia. I know... I know. Where I grew up, though, it was just, 'Hey Jude, don't make it bad...'"

"Take a sad song, and make it better…" she sang with her soft, pitch-perfect voice. The sound of a clarinet rose up from below their apartment building. They peered over the balcony and down to the dirt ground. Three musicians had gathered underneath someone's window. One struck a flat drum with the heel of his palm and the tips of his fingers *'bum clang-a-lang'* and the other began to squeeze a small accordion. The music had a touch of lament in a catchy sound of celebration. People came out on to their balconies or looked out of windows. A crowd came out onto the pavement by the Don espresso café. Alex lifted her hands above her head and began to click her fingers.

"That reminds me," she said. "We have an invitation to a wedding from someone in my women's group."

"We wouldn't wed like this in Yorkshire," he said broadening his accent for effect.

"You and Yorkshire! You are like that man in *My Big Fat Greek Wedding*… who thinks that Greece is the source of all civilisation. Only he had a point!" Alex laughed rising to the sport. "Whatever came out of Yorkshire… except puddings? Black ones… and those like Frisbees full of gravy."

"Sean Bean. He comes from Sheffield. He was fantastic as Boromir in *Lord of The Rings*." He reached to the table and lifted a bread ring up towards the clouds that now seemed lit from within by brilliant moonlight. "Tis a gift… a gift to the foes of Mordor! Why not use this Ring… against the enemy?"

"Hey, we should watch that again soon," she said.

Jude sat on the balcony long after they had cleared the dinner plates away and Alex had gone to bed. He thought about his dad and he prayed for him. He prayed that Alex would have the strength to labour gracefully amongst those who pecked, and that he would too. It was sometime after midnight, as the musicians played on below, that the sudden loud 'crack' of a rifle shot reverberated around the apartment blocks. He started and then drew a deep breath as his heartbeat quickened. The terrible sound of a dog howling out its last breath in the night followed. *Shënomadh*'s dog man had culled another stray.

Chapter 10

Outside the Blue Café under the shade of a silver birch tree Jude sat with Shpetim Gurbardhi watching the passers by on the high street. A horse cantered past pulling a cart piled high with rattling plastic kitchenware, buckets and brushes, and two gypsy girls sitting with their legs dangling off the back. A white car with four young men slunk low drove by, the windows wound down to protect them surely, he thought, from the Greek bouzouki music they'd amplified to a glass-shattering level. At a nearby table was a man with a grey bandit's moustache and a dark beret. He looks like he's walked out of the pages of history to join his comrades for a coffee, before hitching on his bullet belt and heading back to some Partisan mountain base, he thought.

Shpetim balanced his slim, chromed mobile phone on the marble table and slid his fingers down the edges before flipping it over. He held it like it was a thing of wondrous value, which he kept checking he still actually possessed.

"How much did your sunglasses cost you?" said Shpetim as they waited for their coffees.

"I don't remember... maybe £10," said Jude. "I can get you a pair the next time I go back to England." Shpetim grinned. "Did you try the Earl Grey tea I gave you?"

"To be truthful, I liked the box," he said with an apologetic look. "But the tea tasted of... cologne." He reached behind him to his suit jacket hung on the chair back and took out a sprig of dried, green plants wrapped in a blue plastic bag. "My mother sent you this. It's *çaj mali,* mountain tea."

"It looks like something you've confiscated," said Jude.

"Jude!" he said smiling through a look of reproof. He then leant closer. "There is a village near here which produces cannabis... it's like a plantation. Most of the residents are involved. So, we had to put a stop to it. Last year, the police approached it. The problem was the villagers had posted a sentry... a ninety-year-old woman with a semi-automatic weapon. What could we do? Send in the Special Forces? There would have been an outcry!"

"You should have sent in your grandad, Petrit. She might have been an old Partisan flame of his. That would have disarmed her," said Jude. Shpetim laughed. His phone rang. It was still set on Lionel Richie. He stood up and walked a couple of paces away from the table, then spun around on the ball of his right foot. Jude watched as Shpetim fixed his eyes on a detail of mottling in the table's white marble surface. His eyes were clear and set as it seemed information and calculations sped through his mind as he listened. He then quietly issued a series of terse instructions. At one point, when it appeared he was being countermanded, he drew his hand towards his chest with fingers and thumb pinched tightly together, and then splayed them out in emphasis. He sat down with a dour face.

"Ah, Shqipëria!" he said dropping his head. "Albania will never become Albania with Albanians in it!" He glanced at Jude. "Don't ask." Fredi the waiter brought two macchiatos in their blue cups and set them down on the table.

"Pizza," Shpetim said to him. Jude nodded quickly to Fredi so as not to draw him in. "I couldn't have borne this work without God Jude... the things we deal with. I thank Him that people like you came here."

"Was it through the children's group... that you came in to the church?"

"My parents sent me for the free gifts, what can I say?" he grinned. "As I stayed, though, the Bible studies just kind of sank in, until they took root and meant something." The lines on his forehead became less angular. His thick eyebrows straightened. It seemed to Jude that the light of the world flickered through his eyes. "And you, was it because of what happened with your mother?" Jude put a spoon of sugar in his coffee and stirred.

"Well, things seemed very bleak and broken after mum died, for sure," he said. "Then when I got to university... some of the literature I was reading didn't help. I went to the student parties... I liked them for a while. There was someone special too that I liked. I thought I could believe in her... but one night I stumbled upon her at a party with a university lecturer. There was a whole group of them sprawled on the floor drunk. It just intensified my sense of the sham, the corruption of life... in contrast to the high academic ideals. Do you know what I mean?"

"Jude. I'm an Albanian and you ask me if I understand corruption!" said Shpetim with a look of amusement. Jude smiled.

"I was thinking... What is there to admire or look up to? What is there that is good or true in this world? I felt whatever it was they were all suffering from, I was infected with it too... I was no saint." Jude spooned up the remaining sugar grains from the bottom of his cup and stirred again. "I was traipsing around the streets of York after a party in the early hours of the morning one time... and I came to the Low Ousegate Bridge."

"The one on the playing card?" said Shpetim.

"Yes... the one we will make the match with," said Jude staring into his macchiato. "I looked down at the River Ouse... black and sweeping under the bridge. I felt dead inside... so I might as well be dead in body. Thankfully, I'd read one good book at that time, *A Tale of Two Cities*. There's a character in there, Sydney Carton, who stands by the River Seine in Paris at dawn and hears the words of Christ. Well, I remembered them, and they just seemed to penetrate me in that moment...

'He who believes in me, though he were dead, yet shall he live!'

"So you left the bridge?"

"I walked towards the Minster... it's a big church there that dominates the skyline... and waited hours until it opened. Inside, I got down in the aisle and prayed. I had a wonderful experience there... a touch of something that welled up warm and enfolding on all sides... and through me... like a rain shower. I lay there until a verger told me to get up because I was disturbing the tourists." Shpetim was looking at him curiously, smiling. "Well, that was the moment my rudder moved, and I began to inch away from the busy shipping lane where most of the traffic is. And here I am... twelve years later, at a café table in your country." Fredi arrived and put down Shpetim's pizza on the table with cutlery and a ketchup bottle. Shpetim began to cover it with criss-crossing lines of the red sauce. He looked up and caught Jude staring.

"Ç' ke? What?" said Shpetim. Jude tried to feign an expression of nonchalance. "It is good you are here, doing what you are," he said.

"Not everyone sees it that way," said Jude.

"So, are you worried about the phone call?" said Shpetim. "Don't be. People make a lot of threats here."

*　*　*

Three metallic green taxi vans were lined up just below the Don Café as Jude walked across the dirt ground in front of his apartment block. He caught sight of Kristo standing by the first one with his attaché case tucked under his arm. He shook his hand as they met and they jumped onto the front seat and shuffled along.

"My auntie Fatmira and her husband Veli are at their house now... The neighbour, Valon he is called, is also working in his garden," Kristo added with a thinning of his lips.

"Let us hope that Valon will meet us," said Jude. "It takes about ten minutes to get to the village, doesn't it?"

"That depends on the driver," said Kristo with a little roll of his eyes. The driver, wearing sunglasses with little circular blue lenses, jumped into his seat and scrutinised Jude briefly. He slammed the door and leant out of the window shouting, "*Shënvogël...* come on. We are going there *direkt!*" He spun the wheel sharply in a U-turn and accelerated down to the main road. Jude looked around the man's dashboard and smiled to himself. There was a convex mirror for an enhanced rear view, a compass ball, an electric fan, a Sat Nav, a six-inch TV screen, a multi-format music player, and a framed photo of his family. Jude's eye was drawn to his CD stack, on top of which was 'Dare' by *The Human League*.

The driver braked sharply and eased the van down into a trough in the tarmac then swerved around the edge of an open manhole cover. He then drove past a long line of unrendered redbrick apartment blocks and into open country. Jude sat up keenly to watch the surroundings. A yellow moped straining under the weight of three youths droned towards them like an exhausted wasp. An obelisk with flaking white paint and a fading red star on it came into view and they passed it, and then the stark, concrete box-frame of a house without a single brick in it. Roadside stalls were laid out with rows of orange and green gourds or jars of golden honey that glowed in the sun. Stretching across the fields were villas in various stages of completion with walls in shades of pink, orange and lime, a smattering topped with blue flags flying the Democratic Party's swirling logo.

Jude took his glasses off to clean the lenses on the corner of his T-shirt, and cocked his head a little to look at the CD's artwork. The driver turned to scrutinise him again, and flipped open the cover and slotted the CD into the player. He said in English: "They made the transition from avant-garde… to commercially successful synthpop with this." Jude looked at him with some surprise.

"Oh, did they?" he said. "I remember them. I was about seven I think when this came out. Are they big in Albania?"

"Oh no," said the driver. "No one's ever heard of them… I did my degree in Computer Science at Sheffield Hallam University. There's a plaque on the wall in one of the computer suites there… marking the place they did their first performance. It was a student bar back then in 1978. Anyway, I got curious… and I bought some of their CDs. Now I love it! It's such a clean sound." He lifted up a finger and began to cue Jude in to the start of the song. Then he sang, *"You were working as a waitress in a cocktail bar… when I met yoo hoo…"* Jude began to laugh.

"And now you drive a taxi van?" he said.

"Well, there are no jobs in Computer Science in *Shënomadh*. And those people up in *Shënvogël* have no use for anything unless you can rear it for food or ride it into town," he said pointing disparagingly to the approaching village. Jude laughed again with the man as he lifted his finger once more to cue him in. *"Don't… Don't you want me,"* Jude sang along with him. Jude then turned around and began to conduct the rest of the passengers. *"Don't you want me baby?"*

As he and the driver sang together, Jude with his odd, squeaky voice and laughter, the exuberant fun of the moment spread and several passengers began to conduct back, smile and clap their hands along. As the van slowed into the village entrance, Jude heard Kristo say in a low voice, "So why didn't you stay in Sheffield!" They stopped in front of a stone hut half-painted in yellow with two metal pumps and a black oil puddle before it in the brown dust. It had a hand-painted sign reading 'Beni's Benzene'.

"My name is Defrim," he said as Jude gave him a 100 *lekë* note and climbed out.

"Mine's Jude… It's a good job you had your Sat Nav on for those 4km Defrim or we might have got lost," he said.

Defrim laughed. "I'll see you about!"

Jude looked at Kristo as they set off walking up the stony track into the village. He realised that he had not shared the levity.

"I'm sorry Kristo," he said. "I should have asked you sooner. Tell me a little about your auntie Fatmira and her neighbour… Valon you said?" Kristo gave a reserved nod. A flock of knobbly sheep shorn pink were driven over the road in front of them by a man flicking a twig. Kristo stopped.

"Before the communists sequestered the land… my uncle Veli's family owned it in this area," he said. "So did the neighbouring family… Valon's. When the land was redistributed in the Nineties, the neighbour said we were given land that was rightfully his."

"And was that so?" said Jude.

"We have the papers that give us legal entitlement… but that doesn't satisfy him. He keeps trying to move the boundary fence! My uncle Veli has pulled it down. They each throw rubbish over the fence on to the other's land. Recently, Valon's cow died… and he is accusing my uncle of poisoning it."

"Did he?" said Jude.

"There's bad feeling between the two families going back to the 1930s… Blerta, in the English class, is a relative of Valon's." The last of the sheep crossed their path nodding and bleating as they scrambled down a loose stone bank. They walked on up the track and turned to cross a little wooden footbridge over a ditch of black water filled with nappies and empty plastic bottles. They climbed up a narrow footpath between a mud wall and a fence of wood planks. A dog barked behind it and tried to push its snout through to snap at their ankles. They came out on another stony track and turned left.

"That's where my auntie lives," said Kristo pointing towards a well-kept, whitewashed stone house with a small apple orchard. A couple was waiting ahead at a gate in the orchard's stone wall.

"I'd like to go to Valon's house first," said Jude pausing to catch his breath. They stopped at the gate to greet them. Fatmira resembled Kristo, he could see, and held out her elbow for Jude to shake as her hands were wet. Veli's brown trousers hung shapelessly from his waste. He drew an old paint tin of white powder behind his back with both hands as he stood aloof.

"He lives at the other side," Kristo said to Jude. They walked further up the stony track and turned right across a patch of grass. Kristo came with Jude to the top of a rise and pointed down. To the left was a single standing wall of what looked like the ruin of an old Orthodox church. Close by, the red roof tiles of Valon's house were crumbling. The walls too had surface cracks and flaking whitewash. The garden was overgrown and a dishevelled stack of dirty hay slumped around a lopsided pole.

Jude strode down the bank alone to his garden gate. He called out, "*O, zotëri!*" There was a sound of boots crunching over stones and a man's head peered around the side of the house. Valon was in his fifties with a red face, bloodshot eyes and an electric blue baseball cap.

"My name is Jude… I work with the church here," he said.

"You are a foreigner?"

"English," said Jude. Valon beckoned him enter the garden and pointed for him to sit on a wooden bench.

"O, Kela. We have a visitor," he called out.

"I… know you have had some difficulties with your neighbours," said Jude.

"You are with them?"

"No, but I know their nephew, Kristo."

"Look at me," he said lifting up his cap and wiping his shirtsleeve across his brow. "I have no sons… My wife has been dead for three years. My daughter is unwell." He tapped a finger on the side of his head. "Mental problems." A girl wearing a knitted, orange waistcoat and pyjama bottoms came out barefoot. Her eyes followed the cracks in the floor as she poured two glasses of raki from a cloudy plastic bottle and served each of them. "They have taken my land," he continued, "from behind the hay stack to the top of the orchard. My grandfather planted it, not them! Leave the bottle Kela." As the girl left, Jude noticed a hunting rifle leant against the wall by the door. "They killed my cow," he said, "in that shed." As Jude turned to look he became aware of how the whole place stank of dung and animals. He lifted the raki under his nose to relieve it.

"It says 'an eye for an eye' in your Bible, does it not?" said Valon.

"Yes… it means a man should not go to jail for stealing… a watermelon for example. It is not an instruction to take revenge. Have you taken your daughter to see a doctor?"

"Who will help us? They have ruined me!" he said looking towards the orchard, his eyes filling with water as he squeezed the raki glass until his knuckles were white.

"Valon, listen to me," said Jude. "My Bible says… If a man strikes your cheek, turn to him the other… Pray for those who persecute you. Love your enemies… You shall not kill. God says, 'Vengeance is mine. I will repay.' These things are difficult, but their rejection is much worse!" Valon was looking at the floor. "I will speak to some people. We will get a doctor to see your daughter." The man looked up towards Jude, though it seemed his eyes did not see him.

Chapter 11

In the back room of *Laleli Teknik Servis* Sheref held in an eye glass tightly as he examined the magnified components in an opened Sony Ericsson. Osman came through with another phone in a plastic folder. He tossed it down, grunted and left. The television was set on the Al Jazeera English channel in the room's top corner, and he listened to news items as they caught his interest. The issue of foreign missionaries and Christians in the country came around again, and he put down the phone on the workbench to watch. "They could be working for Western Governments," a man in smart, dark suit was saying. "These churches may be fronts for their intelligence agencies... They may use their converts as agents and agitators after they leave..." What were these people doing in his country, he thought? What was it they were spreading? He had seen how they lived. Oh yes. He had been to their student parties with their drugs and low morals. This they thought fit to export here? The arrogance... the hypocrisy of it. These people are phoneys... I know! He put the eyeglass back in and tried to position a tiny microphone with a pair of tweezers but his hand was shaking. He let the phone drop to the workbench and the eyeglass fell there and shattered. They are undermining us, like Omer had said. They want to take our country from us... They should be stopped.

He left the service room twenty minutes later and set off walking quickly towards Aksaray. He'd seen the electronic sign outside the shop displaying '11.04am... August 16th... 26°C' but it felt much hotter. The streets were noisy with the rumbling of traffic. A short, mustard-coloured bus blasted its horn at him as he marched in front of it. A man came towards him swinging a silver tray with tea glasses on a chain shouting "chai chai chai", but Sheref did not meet his eyes. He'd seen a silk headscarf on a mannequin in a clothes shop window. It was sea blue with anchors on it. He wondered if his sister Hanife would like it for her birthday? For a couple of minutes, his mood lightened as he thought of her. He stepped inside and had it gift-wrapped. Back on the street a shoe shiner sitting on a wooden stool with an open case of laces beckoned to him. Porters towing two-wheeled carts piled high with bundles strode along the road almost keeping abreast with him. Another man squeezing juice from pomegranates with a chrome hand press called out to passers by from behind his stall and caught his ear. He had, though, not seen or heard from Omer since they drove over the Bosphorus Bridge with Kadir for the meeting. What had that all amounted to? He did not know.

Across the road was a row of blue public telephones in booths, and behind them a Call Shop displaying flags in the window of countries to which discounted international calls could be made. He entered it and walked to the rear where four numbered wooden cubicles held computers with Internet access. He pointed to them as he passed the shop assistant, and sat down in the one closest to the back. He turned his eyes away now from the bustle of the streets towards his own private panorama. There it seemed like a lid of darkening cloud stretched away in all directions to the horizon. The *Google* front page sat facing him on screen. He slid the mouse until the arrow was over 'maps' and clicked. He typed in 'Leeds' and zoomed the slider in on the streets he knew so well around the Burley area. His mind fell back there. He was in his second year. He'd started somehow to lose his focus. He'd got distracted in part by the crowd he'd hung around with at the Taksim Takeaway. Then, that incident late one night with those local thugs had happened.

He remembered too taking out the crisp, white envelope from the student pigeonholes with 'Mr. Sheref Dushman' printed on. He'd unfolded the letter inside expelling him for a third incident of plagiarism. Why had he done it? Why? The first time, he knew... he had just been lazy. The second he'd been late in starting the assignment and he'd needed a quick fix. All students plagiarised a little, he'd thought. Surely the professors knew that! They'd make allowances! The third time? He had wanted high grades. He had found the perfect answer ready-made on line: an innovative development in using touch-screen technology. It was brilliant. He could get an easy stride ahead too. But he'd been discovered... or snitched on.

The letter was from the PA of the Dean of the Engineering Faculty. The phrases rang out like a trial judge handing down a sentence of hard labour in some penal colony. *'He had received prior warnings... The submission in question was a crucial piece of work... Confidence had been lost... Standards needed to be maintained... Regrettably, the University Authorities had to notify him...'* He remembered his father exploding down the phone at him from Istanbul after he had telephoned the Vice-Chancellor to see if an 'understanding' could be reached. Did Sheref comprehend the humiliation he felt at this man's curt rebuttal? Fool!

Hot needles began to prick at his eyes. He inhaled sharply through his nose again and again until he his face contorted into a snarl he saw reflected in the computer screen glass. Now, he felt his emotions swirl into a charge of energy. He began to think and type furiously, hammering the 'enter' key into his searches, and consolidating his thinking in recent weeks.

He scoured Jude's mission agency's web page for information about him. He memorised his face and his wife's from photos there. He checked back with *Google* maps and located *Shënomadh*: it was about 30km to the north west of Lake Ohridsko... He would avoid airports: too many CCTV cameras and security personnel. He would go overland by train or bus, entering Albania at a remoter border point where security was probably slacker. He would scrutinise the route on his way there noting police checks and how passport and customs officials worked, for gaps, slack points and route alternatives if he needed them for his return. He began to search for times, connections and fares.

He looked up now to the flags of the nations in the front window. He would carry nothing incriminating. He would turn his mobile phone off. He would not use his visa card. He would pay cash and carry enough in a body-belt to buy his way out of trouble. He would say he was a tourist if questioned. He would select museums and sites of special interest and have them marked up in guidebooks. He would also take a camera and collect some postcards to furnish his story. He would have a simple disguise ready: a hat and some mirror-lens sunglasses. If an alternative return route became necessary, he could head for the mountains bordering Greece and slip back that way by night. Then he could come across the Aegean Sea by way of the islands paying or working for his passage on freighters or private yachts.

He closed the open windows on screen and sat back in the chair with a self-satisfied turn of his lip. It was mid-afternoon and the sunlight was bright out in the street. He felt hungry. He paid the assistant for the session and left. By the blue telephones he noticed a man selling portions of rice and chicken from a mobile glass cabinet. He walked over to him. The rice was sprinkled with sultanas and a few almond flakes. The man's eyes looked oriental, but not quite.

"Where are you from?" said Sheref tossing two lira coins in his tin.

"Turkmenistan… Ashgabat," said the man.

"You're a long way from home."

"You go where you have to," he said with a stoic shrug. Sheref looked at him. He finished his plate of rice and threw another coin in his tin.

"You're right," said Sheref and he went.

* * *

With his cheek pressed deeply into the pillow Jude lay on his front. He could not get into a comfortable position. He reached for his mobile phone on the bedside cabinet and checked the time. It was 4.08am. He held its lit face over Alex and saw she was sleeping deeply. He slid it under the pillow and dropped his head. He thought about how the culture had worn her down as she tried to help the women economically as well as spiritually. His mind moved to Spiro: would Mehmed's book be ready for the biennial conference? It drifted to Valon's daughter, Kela, in *Shënvogël* and if the local doctors would really help her. He spun over and lay on his back. He heard a man singing drunkenly down in the stairwell, and somewhere the raised voices of a couple rowing. A taxi van rumbled down May 5TH Street, hunting for passengers for its early morning Tirana run.

On the dressing table was a photo in a clip frame that Alex had taken of light shafts on the grey sea off the cliffs of Bournemouth, where her parents had run a bed and breakfast establishment. Streetlight came through a gap in the curtains and reflected off its glass surface giving a point for the eye to fix on. In that moment, the noises around seemed to fade down. The curtain fluttered by the open window. The particles of air seemed almost charged with something. Alex turned over and sat upright.

"Jude... I just had a dream," she said breathily. "It was very vivid. Can you get me a glass of water?" Jude kicked off the sheet on his side and felt the floor with his feet for his slippers. He switched on the side lamp and watched Alex push herself back against the wall. She wiped her face with her hands, her magnified shadow moving against the orange glow on the wall. He felt his way through to the kitchen in the darkness and fumbled for a glass in the cupboard. He filled it from the tap and returned. He handed it to her and sat down on the edge of the bed. "So what was it?" he said.

"Wait," she said. She was breathing heavily. She drank several gulps and then caught her breath. "There was a man trying to wrap himself in a flag... as the breeze seemed to lift it off him. It was a red one... but not the Albanian flag. It had a white crescent and a star on it."

"It's the Turkish flag," said Jude.

"I also saw one of those blue glass 'evil eye' charms they sell in the market here. Only it was big, like a moon... and it was riding through the night as it passed over the lights of towns below it... Alexandroupoli, Xanthi..." She seemed to pause midsentence.

"Those are Greek towns," he said.

"There was a man looking at a name on a computer screen... It was your name Jude."

"The same man with the flag?"

"They had no clear form. I don't know." Jude ran his hand back through his hair. "And what do you make of it?" he said as he looked at her. She held her gaze forwards as if looking beyond their bedroom. She cast him an anxious glance sideways.

"Let me pray. That's all I can recall of it," she said. She lowered herself under the sheet and closed her eyes. Jude lay down on the bed beside her. He felt her reach for his hand and he slid it to her. He turned off the side lamp and looked up at the ceiling. He knew that God had used dreams to speak to Alex in the past. He remembered her 'Clapham Junction' dream when she came to faith, but what did this one mean? Did it mean anything at all? How on earth was he to know? When he fell asleep, before Alex, sometime around 5am, the dawn light had crept into the room.

Chapter 12

Jude left the apartment just after 8am. He'd made an instant coffee for himself and Alex. He'd taken out his walking boots and packed a small rucksack with water, boiled eggs, apples and chocolate. He'd kissed her on the nose as he'd left. He was heading for the mountains behind *Shënomadh* to seek God: to pray. He strode through the cobbled streets close to Shpetim's house, and up a dirt track that wound steeply towards the first ridge of hills visible from the town centre.

The track was smooth enough for a car for the first 2km, and he soon found a steady rhythm to his stride that freed his mind to focus on a prayer.

"Lord, I commit this morning to seeking you… I bring to you all the concerns of my heart. I lay myself open to hear from you. Amen," he said loudly and unselfconsciously as he swung his legs towards the solitude. He looked back across the rooftops of the grid of communist-era apartment blocks below him to see if he could pick out his own. He flapped his arms above his head in case Alex was watching.

A long-slumbering feeling of freedom and exhilaration from the landscape arose in him, and he remembered a walk with Jack in the Yorkshire Dales through The Valley of Desolation to Simon's Seat. He thought of that winter trudge across the dark, peaty moorland and Jack racing ahead with no breakfast in him but some snack bar - probably a *Curly Wurly*. He thanked God for the Albanian climate. The sky was a dome of azure and the air was still, though fresher than it had been in recent August weeks. The slopes were covered with a dry, straw-like grass and the faint sound of goat bells came across them. A lizard flipped up on a nearby stone.

He took a track that forked off up a pass through the hills before it continued down into the next valley. It was passable only by pack mules and those on foot. The ground between the clumps of oak scrub was covered with rocks and stones of all sizes, and a stream now trickled down through them. He pressed on, occasionally running up rocks and jumping across gaps, until he came to an open space with a fording point where the mud was caked hard but for a thin, dark stripe in the centre. He sat on a low rock and took out his bottle of water and an apple.

Shortly, he heard the whinny and clumping of an animal, and a tall, heavy-limbed man came into the opening leading a chestnut mule saddled with a creaking wooden frame. The man did not see Jude until he let the animal drink. He had a face that looked like it had remained frozen in position after a bank-robber's stocking had been torn off it, thought Jude.

"*Mirëdita!*" he called out.

"Good day to you!" replied Jude thinking he seemed friendly enough.

"What are you doing up here?" he said raising a hand quizzically.

"Walking… and you?" said Jude.

"I'm going to cut firewood," he laughed. He took a few paces towards Jude and then he noticed his expression change. He reached into his trouser waist, drew a pistol, and pointed it towards him. A single round cracked out. Jude saw something arch up into the air from the corner of his eye. He dropped his bottle of water. The man strode past him quickly and stood looking at the ground.

"Snake," he said. "You need to keep your eyes open up here son!" Jude's heart was thumping.

"What kind of snake?" he gasped jumping up and walking tentatively over to the man.

"A poisonous one," said the man wrestling off the branch of a bush and then lifting up the limp, brown creature with it at arm's length. The bullet had blasted half its head off, but the remaining eye seemed to stare at Jude with a cold defiance. He shuddered as the man flung it over the bush. They sat down on the rocks and chatted for a while. Jude tossed over an apple to the mule and it felt it with its huge lips then crunched it.

"You're a fine shot!" said Jude.

"Police," he said. "See that rock up there?" He pointed the pistol and another round cracked out of it. There was a 'ping' and a 'whiz' and the bullet thudded into the dirt by Jude's feet sending up a little squirt of dust. The man slapped his thigh and roared with laughter. Jude thought, he has saved me from hospital to put me back there with a ricochet.

The man took his mule by the rope reins and Jude followed him. They kept to the course of the stream up through the pass until it opened out over a dry, grey stony valley beyond. A pine forest clung to the facing valley wall, which was topped by a cairn-shaped pinnacle of rock. Further to the right along the same ridge, perhaps 2km away, was a towering, white, concrete cross set on its own summit. The path wound down onto the valley floor and then divided there with a separate path up to each point. The shadow of a single large cloud now edged across it. He decided he would head for the pinnacle. He parted company with the policeman as they climbed through the pine forest.

"Whistle for me if you meet any brown bears," said the man laughing.

"No trick shots… and I'll do that, okay?" said Jude.

At the base of the pinnacle he pulled himself carefully up onto a rock with the branches of a red sloe berry bush. He traversed the side towards a ledge he had seen, and threw his rucksack onto it. He sat down there with his back resting on the rock face and looked out over the view. A patchwork of greys and browns stretched out across the rough, undulating landscape. A mountain with a dome-like top was crowned with a wispy tiara of cloud perhaps 30 km away.

He took out his food and began to nibble as he thought and prayed there intermittently. He remembered a conversation he'd had in the past with Alex. 'Look… Joseph had dreams… and so did Nebuchadnezzar, but you can't take every nightmare as divine revelation. It's the way the subconscious mind sifts through experiences and feelings...' he was saying. And she had not tried to counter the argument, nor had she indulged in any self-satisfaction later. Without Daniel's gifting, what am I to make of last night's, he thought? Had those boys on the Istanbul waterfront actually reported them to the police? Had some official been checking up on them? But why the Greek towns? Why his name particularly on the computer screen? Maybe she was frightened about what had happened to Jaap and it was all getting mixed up. Even if a little Turkish dust had been disturbed, what matter? He had no plans to return, but Jaap did, so he would mention it to him. His real concerns were the threat on the phone, Spiro and production deadlines for the book.

He took out his pocket New Testament and Psalms. He felt drawn to read *Psalm 27*, which he shouted out loud:

'The Lord is the stronghold of my life - of whom shall I be afraid? For in the day of trouble he will keep me safe in his dwelling; he will hide me in the shelter of his tabernacle and set me upon a high rock...'

He then read sections of *Psalm 139*.

'O Lord, you have searched me and you know me... you perceive my thoughts from afar...'

"Speak!" he shouted. He sat waiting, watching, listening... He caught sight of a possible golden eagle hovering on a thermal way down the ridge, but nothing rose within him. There is no sudden strong wind for me today, he thought, no shaking ground, no fires flaring up, nor even a still quiet voice in my mind! Yet, I know I have been heard.

He smelt a difference in the air. Drops of water struck his cheek and he turned his head upwards to see that dark clouds had come over from behind. He gathered up his eggshells and chocolate wrappers and stuffed them in his rucksack. He slid his way around the rock surface to the sloe berry bush and jumped down. The shower was now coming on heavily. Large drops of water, though not cold, pattered on his shoulders and soaked his back. He ran under the canopy of pine trees and back down the path slipping on the carpet of soft, brown needles.

A small, stone hut with whitewashed walls, an Orthodox chapel, offered more shelter. He leapt through the entrance door and sat down on a stone ledge inhaling deeply to catch his breath. He brushed the water off his hair and then wiped the lenses of his glasses. The room smelt of burnt wax and musty incense. A single candle flickered in a red glass holder before a row of icons. As his eyes adjusted to the darkness he made out the bearded form of a saint. He had large, round eyes and a gaunt face and there was a fishing net and a cockerel in scenes around the border. The thought came to Jude that Simon Peter, the rock, the first and eldest of the disciples, had died a martyr in Nero's Coliseum. A peal of thunder rumbled out.

* * *

Sheref sat at a café table facing the glistening pastries arranged behind a glass counter. A Turkish coffee sat before him on the cream plastic table but he had not touched it. Omer had telephoned him asking for a meeting. What would it lead to this time? More of Kadir's provocations? He fiddled with his mobile phone as he waited. The back light was worsening; he must take a look at it. He shuffled his feet a little under the table. Two young men serving the customers had looked at him twice now. What was it? He looked at his clothes and his reflection in one of the mirrors that rimmed the walls all around. He smoothed his cropped brown hair backwards and glanced at the small scar on his forehead above his right eyebrow. He noticed the skin around his eyes was grey and sunken, and his face looked thinner and drawn of colour.

Behind the glass counter were metal trays of baklava, spinach and egg rolls, golden-brown bread rings, biscuits powdered with icing sugar and piles of white boxes for customers to take them away in. He was unappetised by them, though, as the nerves jangled in his stomach. His eyes followed the mirrors to a door that led to a kitchen at the rear. There he saw the reflection of Omer entering off the busy Ataturk Boulevard. He turned around as Omer slid along the cream plastic upholstery to sit beside him at the table. Sheref nodded minimally to him.

"What will you have?" said Omer inclining his head towards the glass counter.

"Nothing," said Sheref.

"Take something. Be natural," said Omer, his eyes languidly taking in all his surroundings.

"Baklava... with ground pistachio," said Sheref.

"So how have you been? You look... tired," said Omer and caught the counter man's eye before pointing to one of the metal trays.

"Do your friends want to tire me more with another drive?" he said. The waiter arrived with some pieces of baklava on a saucer and a coffee for

Omer, who waited for him to leave before speaking. Sheref felt something tap his thigh. He glanced under the table to see a white envelope resting there.

"There is a message for you inside," Omer whispered almost inaudibly. Sheref pulled back the flap and on the top of a thick wad of fifty euro notes was a typewritten message. He drew it out. *'Prove your capabilities, and you will be given important assignments for your country. Gazi.'* "Now pass it to me." Omer took the slip of paper and folded it into his pocket. A smile began to spread through Sheref's feelings though his face remained unmoved. His appetite was returning. He put a piece of baklava in his mouth and licked his fingers.

"Did you decide on your route?" said Omer.

"Through Greece," said Sheref.

"*They...* do not give visas away, you know," said Omer. "When you're ready... give your application and passport to me." Sheref nodded. Omer drank half of his coffee in one gulp and set the cup down. "*Iyi şanslar,*" he said coldly. He stood up and left.

Sheref sat sipping his coffee. He took a second baklava and savoured it. He ran his thumb and his forefinger around the outside of his mouth to clean the syrup off. He saw himself now like a fighter rising up off the ring floor in Edirne, oiled and stepping forwards.

"Oh friend. Did you finish your coffee?" one of the waiters called over as he dried a cup with a tea towel. "Old Yagmur will read your cup for a lira." He pointed to the door in the café rear. "Just take it through." Why not? thought Sheref riding on the crest of the moment.

A woman wearing a grey headscarf and thick, black eyeliner squatted on a stool next to the sink. Her brow trickled with sweat as she scraped the burnt pastry scraps off the bottom of a metal tray with a spoon. She eyed him shrewdly as he entered with his cup, beckoned him closer, then wiped her hand on her dress and held it up to him. She looks like an Azerbaijani, he thought. He put a lira there and then the cup. She lifted it close to her face. Her eyes widened and she gave a startled little grunt then pulled his hand roughly towards her and examined his palm.

"A guide is helpful to the tourist, is it not so?" she said archly. Sheref felt oddly penetrated by her words. What had this seer understood? He stared at her, suddenly feeling like a section of some inner wall was breached. "Do not close your heart. Open it! Listen to the voice… Take this. Protect yourself from evil." She held up a disc of blue glass that had a large, white tear drop in the centre filled with a light blue disc and a dark blue one in centre of that. It was hung on a keyring. He reached for it but she drew it back. "One lira," she said holding up a bony finger.

"Put your finger down hag… before I snap it off," hissed Sheref. He threw a coin on the floor and snatched the keyring. Her lips parted around the black crevice of her mouth and a mirthless laugh echoed out.

Chapter 13

As Jude and Alex climbed the stairs inside Jaap's apartment block their footsteps echoed in the stairwell. Jude noticed they were made of a speckled marble with an orangey tinge and he smiled to himself. The block had been built in the last five years and offered a much more agreeable living environment than the communist-era ones, he thought. Jaap's front door was of a light-coloured, varnished wood. He rapped on the shiny brass doorknocker and pulled a comic face at Alex as they waited.

The latch was turned with several 'clanks' and Jaap van Halen opened the door and gestured them enter his hall. In his early-thirties, with a thin, blonde moustache and a small paunch, his high hairline offered no cover for the gash he'd sustained in Istanbul. It was still red and sore and drew Jude's eye immediately.

"Good afternoon Jaap! The wounds His chosen ones have taken for His sake are the medals of honour in heaven," said Jude trying to bring a smile to the

Dutchman's face. "The writer Rick Joyner said that… you should reckon that one a George Cross." There was a flicker of amusement below his moustache. As they changed into house slippers Jude noticed Jaap's beloved, brown leather pilot's jacket hanging up, and his wife Odguda's stout, brown leather shoes, which she wore religiously, even into the summer months. He remembered how he had been astonished that she had never heard of the legendary rock guitarist whose name she now shared. But he had liked Jaap from the moment he had chanced a little air-guitar in jest, and Jaap had replied with a touch of his own fingerwork up and down an imaginary fret board, out of sight of his wife. She had a muscular neck and arms, was sweet in nature, but frowned in disapproval a lot, he thought.

Odguda came through from the lounge with their three-year-old boy Uys following.

"*Hallo* Alex. *Hallo* Jude. Come in," she said. "I am just making some coffee for us. We brought it from Amsterdam… maybe you will like it." Jude followed Alex through to their lounge and sat on the couch. Alex gave her the sultana and walnut flapjacks she'd made, and went with her to the open kitchen area. Jude liked their house. It was clean, well-ordered and peaceful with its teak wood furniture, a homely watercolour of windmills by a canal, and a print of Rembrandt's *Return of the Prodigal Son* on the wall.

"I brought two packs of *UNO* cards for us to play with," said Jude taking them from the side pocket of his cargo pants.

"Good man Jude," said Jaap patting him on the shoulder.

"Play *UNO*? Is it gambling, Jaap?" Odguda called from their kitchen.

"*Nee*," said Jaap, a pained expression glancing across his face.

"No euros necessary Odguda," Jude called back. "But if I win… it will cost you a packet of *stroopwafels*." Uys ran up and stood by Jude, holding out a blue, wooden toy aeroplane for him. His little eyebrows were blonde to the point of invisibility like his father's moustache. Jude got down with him and drew the plane backwards on the floor before releasing it to shoot off across the tiles straight under a cabinet.

"*Papa*," he said with a frown just like Odguda's. "The *Engelsman* has lost my aeroplane!" He ran to the cabinet and lay on his side peering beneath it.

Jude turned to Jaap smiling and mentioned the girl Kela in *Shënvogël*, and if he had any Dutch contacts that might help her. He nodded thoughtfully.

"How've you been? What are your thoughts about Turkey now?" said Jude shortly, pushing the glasses up the ridge of his nose. "I heard there were more incidents there."

"Jude… in recent years, there has been a wave of persecution there. That I knew before we went," he said sitting back and letting out a sigh through pursed lips. "Church buildings have been vandalised and sprayed with graffiti… Petrol bombs have been placed and ignited to intimidate worshippers… Missionaries and pastors have received threats by phone and letter. A pastor awoke one morning to find a huge, red swastika painted on his apartment door… another had his son kidnapped." Uys ran back with his plane and lay over his father's lap. "Go help *mama* with the biscuits," he said rubbing his hair softly and pointing him bodily towards the kitchen. "And it gets worse... vigilante groups have threatened church workers. Some have been assaulted too... I thought we'd be fine by the ferry piers." He paused as if remembering, and moved a hand towards his head before suppressing the urge. "Other religious minorities there have not escaped it either. A few years ago, a young man of sixteen... shot a Catholic priest at his church in a town on the Black Sea. Recently, a Turkish pastor, a German mission's worker, and a new Turkish convert were murdered at a Christian publishing house in Malatya by a group of young men. I fear there may be more killings there..."

"I didn't realise the extent of it," said Jude.

"The Turks are a fine people," he said shaking his head. "It grieves me that this has come from elements in their society... but it's by no means the worst place for such things. There are maybe... thirty countries where the climate is more severe."

"Jaap," said Jude working up to the thing he felt strangely awkward about saying. "Alex has had this dream... a couple of nights ago." He recounted what she had told him. Jaap sat quietly thinking for a few moments. Then he shrugged his shoulders.

Alex came through with flapjacks and *stroopwafels* on a plate.

"Come on you men... Make yourselves significant!" she said. Odguda followed her with the coffeepot and cups. Jude poured. He sipped a mouthful and coughed.

"That's some good strong stuff!" he said. Jaap placed a *stroopwafel* on top of his steaming cup.

"It softens the syrup. Go on, try it," he said.

"Right," said Jude dealing the *UNO* cards around the coffee table. "The object of the game is to get rid of your cards first. Play your action cards... the 'Skip' card, the 'Reverse' card, the 'Draw 4' card... to foil the other players!" Ten minutes later, Odguda slipped her last card onto the central pile and looked up.

"I've won!" she shouted, and thumped Jude on the arm. Jude rubbed it. She packs a punch, he thought.

"She's cleaned the floor with us Jaap!" he said with a wink.

"*Ja, ja,*" he said a little wearily. Odguda stacked up the side plates and carried off the coffeepot to brew a re-fill. Uys followed her swinging on her skirt.

"Jaap. Do you mind me asking?" said Jude lowering his voice. "Odguda. She seems quite... strong. Does she work out?"

"Only on my opinions," he said with a rare smile.

"You didn't tell me how you've been," said Jude.

"I've been fine... but she's been troubled by what happened in Istanbul. She keeps checking on-line vacancies for pastors in the Amsterdam area. She thinks that maybe we need to take time out with Uys... change focus even."

"But your heart is not in that, is it?" said Jude. Jaap looked at his hands. "Maybe she is right... about the break at least," he said.

* * *

Sheref rode up an escalator inside the Kanyon Shopping Mall pressing frustratedly at the buttons on his mobile phone. The number finally took and he heard Hanife's ringing.

"Are you coming?" she answered.

"I'm here... where are you in this place?" he said.

"I'm at the Burger King. It's on level... K1." Sheref slipped it back in his pocket and looked all around him as he rose. Crowds of shoppers were descending on his left carrying their new purchases in smart, plastic shopping bags emblazoned with designer brand names. The sound of amplified pop music was mixed with the shouts of children and the public address system declaring some one-day-only special offer. As he stepped off on the next level he noticed a shop with an amazing display of Turkish delights. He quickly chose bars of a glassy green type filled with hazelnuts and the assistant boxed up two kilos for him. It was expensive, but why not use up some of his euros on this, he thought? He strode past a row of display boards for *Turkcell*, where three sales girls were hovering with clipboards. They were so pretty and he felt a loneliness stab through him. One stepped towards him, hesitated and spun back to her colleagues. He snatched a free promotional backpack and left.

He peered in through the entrance of the burger restaurant and saw Hanife sitting with a group of her friends. He waved and beckoned her to come. He didn't want to join the group. He remembered turning seventeen... the optimism of the time. That was four long years ago now. They were young things. What did he have in common with them? Hanife ran up smiling and he gave her the box of sweets.

"Happy Birthday!" he said. "Let's get a coffee at the Starbucks."

"Come in and join us. Stay with us," she pleaded. "You know Fazil… and Shelale, come on!" He refused. She waved back at them and shrugged her shoulders. They walked together along one of the mall's vast curving walkways and down in an elevator. A man could get lost here, he thought. They crossed a wide plaza into the café and sat on a dark leather sofa. Sheref went to the counter and paid for two caffelattes, hers with a shot of amaretto flavouring. He knew what she liked. When he returned, she was lifting up the flap of the box of Turkish Delight. She looked at him, her brown doe-eyes wide with joy. She was wearing a sky-blue T-shirt with matching plimsoles and black flares. He put down the coffees and sat opposite. Her headscarf was pulled off and resting down the back of her head.

"Oh… so you go to Burger King and Starbucks and suddenly you're emancipated! Ah Hanife, Hanife," he said teasing her as he touched her on her button nose. "I've got just the thing to go with your T-shirt." He handed her the gift-wrapped headscarf he'd bought in Aksaray. She tore off the paper, draped the scarf over her head, and turned her face sideways imitating a model's pose.

"I like the anchors," she said. She then folded her slim, brown arms on the table surface and rested her chin on them.

"Why do you stay out so late?" she said. "Why don't you eat at home with us in Merter anymore?"

"You know why!" said Sheref tearing open a sugar sachet and tipping it into his latte.

"*Baba* will come around in time. You know how stiff-necked he is," she said. "Please… go see him at the Bazaar."

"He was always distant from us Hanife… and his expectations sky high. I was just a stepping stone to his aspirations in the West… that sank. And mum… wrapped up with spending his money… or her women friends. There can be no return to the way things were. There is no bridge back… I'm lost to him, now," he said, suddenly feeling the needles prick at the backs of his eyes. He tried to suppress it. She reached out a hand and stroked his cheek. "I'm going away soon. I won't be around for a while."

"Back to England?" she said.

"No… you remember how *baba* said his family name came from the *Arnavutlar*, way back. Well, I'm going to go there. But don't tell anyone."

"Albania. Why are you going *there*?"

"A break… tourism," he said looking down at the torn sachet on the table surface. He could not look at her and lie. He lifted his gaze slowly to meet hers. The birthday happiness was ebbing from her face.

"Look at your eyes Sheref," she said. "Have you been sleeping? Your shirt is dirty. You look different, more hunched over… You've bitten down your finger nails." She reached to touch his fingers.

"I'm okay," he said slamming his fist down on the table startling her. Other customers turned to look at them. "*Ben iyiyim*," he said in a softer tone. "I'll… call you."

"When are you going?" she said, a tear glistening in the corner of her eye.

"Friday evening…"

Chapter 14

Shpetim was leaning over his wooden gate as Jude strolled up the cobbled street to his house in the fading evening light. He greeted Jude with a strong handshake and touched his cheek to Jude's on both sides. He lifted Jude's black bag from his shoulder and insisted on carrying it into the yard.

"*Ç' kemi?* How's the book coming along?" said Shpetim.

"Well… I'm ready. Spiro, I don't know," said Jude. Shpetim smiled at him knowingly. Skender, Luan and *xhaxhi* Petrit were sitting at chairs around the table, and Luan stood up and moved one into position for him. Mrs Gurbardhi was flicking water from a plastic bottle around the flagstones to dampen down the dust. She wiped her hands on her pink pinafore and smiled at Jude before saying "Good evening" in English. A raki bottle and eggcup-sized glasses were spread around the tabletop. Skender started to fill a glass for him. Jude declined, but he insisted and poured him one anyway. Jude sat down with them and they chatted.

Mrs Gurbardhi came down the steps of the house carrying her large, round, metal tray. She balanced it on the edge of the table and began to lift off the saucers of *mezet* she had prepared. There was white cheese, olives, a green salad, and some sliced liver fried with oregano.

"I have prepared some *kukurec*. Do you like it?" she said.

"I'd like to try it," said Jude. She watched eagerly as Jude pushed his fork through a piece and put it in his mouth. It was a chewy, offal-like substance, which he did not take to. "I didn't taste the like of it before," he said having searched quickly for a phrase that would not offend. She nodded contentedly and went back up the steps.

"Did you bring one of those films for grandad Petrit?" said Shpetim.

"Yes… just pass me my bag," said Jude. He lifted out his laptop and set it on the table top before rotating it to face Petrit. "It's called *Ice Cold in Alex*. Anthony Quayle plays a South African soldier… in the Libyan Desert." Jude placed a piece of white cheese in his mouth whilst he waited for the laptop to start up. He chose a scene where Quayle, John Mills and others were trying to push an old ambulance up a huge sand dune. Petrit leant in close to scrutinise it.

"Is it him?" said Shpetim eagerly. All eyes were on the old Partisan.

"I don't know," he said. "It's been a lifetime since I saw him. We had walked all the day to get to the cave…"

"Yes, yes... We know the story," interrupted Luan. "Look hard!" Petrit lifted his stick and jabbed at the screen. A smile began to form on his face.

"Will you look at that!" he said. "I remember... the eyes." Jude sat back in his chair smiling. Shpetim laughed and put his hand on the old man's shoulder.

"Go get your souvenirs!" said Shpetim.

Petrit shuffled back down the house steps ten minutes later with a frayed, brown envelope, which was passed to Jude. He lifted out a black and white publicity photo of Joan Fontaine. It was in good condition except for a diagonal tear from the top left corner halfway to the centre. He tipped the envelope sideways and a gold sovereign rolled into his palm. It was in near mint condition and had Queen Victoria's head on it. Jude ran his thumb softly over its face.

"Where did you hide these... all those years?" said Jude thinking they could have cost him internment. Petrit touched his nose.

Jude nibbled on the *mezet* with the others and listened to the table chat. Skender poured himself another raki. Luan was showing off his new LG phone.

"Did it fall off the bottom of a Greek lorry?" Shpetim asked his brother.

"We usually say *back* Shpetim," said Jude.

"Bottom, back... it's stolen," said Shpetim.

"You're saying that because it's better than yours!" said Luan beginning to puff up his chest.

"Shpetim, get your cards. Let's play that game you like... *spathi* is it?" said Jude trying to steer them away from another wrestle in the bush.

Shpetim produced a pack of cards and began to deal them out. It was a mixed selection of different packs Jude had brought for him, and the pictures were of more interest to Shpetim than playing the game. He quizzed Jude. *How many litres of petrol does this Triumph Spitfire need to go 100 km?* —I don't know. *What rank of soldier wears this hairy hat?* —It's a bearskin. It's for regiments that guard the Queen. *What kind of meat do they serve in this 'Dog and Duck' restaurant?* —It's a pub, Shpetim.

Jude leant back in his chair. He looked up through the vine canopy to see a southerly star, maybe Jupiter, blink. Insects were flying in a cloud around a white streetlight a hundred metres away. A dog barked from the depth of its big stomach and whined beyond the yard wall. He checked the time on Luan's phone; it was 11.06 pm; he thought he should be going. Skender poured himself another raki. He took out one of his *Karelia Slims* cigarettes and lit it. He looked heavily at Jude.

"You say you are here in our country to witness to God, Jude... but where was God for the Albanian people all those years?"

"He was present, *xhaxhi* Skender," said Jude, "but... you know... the communists prevented His servants from working here, particularly after '67. They had no freedom to come and go again until the Nineties."

"Freedom," he scoffed. "Look at this 'freedom' we have? Freedom to throw our rubbish in the streets? Freedom for our young women to show as much skin as they can? Freedom for employers in restaurants to pay people 100 euros a month... for seven-day-weeks? These things too the communists prevented."

"*Babi*. You would not go back to those days, would you?" said Shpetim. "Don't let nostalgia cloud your sense about the way things were… There is a hope beyond these times. Won't you just listen to me… once… when I try telling you about it? Before it's too late!" Skender raised his hand to brush off the suggestion. Shpetim stood up toppling his chair over backwards and then strode off up the steps. The front door of the house slammed behind him in an angry full stop. Luan got up and went after his brother.

Skender's shoulders hung low. He swayed a little and his red eyes moved sluggishly towards the bottle. He poured himself another glass of raki.

"My boy Shpetim is right. You know how we old people get sentimental for the past… Let me tell you something that may shock you Jude," he said. "There was an old Orthodox church at a village nearby… *Shënvogël* it is called. We ordered the villagers there to help us… They were too afraid to refuse! We had our own Cultural Revolution here, you know?" He drew and exhaled cigarette smoke like the figure of the north wind on some old map. "I remember seeing the frescoes across the little, domed ceiling… the carved wooden screen inside. I thought how artfully they had been made. But I was zealous in carrying out my ideological beliefs. We believed they had kept us mired in backwardness. *Xhaxhi* Enver had declared we were to be the world's first atheistic state…" He lifted his glass to his lips and tossed his head back to slug it down. "We smashed the windows with the butts of our rifles. We tossed in hand grenades. We started a fire with branches and petrol... The roof tumbled in with a great crash. When I heard that sound... I had a feeling on that day that it was a shameful thing we had been ordered to do. I... have never told a foreigner this." He did not look at his father, Petrit. He was looking at Jude. He was blinking.

"May I tell you something too... *xhaxhi* Skender," said Jude. "When I was seventeen... I played around sometimes with a group of boys outside a Fish and Chip shop in my home city. One evening, the son of a local vicar came along... He was bullied regularly at the school... everyone knew he was a soft target... The boys I was with mocked him and pushed him around. They stole his food, threw his chips at him and someone... put mushy peas up his nose and smoothed them with a chip fork. I was there laughing at him too. The boy suffered from depression, and some years later took his own life." Jude lifted out his wallet from his back pocket. From the pouch for coins he took out a nail. It was metal grey with a square shaft and a tapered head like the type used to shoe a horse. "I carry this," he said. "It reminds me that my sins too nailed Christ to his cross... and there he forgave me too." Jude lifted the raki bottle up as if to pour himself a drink and slipped it down by the leg of his chair. "There now, we have both made our confessions..."

* * *

Jude unfastened the handle on his balcony window, rested his elbows on the ledge, and drew the night air into his lungs in invigorating draughts. It was warm and tasted a little of toasted peppers.

In the surrounding apartment blocks residents had closed their curtains to create a patchwork of illuminated squares in a black backcloth. Along a distant mountain road a line of white lights hung like bunting. Two rubbish bins had been set ablaze below and thin plumes of smoke rose up from them. A car with a broken headlight drove slowly down May 5TH Street and turned right at the bottom.

The dinner of fresh, stir-fried vegetables and rice he had cooked was sitting comfortably in his stomach. Alex was clattering the plates as she finished off the washing up and singing in her deepest voice, '*Swing low, sweet chariot. Coming for to carry me home…*' He smiled as he remembered her singing it in the worship group in that disused church building in Clapham, where 'The Safe House' had been established. He thought briefly of the dream that led her to that fellowship and then their meeting there back in '98.

"Jude? You can't see anyone unusual down below tonight, can you?" she called over to him.

"It's dark, why?"

"I saw a man standing in a doorway next to the Don Café... grey shirt... black, well-shone shoes…"

"What's unusual about that?"

"Nothing concrete… anyway, are we watching *The Fellowship of the Ring* tonight?"

"I'll get it ready," said Jude looking down to the café. He could see no one. He turned around, walked across to the sofa, sat down and began to rifle through the DVD stack.

"Would it please Mr Rochester to take something to follow his dinner," she said imitating the heroine of the Charlotte Brontë novel again. "In his library perhaps? After walking Pilot?"

"It would so, my Jane," said Jude, a smile rising across his face. "But I should not chance the dog's life on these streets! And I desire not wine, nor cheese... I was thinking the other day that I fancied a trifling confection called a *Curly Wurly*!"

"I could consult with Mrs Fairfax the house-keeper? Or would these suffice?" She stepped into view from the kitchen. An eyebrow was arched over an impish eye as she held up a box of *After Eight* mints and the packet of *Lavazza* coffee.

"Fantastic!" he said wiggling his glasses like he'd seen Eric Morecambe do on her father's old television set.

Alex brought the items through after ten minutes on a tray that had a pencil design of Bournemouth Pier on it. Jude switched the main light out and Alex sat on her calves next to him and snuggled up in the glow of the TV screen. They watched keenly to scenes where the Black Riders were racing to The Shire. He felt a little shudder as a great, black-cloaked spectre sitting on one of hell's horses galloped closer in pursuit hissing, '*Shire... Baggins'*. Frodo was real-ising suddenly that with the 'The One Ring' now in his possession he must flee.

"Can you stop it... whilst I go to the bathroom?" said Alex. Jude rolled his eyes, pressed the remote and poured out the coffees to use up the waiting time. She seemed to be taking forever so he flicked the channel onto *TV Shënomadh*. The local news bulletin was being broadcast and the reception was weak and fuzzy. A cold-faced woman with a tight, black bun of hair on top was reading the news before a back-projection of the world that shimmered around her edges.

"A man was shot dead in *Shënvogël* today…" she said. Jude closed his eyes. "The victim, Veli Fitore, was involved in a dispute over land with his neighbour." He opened them slowly bracing himself for the full horror of it. Images of a man's brown, bloodstained trousers flashed across the screen. "*Shënomadh* Police have arrested local hunter Valon Malikuqi of the village. Our reporter, Lali Lafazani, was there." More pictures of a man being marched in handcuffs past a crowd of staring people to a waiting police car were shown. His head was pushed roughly down to bundle him onto the rear seat, knocking off his electric-blue baseball cap. Kela! thought Jude. What would become of her now?

Chapter 15

Jude's eyes fixed on the Union Jack cover of his mobile phone, which he'd placed on the living room coffee table in front of him. It read 10.30am, Friday, August 22nd. He'd just called Spiro seeking a meeting. Jude must make progress with Mehmed's book: he was running out of time. Spiro had agreed to come over in around twenty minutes. He'd put out the interview tapes and his laptop ready on the coffee table in case he could stay to work on it now. He reflected on how much easier things had been when he'd worked with his own language, when he wasn't so reliant on others to do the editorial work for him. In fact, he'd done it himself on the pieces of writing he attempted after university in England. *People's Friend* had said he'd delivered a well-polished piece when he'd submitted that historical romance short story they'd published. The editor at BBC Radio Four had used his topical comedy sketch with no alterations. But that was there, not here, he rued.

He picked up the phone and scrolled down through the numbers in the contacts list to pass a little time. He'd heard nothing from Edona, but he was sure she would have contacted him if there had been any more 'office workers' hanging around her Tirana apartment block. It would be good to speak to Mehmed again, he thought, but he would wait until he had some positive development to pass on. It was Kristo's name that left him feeling heavy-hearted. He'd called him the day after the news report on *TV Shënomadh,* and Kristo's words had felled him. "What *good* did your visit do?" he'd said. It seemed that it had done no good at all. Yet he or Alex must look into what had happened to Kela. He had talked with Alex about it that morning before she left, but she too had seemed upset with him about something.

Jude closed his eyes and tried to pray, but it felt like a struggle. He began to say the words of *Psalm 23* out loud,

> *'The Lord is my shepherd. I have everything I need...'*

...but the formal 'rat-tat-tat' of Spiro's unmistakable knock interrupted him. He took a deep breath and slid his glasses back up the ridge of his nose with his forefinger. He walked through to the entrance hall and turned the latch in the door.

Spiro stood looking uncomfortable. He stepped inside again with a single stiff stride.

"Thank you for coming Spiro. Come on through to the living room," said Jude. Spiro walked ahead of him and sat down on the sofa. He laid his bag and keys on the coffee table a little theatrically. Jude sat facing him in an armchair. He could see that though Spiro was physically present his eye contact was noticeable by its absence. "I wanted to talk a little about Mehmed's book. I wondered how you had been progressing," said Jude.

"Well… as I said to you the last time we met… I have already done about twenty percent," he said, his eyes remaining on Jude's Ansel Adams print.

"So you are in the same place… as last time?" said Jude restraining the urge to run his hand back through his hair. "It is just that there is not a lot of time… to complete it. I'd understood you knew it needed to be ready by now. Is there some problem?"

"I've had work to do. It is… well-paid," he said turning to look at Jude directly now.

"We agreed a fee… this is not a well-funded development agency here," said Jude sensing the volume of his own voice rising.

"But you could…" Spiro began.

"What about the privilege of service you mentioned when we started?" said Jude. "What about doing something because you love the Lord?" His frustration had suddenly barged the security guard aside and kicked open the door. "Do you think He said to the first disciples, 'Come follow me… by the way, the wages are ten denarii a week. It's about the same as being a Roman procurator's clerk… is that sufficient for you?' Haven't you heard the teaching about seeking His Kingdom first… and all things will be given to you as well?" What about… putting your hand to the plough without looking back?" Spiro's eyes widened. He stood up and drew his shoulders back stiffly. He turned to the table and gathered up the things before him. He brushed another invisible fleck of dust from the sleeve of his brown suit jacket. He walked through the living room to the front door without saying anything. The latch clicked behind him.

Jude had not moved from the armchair. He sat breathing heavily. His heart was thumping. He put his hands over his face and then drew them down across his mouth. He took a deep breath and stared ahead. I've really blown it now, he thought. I lost control; I said it in anger; I've burnt the relationship... It was then he noticed something. Where were the interview tapes? Oh no, he thought, Spiro's really got me to ransom now!

* * *

It was dark in Istanbul as Sheref passed by the windows of the Orient Express Restaurant in Sirkeci Railway Station. The pink facade of the grand, Ottoman art nouveau building was bathed in the warmth of lighting, though he felt a little chilly, perhaps from the evening breeze off the Bosphorus, he thought. He hovered on the station platform and looked around. Light fell across his path from a row of high, circular windows, their patterned glass throwing shapes down across the shining marble-floor. A large round clock hung from the platform roof by a long row of steel columns. It read 8.30pm. The train ahead had only two long, blue carriages, each with a white stripe down the side, and an engine rumbling in readiness at the front. He read a white sign slotted into a carriage door as he approached, 'FILIA-DOSTLUK'. Yes, this is it, he thought, 'The Friendship Express'. There seemed to be few passengers waiting for it. A couple of backpackers hovered in the shadows. A cat hissed and scampered away beneath a bench.

Sheref pushed his ticket at the guard, who nodded his consent. He stepped over a yellow line on the platform edge and up into the carriage's corridor-aisle. He shuffled past three doors until he came to the compartment he had reserved. He found a light switch and dropped his backpack on the bed. He glanced around. It was a two-birth room with the upper bed folded back into the wall. It had a washbasin with soap and a white towel, and a wall cabinet with a mirror. It would be his alone for the twelve-hour journey through the night to Thessaloniki in northern Greece. He had paid the first class supplement to ensure it.

He felt the gentle motion of the carriage moving just after 9pm. He got up and stepped back into the corridor-aisle. A metallic screech came up momentarily from the tracks outside and then a jolt pushed him gently against the cold glass. He reached up and slid open a small window to see out better. A prick of light dropped from red to green ahead. Soon the train began to turn to the right and the black sea twinkled into view. Across the water the Maiden's Tower cast a finger of light over the surface towards him. Ahirkapi Lighthouse came quickly into view flashing its white beam way out over the Sea of Marmara towards the freighter traffic dotting the darkness with little clusters of lights. Sheref smelt the salt in the air. He closed his eyes as the train rocked and he remembered riding in a horse drawn carriage on Buyukada in the Princes' Islands with his family when he was a boy. The carefree happiness of the day came in again on time's tide and then quickly washed away leaving an emptiness.

Soon the train had built up speed and they were out beyond the airport into the suburbs. The rhythmic vibrations clattered beneath his feet. Tower blocks chequered with lights rose up high around him. The minarets of passing mosques needled the stars, and he saw the Turkish flag raised high on a white pole arching like a great crimson hand waving at him. He stepped back into his compartment and closed the door behind. He turned off his mobile phone and slid it in a side pocket of his backpack. He took out his guidebook of Greece and a pen and marked up 'Kastra' and 'The White Tower' in Thessaloniki. He unfolded a road map of Greece and followed the train line the full 700km, to the border, past Alexandroupoli, and as it wound below the foothills of the Rhodope Mountains through Xanthi, Drama and Kilkis. He lay down on his back and stared at the wall.

The train began to slow just before midnight. He lifted up the blind on his window and saw a sign with 'Uzunkopru' pass by. It drew to a halt. There was a knock on his door shortly and a grey-haired, Turkish border guard gave a quick examination of his passport. He stamped it and continued down the corridor. After twenty minutes, the train eased off and Sheref kept alert. The noise of the wheels on the tracks changed to a higher, hollow tone as they passed over bridges and he caught glimpses of marshland. He saw another sign reading '*Hellas*'. As the train stopped again a feeling of malaise crept through him and he swallowed. He was crossing over now. A knock on his carriage door came again and he opened it. Two men stood there. One wore a dark blue bomber jacket with the flag of Greece as a badge on his arm. He kept one hand resting casually on a thick, black, holstered pistol, and Sheref felt the cold hostility of his stare.

"What is the purpose of your visit here?" he said thumbing at the ink on his visa and flicking near the edge of his photo with his finger nail.

"Tourism," said Sheref rubbing his eye.

"Your bag… please," he said. The other man searched his backpack roughly. He lifted out the guidebook of Greece, turned quickly through the pages and glanced at him, Sheref thought, with an unspoken question. He nodded at the first man and they went. He'd left Sheref's things scattered on the bed.

He lay in his compartment without sleeping for around an hour. Then he stepped back out into the corridor-aisle to see. The train was hurtling along at a pace now and he stood there swaying. He looked to his left as one of the backpackers came out of a compartment. They passed though a cutting and the clattering suddenly amplified off the walls. She returned inside when she saw him. He watched the train's window lights passing along the adjacent tracks. The three-quarter moon seemed to be racing along with them. Below it the lights of distant towns looked like constellations on the ground, tight groups of white pinpricks broken with the occasional neon orange, a red or a blue. A car's headlights rose and flashed and seemed set on a collision course with them until they passed underneath the tracks at the last second. The night air smelt similar but a little different here. The Aegean Sea must be close, he thought. Then he heard the sound of a deeper horn. The carriage jolted and the whole train shuddered as an oncoming train passed. The air buffeted his face through the open window. He returned again to his compartment and drew down the blind. He drank from a bottle of mineral water and switched the main lights out leaving only a strip light on above his head. He lay on the bed but the creak and rattle of loose fittings kept him from deep sleep.

Sheref awoke suddenly with a sensation of being pressed against the wall. There was a screeching sound as the train drew to a rapid halt. He sat up and ran his fingers around the edges of his lips. His mouth felt dry again. He smelt a faint odour of burning. He drew up the blind to peer outside. Away perhaps two or three kilometres on the mountain side he could see two lines that looked like long lava flows down black rock. Above the tongues of orange fire the smoke was swirling up across the face of the moon. It seemed to him that its silvery disc at once turned blue with an eye-like pupil in the centre and then back to silver. It's a wildfire, maybe close to the tracks ahead, he thought. He sat back down on his bed. It was then that he felt the hairs rising on the backs of his hands. There was a presence in the compartment with him. He heard the faint sound of breath being exhaled. It drew out into a snarl deep from the throat. He switched the main light on quickly and saw nothing. He went to the sink and splashed water on his face and lips. He looked at himself closely. His eyes were heavy-lidded, and he touched his nose at the point where it was a little misshapen below the bridge. Hanife had said he looked more hunched; he pushed his shoulders back. In the mirror behind him he thought he saw a grey, wolf-like form. He spun around and saw nothing. He pressed the heels of his palms into his eyes.

He lay back down on the bed and listened to the hum of the stationary engine. He checked the time on his watch. It was 5.30am and he felt tired. The train must be somewhere between Xanthi and Drama, he thought. He closed his eyes and felt his rib cage rising and falling. He slid into sleep. There he saw himself wrapped in the red flag of his country, stroking down the creases across its white crescent. He saw himself walking out before a stadium full of football supporters dressed in the black and yellow strip of Fenerbahçe, and holding his arms aloft as the crowd roared its approval. He saw himself standing before three senior military officers in full decorative dress as he was saluted and a medal pinned to his chest.

Chapter 16

Alex Kilburn ran cold water over her hand and forearm from the kitchen tap. It stung but it was soothing. She dabbed it dry with a towel and rubbed on a little antiseptic cream. She had started to take a shower when the hot water pipe on the bathroom wall had broken away scalding her. She returned to the bedroom, dressed quietly as Jude slept, and checked the face of his mobile phone: it read 7.34am, Saturday, August 23rd. She touched his hair and tried to push aside her feelings of annoyance with him.

She stepped quietly back to the kitchen, made a mug of peppermint tea, and set out Jude's pint mug for him ready with two tea bags and a big spoonful of sugar in the bottom. She then sat down on the sofa, took her Bible and turned to the reading-plan. It was *Proverbs 31* today.

> *'A wife of noble character who can find? She is worth far more than rubies.'*

She read on and thought that though she might not be ...

'like a merchant ship bringing food from afar'

... she could at least go down *Shënomadh* bazaar. She wondered too when they might have a child? She decided she would use the verses as a Bible study with her women's group. She prayed a little and remembered what was troubling her: the dream. God has given me that for a reason, she thought. There is some sort of danger from Turkey, connected with that mission trip, and it's approaching. It was Jude's name on the computer screen, not Jaap's, nor anyone else in the team. Why? She remembered too the text books and periodicals she'd read in her third year at university for the module on 'Politics and Society in Post-Communist Eastern Europe'. How much it had impressed upon her the dark faces of power and the dangerous people behind it. There was that threatening phone call Jude had received too. She needed to watch, to be alert, to be vigilant... She stretched out her hands and lifted up her palms offering it all to Him who was with her *'always, to the end of the age'*. She checked the refrigerator then let the latch on the front door close quietly behind her.

As she walked across the dirt ground in front of their apartment block, she realised that an itch in her spirit had been increasing. Was something imminent? She crossed over May 5TH Street and between the three tables on the pavement into the *Don* café. She felt the eyes of several men on her.

"Is the owner here please?" she said raising her voice. A rough-shaven man with a surly expression nodded. "Can I ask you something?" She heard a snicker. The owner stood up and walked across. "I live with my husband, Jude, in that apartment block." She pointed. "Earlier this week... there was a man wearing a grey shirt and shiny black shoes standing outside here. Did you see him? Is he from around here?"

"I know who you are *zonja angleze*. I have seen you… and your husband. I saw the man, and he was not from this neighbourhood, was he?" he said turning to the other men. Several of them clicked their tongues to make a 'tut' sound.

"Thank you," she said and left. She walked along the pavement past three parked metallic-green taxi vans. A driver with circular blue lens sunglasses waved to her but she ignored him.

She came to edge of the bazaar after a ten-minute walk. She passed a row of stalls heaped high with jumbles of shoes, and another covered with music cassettes where an Eastern sounding singer was amplified to distortion through a pair of battered speakers. A man swinging a squawking turkey by its legs walked past her, and the smoke of charcoal-grilled *qofte* sausages blew into her eyes. A dark-skinned woman with matted, black hair wandered across the road looking everywhere and at no one like a wide-eyed child in an adult's body. She made directly for Alex holding out her hand imploringly. Alex gave her 200 *lekë* and noted she was wearing a floral-patterned dress over the top of her trousers. She passed a stall selling penknives, flick knives and kitchen knives and entered a shop. It had hand-painted vases, cheap ceramic ornaments, and illuminated plastic models of mosques and churches. The owner came over to greet Alex warmly.

"Good day Mr Zanati. Are your family well?" she said.

"Ah, *zonja angleze*... I am glad that you have come. Your three pine cone baskets have all sold," he said. "I would like you to bring me a further twelve. Can you do that?"

"Could you give me around two weeks?" she said.

"No longer," he said wagging a finger with a smile. "My customers have been asking for them now!" Alex felt like dancing right there in the shop. She couldn't wait to tell Jude. She chose a small gift to take to Diellza's wedding that evening before Mr Zanati came through with a receipt and payment in a clean, white envelope, presenting it with a ceremonious delight.

She walked further to a stall where a woman was selling picked peppers stuffed with white curd from several large plastic buckets. The other sellers were hustling Alex for her trade but her resolve was fixed. This woman kept a clean stall and was honest. As she chose a jar of pickled green chilli-peppers and two packs of Macedonian white cheese, she reflected that Jude had been eating much more of them than usual. A time when she'd first met him came into her mind and he'd been having some difficulties with his father. They'd gone together to a tiny surgery in Clapham where an Indian doctor had prescribed him tranquillisers for seventy-two hours.

She gathered more items around the market and left. Fifteen minutes later, she was climbing inside their apartment building, the plastic bag handles cutting into her fingers as her feet shuffled up the last stone steps. She put them down outside the door and shook her hands to get the blood circulating. The neighbour Julieta opened her door and looked out.

"These thyroid pills... what does it say here?" she said. Alex walked over.

"Two in the morning and evening," said Alex reading the bottle's label.

"When does your women's group meet? Can I come?" she said.

"Tuesdays. Yes, bring a cake," said Alex restraining a second urge to dance on the spot that morning.

* * *

Jude awoke just before 9am feeling heavy-headed. He had taken the opportunity for a Saturday morning lie-in, but the extra hour had not left him feeling refreshed. He pulled on a shirt and trod through to the kitchen where he found Alex gone but his pint mug ready with two tea bags and a big spoonful of sugar in. When the kettle had boiled he filled it with hot water and milk, and slumped down on the living room sofa. A large manilla envelope with Royal Mail stickers on it addressed to him was on the coffee table. He tore it open and drew out a newspaper. He thumbed through it casually to the entertainment section. The house phone rang next to him. He lifted the receiver to his ear.

"Is that you Jude?" he heard. He felt a sudden upsurge of mixed emotions.

"Yes. It is dad." He put down the paper and sat up.

"The line's terrible."

"Sorry about that… are things okay? What have you been doing?" said Jude.

"Yes, fine, well, I've done a few local walks… it's been a few months since I was up in the Dales, you know. I went down to the cemetery on the 2nd, on your mother's birthday… put some geraniums there… She always loved them." Jude heard him pause and breathe. "Oh, and next Saturday, I'm meeting up with members of the English Civil War Re-enactment Society. We're doing the 'Battle of Marston Moor'… for the crowds at Roundhay Park."

"That sounds like fun. Whose side are you on?"

"Why the Roundheads of course! And how is your little publishing project coming along?" Jude hesitated, but he wanted to unburden himself.

"It's been a bit… difficult, dad. There's this local man helping me correct the manuscript. I don't know if he's going to do what he agreed to."

"Don't trouble yourself unduly over it. These things in life… that we put such stock in… are far less important than we imagine them to be. We all need to think we are significant, when in truth, in the grand scheme of things, we aren't. It's just our vanity. How many books have been published in this world?"

"But… it is the message here that counts, dad," said Jude feeling a little reduced. "It has like… fine shavings of gold in it. It has power… to stop a person withering, sinking, or destroying themselves… or someone else. Mehmed's story could stop an action that has a chain reaction. What if it could transport a person out of the mist around them? What if it can… tip a heart into eternity? Isn't it worth it?"

"I know that your faith is important to you. It gives you your orientation. Religion is an ennobling influence on societies, I'll grant you that…"

"This is a discussion I'd rather not have with you now dad, okay!"

"As you wish. Look... give my love to Alex. When are you back here next?"

"I don't know. Maybe Christmas... Look... erm... don't go sticking your pike in too many Cavaliers, will you?"

"I shall try not to Jude."

"I'll call you soon dad." Jude put the receiver down. He walked over to the refrigerator. There was not even a crumb of white cheese to nibble on. He swung the door closed with a little too much force and a bowl clattered inside. He sat back down on the sofa and unfolded the newspaper. He felt like he was slowly leaking air. He turned to the entertainment section again looking for something diverting. He heard the latch on the front door turning. Alex was back from the bazaar.

* * *

As Alex stepped into the entrance hall she noticed something grey on the bathroom floor. She went in to see that a metre-wide circle of plaster and brick pieces had dropped off the ceiling. The whole room was filthy with dust. She carried the bags through to the kitchen past Jude, who was sitting reading a newspaper on the sofa.

"Jude. Have you seen the bathroom?" she said.

"No. I've been looking at this *Daily Mail*. It came from England... and has got no bites in it," he said. She looked at him. His hair was dishevelled and he had a brown five-o-clock shadow. He was sitting in shorts wearing one of his baggy, white shirts with a loose tan thong for tying up the neck. He was touching the chip in his front tooth as he read. He barely looked up.

"Is everything okay?" she said.

"Yeah… well," he said.

"Jude. Mr Zanati at the market has just ordered twelve pine cone baskets! Isn't that great?"

"Oh right," he said. That's it? That's all you have to say? she thought, as she thumped a block of white cheese down.

* * *

Jude walked along May 5TH Street feeling like he needed a friend. He sent a text message to Jack to see if he was at home for a link up via web-cam, and set off walking towards the Planet Internet café. The Saturday afternoon sun was hot on the skin of his arms and he felt the heat off the paving stones through his sandals. As much as possible he kept to areas of shade. There against a wall a man was selling sunflower seeds off a wooden tray balanced on a plastic crate. He was sitting expectantly with a glass ready wearing black sunglasses like some old, blind blues player. Jude dropped a 50 lekë coin in it as he passed.

In the café's basement the darkness was a welcome relief to his eyes. He felt the air-conditioning's cool waft and as his vision adjusted gradually he made his way to a cubicle in the corner. He felt his mobile phone vibrate and as he checked it he smiled to himself. The text message read, 'Jack is in the house'. He pulled his chair in close and typed Alexandria777. He thought over what his dad had said about 'significance in the grand scheme of things' and if, in truth, he might have a point. He pressed the green dial button and a black window sprang up in the centre of his screen. It cleared to reveal Jack's terrier Billy Boy sitting with a Leeds United scarf tied around its neck.

"Well now, Jack," said Jude laughing. "You've been eating some prime cuts. That's a nice shiny coat you've grown... but don't let your tongue hang so!" Jack's head slid in from the side of the screen with a big grin on it. He lifted down Billy Boy and sat facing his web-cam.

"How's it all going out there? Where did you say you were? Alabama?" said Jack.

"No. That's just south of Doncaster. Your geography... don't you read my prayer letters? I've been serving in Algeria for over three years now!"

"Oh, sorry about that," said Jack.

"I had a chat with my dad this morning."

"Mr Motivator?"

"And Alex has had this dream."

"Go on."

"It was about some danger coming from Turkey... looking at my name."

"What... like in that film *The Day of the Jackal*? She saw someone coming over the Trans-border highway... with a custom-made sniper rifle concealed in the exhaust pipe of his sports car? Or more like the remake with Bruce Willis? That sort of danger?"

"Yeah right! More likely it's some official with a bee in his bonnet... after we went there."

"Jude, when Alex dreams, you wake up and drink a double espresso, my friend."

"Well… you were right about not everyone being happy Mehmed is telling his story. Someone called me up and threatened me over it."

"Now you're really pulling my leg! Are you walking around out there with a target sign stuck on your back?"

"What can I say? Gandalf… I wish The Ring had never come to me?"

"I'll tell you something Jude… there was a story on the BBC about this man from Albania. A few years ago… he followed another Albanian all the way to London seeking to avenge his brother's death. Well he found him in a house in Hounslow… stabbed him in the living room, and dumped his body under the flight path of Heathrow Airport. Detectives thought he fallen out of a plane's undercarriage until they worked it all out! I've been thinking a lot about your book since then. We've been praying for you in the house group. I'm going to pray again for you this evening… with Lindsay, okay?"

"Thanks Jack."

"You keep your head low… Now, there's a Leeds United match starting on the TV. It's been a while since I went down Elland Road, but I still like to keep an eye on them."

"Okay… well make sure you teach Billy Boy how to behave like a gentleman in defeat," he said. Jack grinned.

"Bye," said Jude. He pressed the red 'End Call' button and the video window turned black. He sat for a while in the darkness of the café corner thinking. He did not want to walk out again in the full glare of the sunlight.

Chapter 17

The 'Friendship Express' came slowly along the last kilometre of its journey into Thessaloniki railway station. Sheref stood in the corridor-aisle peering through a small, high window and swaying slightly with the motion. He watched the cage-like metal frames that carried overhead electricity cables, and the dense, concrete buildings of the city centre slide past. The sun was glaring off their white surfaces, and he could smell the sea in the air mixed with the fumes of countless vehicles. The train jolted suddenly as it crossed some points and a metallic cracking mixed with a high-pitched hum like the sound of a finger round the rim of a wine glass rose up from the tracks. He checked his watch: it read just after midday. The journey had taken fifteen hours with the delay caused by wildfires - three hours longer than scheduled. He had slept for only an hour and a half and he was fighting now to keep his eyes open.

The brakes gave out a short screech and the train stopped. He opened his carriage door and jumped down onto Greek ground for the first time. Through the sensation of novelty came a stab of unease. He walked along a shaded platform past other carriages sprayed large with rainbow-coloured graffiti lettering. He crossed the tracks on a wooden boardwalk and went down a flight of steps. In the underpass the noise of suitcase wheels trundling across the gleaming white marble accompanied him. He came to the ticket hall, cavernous with long, high windows pouring light down across the shiny black floor. There were not many people in it. By the exit doors a little, black, nineteenth-century steam engine on display caught his eye. It was similar to ones he had seen in a museum in Leeds.

He took out his sunglasses, mirror lensed and cracked on one side, and put them on. He felt like his face was covered. He'd decided he would check in to a hotel for a few hours rest and then telephone the city's 'KTEL' bus station to check actual service times to Kastoria against his Internet research. He turned left and began to walk along the busy road flowing with traffic. He drew out his guidebook and flicked to the page with the city map on. A lorry rumbled past wafting him with hot air, and he looked around until he caught the street name on the wall of a building. Yes, he was on Monastiriou Street. He walked a short distance to a table outside a restaurant and sat. When the waiter came, he ordered two cans of cola, a bottle of water and two meat kebabs in pita bread. He spoke in English and the waiter understood. When the kebabs were brought they tasted passable, he thought, but not like Turkish ones: they needed fresh, green chillies or ground, red powder to spice them up. He slid his camera out and took a few shots of nearby buildings. He paid with euros from his money-belt and pushed the drinks into his backpack. He walked on a little further and came to a shoe shop with postcards outside. He rotated the stand and chose one of the narrow streets of 'Kastro' and another of 'The White Tower'.

He continued walking until he noticed a sign saying 'The Ruby Club' with a smiling girl in a red bikini painted large on a hoarding above. He felt drawn to look quickly though the window, but it was all blacked out and locked up. Nearby was an 'Erotic Supermarket' and he noticed men standing around in doorways sizing him up coldly. He quickened his pace. On a side street to the right he caught sight of a flashing sign reading 'Hotel Persephone'. He walked towards it, and pushed open the glass entry door to the reception area. The girl behind the counter had dyed-blonde hair tied back and cherry eye shadow. She was pretty even though she wore a world-weary expression, he thought. He knew she knew he was staring her.

"Do you have a room... for me?" he said.

"Forty euros for the night... and your passport," she said. She kept her eyes lowered, moving uneasily as if to leave. He handed them over. She kept the passport and handed him a key on a heavy, metal disc with the number 215 on it, and two remote controls.

"TV and air-conditioner," she said. "Press zero for an outside line in your room... no guests allowed." She did not look up as he wished and immediately made a call on her mobile phone. He entered a tiny mirrored lift no bigger than the width of a single door and pressed the button for the second floor. He found his room. He closed the door behind him, threw his backpack down, and lay across the bed. He was asleep within minutes.

He awoke and turned over to look at the ceiling. The ornate plasterwork around a light shade of cascading glass droplets was painted gold, as was the room's cornice. He lifted up his arm to bring his watch into view: 7.10pm. He must call the bus station! He reached for his guidebook and the number he had circled. When he dialled it there was no answer. He would just have to go there early in the morning. After rubbing his eyes looked around. The walls were the colour of the café lattés at the Kanyon Mall. There was a portable television set on a scuffed wooden table and a painting of sunlight falling on a wilting, red rose. The bed-linen was crisp and white. It was okay here, he thought. There were white towels and tubes of clear shampoo and shower gel set out. He would use them.

Thirty minutes later, wearing a white hotel dressing gown, he walked to the window and drew back the curtain a little. The lights of nearby hotels and shops were flashing pink and blue in the dusk. The Ruby Club lights were blazing red and the front door was now an open square of white light. He sat on the bed and wondered if the reception girl was still on duty. He remembered one Saturday night in England after he had left the Taksim Takeaway with Gul. They were walking down a road of red-bricked terraced houses. They heard the heavy bass sound of music and laughter, and they passed an open door where he saw faces from the university. They were drawn into the crowd and to the kitchen table loaded with bottles. He filled a plastic cup with red wine. He walked to the stairs and climbed through the other students sitting there. He saw pills being passed. He pushed open a bedroom door and saw couples together on the floor. A pretty girl with lilac lipstick and wavy blonde hair tied back with a headband was sitting in a corner. He sat down next to her. She seemed so friendly, willing he thought. He moved closer and tried to kiss her. She stared at him and smirked, then stood up and walked away. He turned to see others laughing at him… He began to breathe heavily now through his nose feeling again the sting of the moment's humiliation. He felt his emotions funnelling towards a fixed point in his mind. Well, now he had the euros, he could do as he wanted, couldn't he?

He dressed quickly and locked the door behind him. The girl in the reception was gone; a middle-aged Greek man with chin folds sat in her place. He stepped out into the evening, and turned along a back alley parallel to Monastiriou Street. It smelt of rotten fruit. He walked on it for a block. By a row of metal wheelie-bins he saw a light on in a parked car with a woman sitting attending to her make-up. She looked at him as he walked towards her. She opened the car door and gave him her eyes directly.

"My name is *Anjeza*," she said. On the back seat was a young girl with a colouring book and crayons. He closed his eyes as he kept walking. He felt a nausea rise into his throat. He could not use her - for all his own hunger. He turned right at the next corner and doubled back on himself.

* * *

Jude lifted his black crushed velvet jacket out of the bedroom wardrobe. It was rare that he wore it, but it would fit tonight's wedding celebration well, he thought. In the entrance hall he took his 'Beatle Boots', black leather with a Cuban heel, like his dad had once worn, off the rack, and gave them a quick wipe. He was ready, but Alex was lingering in the bathroom. He heard her singing quietly, *'This train is bound for glory, this train...'* and then the clatter of some small item, lipstick probably, being dropped into the sink. He walked out on to the balcony and waited. Dusk was here: a light patch of sky slashed with grey-pink wisps was being chased over the ridges by the darkness. The red rear lights of three taxi vans glowed below the *Don* espresso café. One of the drivers waved up to him and Jude lifted his arm.

"Who's that?" said Alex as she stepped out.

"That's Defrim... the gizmo guy. He's got more gadgets on his dashboard than Bond's Aston Martin," he said. Alex was wearing a purple Asian kurta. "You look nice," he said. "What about me?"

"You look like Austin Powers," she said. "Let's go."

The wedding party had hired a room next to a patisserie, a block further than the Planet Internet café. Its windows were wide open to let in the cool evening air, and groups of people were gathered at the doors. Alex waved and greeted several women she knew with a kiss on both cheeks as they entered. Long tables were ready laid with plates of food, and they sat down at a corner near the door. Each guest had a slice of pork, yoghurt sauce, mixed pickles and some Russian salad on it. Baskets of bread, potato fries and bottles of mineral water were also placed at intervals.

"Jude, if they set these out earlier in this heat... you should be careful," whispered Alex, waving across the room at Diellza, who was sitting with her new husband at a central table wrapped up in a dress of white gauze.

The other guests settled and the eating began. Alex nibbled bread and drank mineral water. Jude felt too hungry for prudence and tucked in. Half an hour later, the wedding musicians took up their instruments. They struck up a single note together and held it whilst the clarinettist fluttered a tune around it. They then switched into a steady rhythm that drew people out onto the floor to form a line holding hands. With three steps and a hop the guests danced and the line lengthened and snaked through the tables. Jude smiled as he watched and tapped his foot. Alex lifted her arms and began to click her fingers in time. Her friends were beckoning them to join the line but he felt uneasy dancing. Alex glanced at him so he rose for her. Holding her hand he tried to keep in time, but he seemed to be hopping when she was stepping. He stumbled for a while then withdrew his hands as the line passed their seating places and he stood there clapping. Alex could have been dancing at Albanian weddings all her life, he thought. She continued without him with a sprite-like ease.

They sat back at the table together and Jude reached for her hand. She let him hold it with little physical response. The musicians now began a new tune that Jude knew as 'The Napolon'. Diellza moved to the centre of the floor, and as she danced with her husband a woman walked forwards and tucked a note of money into her dress. Others then followed decorating her with currency like they were pegging it freshly printed on a drying frame. Another woman ran forwards with a flaming handkerchief for her.

Diellza twirled it around as she danced and then tossed it as it began to scorch her fingers. It landed on the table in front of Jude and Alex and caught the side of a breadbasket. A tongue of fire rose up. Jude grabbed a bottle of mineral water and poured it over.

"It's okay," he said to those nearby. "It's only the basket." He raised his eyebrows as he glanced at Alex, but she was looking pointedly at him.

"Did I say something?" he said.

"You don't value my work, do you?" she said in a low voice.

"Pardon?" he said.

"When I told you about the basket order from Mr Zanati this morning… you just said, 'Oh right'."

"Alex, I've said we could go together to gather pine cones." He was a little taken aback and pushed his glasses up the ridge of his nose. "There's a place below the rock pinnacle I've seen… I'm sorry. I was distracted, with dad… and Spiro's self-interested games." She turned to face him and looked levelly.

"You know what Jude? Maybe, if you'd grown up here like Spiro… if you didn't have a steady income like we do from the Safe House… you'd try to get the best you could from a deal! You should have a bit more sympathy with people's social conditions… We could leave tomorrow, but they couldn't," she said gesturing around her with her eyes.

"What! So you're on his side in this are you," he said feeling his voice rising a little in anger with her. He was going to answer that. "And that excuses someone from a day's work, does it? Not the usual… five people to dig a hole… one to hold the spade and four to argue over it… type work. I mean focussed personal effort for a continuous stretch of time." He was beginning to feel a little unwell. "Look, can we go outside and get some fresh air."

"I don't want to leave so soon Jude," she said huffing a little as she screwed up her nose. Jude got up and walked to the door and she followed him. Outside, he leant against the wall and breathed in deep lungs-full of night air. He could feel beads of cold sweat forming on his forehead. He set off walking towards their home. Alex stepped up by his side to keep abreast.

"Don't you think He cares about the conditions people live and work in then?" she said.

"Yes, but He saves individuals... He changes their hearts. He makes them the salt of the earth," he said irritatedly.

"Jude, when was the last time you read the book of Amos? Don't tell me that God has no heart for these things!" she said, her voice full of emotion.

"And you the third chapter of John's gospel?" he shouted.

"Most people would say the gospel has a bias to the poor, actually," she said, her voice breaking.

"Well I thought all had sinned and fallen short," he said dryly. She stopped walking and stood facing him in the road a couple of metres away, her chest rising and falling as she breathed.

"I cut my hand on the drawer, Jude, and this morning I scalded it on the shower pipe... I cleaned up the bathroom ceiling whilst you were chatting to Jack at the internet café. One of us could have been badly injured! You've been too busy to care... staying out late with Shpetim." She was red faced now with tears in her eyes. "And you, talking about a day's work, you… you couldn't fit a spanner to a nut!" The lights of the apartment buildings were now turning around Jude. He could hear a high-pitched note rising in his ears. He turned to walk away. His leg dropped down into a large hole in the pavement. He slumped forwards and his shoulder struck the ground. His glasses skidded away. He looked up at Alex as she ran towards him. Then he vomited.

Chapter 18

In the upstairs room at *Shënomadh* Church Jude shuffled with Alex along a row of chairs in the rear half of the seating. Two of the worship musicians were squatting down together on the plinth tuning up their guitars. Ahmeti, a dark, skinny, young man whose pyjama-striped shirt hung on him like a sail, was flicking a little anxiously through his sermon notes. Two electric fans standing either side of a lacquered wooden cross on the wall were spinning in their metal cages sending a cooling breeze the full length of the room. Jude looked through an open window. A hyena-like mongrel had sprawled itself brazenly on top of the gun-bunker outside with not thought for the town's dog man. Shpetim ambled past, mobile phone pressed to his ear. He made a sharp start towards the creature and it scrambled off.

The rows of chairs were soon full and Jude nodded and smiled to his student Mira and her daughter Lule, who were sitting nearby on the left. Jaap stood up and welcomed everyone before making some announcements. When the worship songs began, Jude rose with the others singing even quieter than usual in his self-consciously subdued voice. He still felt queasy from last night's food poisoning. It seemed to him also that way down at the tips of the roots of his nerve ends a jangling presence had entered. Alex was standing next to him, yet it felt like she was two rows apart.

Fifteen minutes later, Ahmeti stepped up to the lectern and began to speak. Jude tried to listen, but the extra effort of processing a second language this morning left his mind struggling to engage with the sermon's theme. Thoughts about the dream and Alex, the book and Spiro, were dancing forwards in his mind jabbing with prongs of concern. He slid out his mp3 player and rested an earphone just above his lobe. He started to listen to an English audio sermon he'd downloaded. He glanced around. Odguda was frowning at him. He pulled it out and tried again to focus. He heard Ahmeti read from *Psalm 91*,

'He ordered his angels to guard you wherever you go. If you stumble, they will catch you.'

He caught himself thinking, well Lord, I would have appreciated an advance warning about that open drain last night… To tell the truth, right now, I feel like another well-aimed punch and my knees might give. I'll be on the canvas looking sideways at the ropes… He then felt something tiny muster in him. He shuffled in his seat. He felt a nudge to lift an arm upward in praise. His mind moved to pieces of the Lord's Prayer. 'May your kingdom come… Your *presence* on Earth!' he prayed in his heart. 'May your will be done… *Your* plans work good things from all these present days. Deliver us from evil… Stretch out your strong arm Lord. You *are* mighty to save.'

He came back into his surroundings. His arm was raised. Ahmeti had stopped. He thinks I'm raising an objection, he realised, and snapped it back to his side. A row of turned heads lingered regarding him with curiosity.

After the service had finished, Jude wandered down the steps to the entrance hall. Spiro was waiting by the room where Jude taught his English classes. He made a single stiff stride towards Jude and stood in his stagy manner.

"Here are the interview tapes," he said swinging them forwards rattling in a carrier bag. "And here is Mehmed's book... the corrections are finished. I've cut some of the repetitions out." He handed Jude a black USB stick. "We agreed the fee, didn't we?" His mobile phone rang in his leather belt pouch. He rejected the call. A wave of emotion welled up in Jude that he wanted to articulate much more volubly than he did.

"Thanks Spiro," was all that came out. He held out his hand to the man. Spiro shook it.

"There is one more thing," said Spiro lowering his voice. "Someone has you under surveillance... I saw him for the first time when I took a smoke on your balcony. He was there again when I left you on Friday morning. I will be at your apartment early tomorrow... to help you deal with your printer. If I see him again, I will challenge him... tell him he will have to reckon with Spiro Krenallari if he continues." He tapped himself on the chest and smoothed his frond of hair. "I have... friends Jude... *Mos ki merak*." He turned to the door and left.

* * *

Jude walked with Shpetim across town to the Blue Café after the Sunday service. They sat outside in the shade of a silver birch tree, but even there the marble-topped table was hot on their hands. Jude glanced around to see if Fredi was on duty but remembered he was at the Elita Café today. Another waiter brought them a bottle of still mineral water, two blue glasses and a metal tub of ice-cubes with tongs. Shpetim took a cube, held it to the back of his neck and rolled his shoulders. They ordered cappuccinos, and they were brought quickly, topped with spiralling towers of aerosol cream and dusted with cocoa powder.

Jude took his phone from his pocket to see if Alex had texted him. There was one from her that read, *Gone visiting*. He wanted to tell her about Spiro then he noticed that Shpetim was admiring it.

"I can do better," said Jude guessing his thoughts. "We'll go to the stall on Portobello Road. It's got all sorts of excellent, tacky Union Jack things."

"What is 'tacky'?"

"It's like those plastic churches with flashing lights in the bazaar."

"They are beautiful."

"Well... anyway... how is your father?"

"He is drinking too much... but grandad Petrit watches your film with Major *Kueill* every evening," he said smiling. Jude took a gulp of his cappuccino. He grinned at Shpetim with a cream moustache.

"Jaap was looking better this morning at the service," said Shpetim with a hopeful smile.

"I was at his house this week. We talked a little more about the Turkey trip," said Jude.

"What did he say?"

"Well… he was telling me about the vandalism of church buildings there… about a Catholic priest who was shot in his church, and how three believers were murdered at a Christian publishing house… things I didn't know."

"I've seen some reports… about a clandestine group there," said Shpetim. Jude noticed his glance. "It is being called 'Ergenekon'. It's thought to be made up of renegades from the security forces… army, navy… There are ultra-nationalist youth groups that may have links with it."

"And so?" said Jude.

"It's claimed they'd planned a string of assassinations… including the leaders of minority religious groups there, and that there are links to the killing of the priest and the three men at the publishing house… There have been arrests of alleged coup plot members."

"You know about these things? So… why? What was their motive? What coup?"

"They are thought to have drawn up a plan… to stir up chaos and fear. Their aim being then… to step in and take over control of the country from the existing government."

"It sounds a little fantastical."

"It's reports, intelligence chatter… It's unproven," said Shpetim. Jude was thinking about it when another thought occurred to him.

"Shpetim? Spiro told me something today…" he said. Lionel Richie began singing through Shpetim's mobile phone. He lifted it off the table and pressed it. A sour expression crossed his face as he listened.

"*O, Zot i madh*! Lord! Blue Café," he said. He stood up and stepped away. He spun around on the ball of his right foot looking apologetic as he spoke into the phone, and indicated with a hand that he had to leave. A police car screeched up in front of them on the high street. He walked forwards and jumped into the rear.

* * *

Jude was alone, lying on the living room sofa with his sandals off, easing his way into a late Sunday afternoon nap, when a knock came on the apartment door. It had a character he did not recognise, but not only for this reason, some sense beyond hearing caused the hairs on his forearms to ruffle like a wheat field in a mild breeze. He looked towards the door. He rose and trod barefoot, through the room into the entrance hall. He listened. It seemed unnaturally quiet. He hesitated. Then he turned the latch and drew in the door. The lights in the stairwell were off and it took his eyes some seconds to penetrate the darkness split by the bar of light he'd let out. He then made out the form of a tall man's arm and shoulder standing in close against the wall to the side. Jude's senses came alive. Danger was edging out of the shadow. He knew it. It's come, he thought in the splitting of a second.

The man took two quick steps towards him. Jude stumbled backwards away from his approach into his entrance hall. The man strode in after him. Jude backed into the living room stubbing his bare heel on a raised edge of floor mat. He thought to turn and run, but he was trapped. He felt his pocket for his mobile phone. He'd left it on the coffee table.

The man swiftly closed the door behind him. He advanced over Jude with his eyes kept closely on him. They then swept around, to the kitchen, and through doors left ajar.

"You are alone in the house?" he said tersely, with, Jude noted instantly, a Kosovar accent.

"My wife will be here any moment... I have friends who will call me," said Jude staring back levelly, but breathing heavily.

"Sit down," he ordered. Jude complied observing the man cautiously as he too was being observed. He had a sallow, clean-shaven face. He was physically lean and coiled with alertness. He was wearing a pressed, grey shirt, black trousers and polished, black slip-on shoes. His eyes were firm, but not cruel, Jude thought.

"I would like your assistance," he said briskly. "There are two ways we can do this. You can give your co-operation willingly... or there are other ways." He placed a hand purposefully by his trouser waist. Jude could see clearly the L-shaped bulge of a pistol below the cloth. "I think that we understand each other." Jude nodded. The man now stood at ease like soldier used to standing to attention.

"The manuscript... I would like to see it," he said.

"You want... to read it here, or to take a copy?"

"You have a computer, I presume, so open it." Jude indicated with his eyes towards the side desk, stood up slowly, and walked to his laptop. He keyed in the password, slotted in the USB stick Spiro had given him after church, and clicked open the file.

"You can relax now," said the man. "Make some coffee for yourself if it eases you. If your wife comes, you will tell her I am a friend of Mehmed's. Act wisely now…" He positioned the chair and laptop so that he could see over the rim of the screen to observe Jude with ease.

Jude walked cautiously to the kitchen and took down his Mr Rochester's Mug from a shelf. He went through the motions of making a pint of tea to give himself something to focus on. Where was Alex, he thought? She'd been out for hours! Maybe it was better she didn't return now to disturb this man. He prayed in the quiet anxiety of his mind that it would be so, and thought. His heartbeat felt quicker, but not racing. This man is controlled, not wild, professional, he reasoned: first the pressure, then the courtesy. He looked to be scrolling quickly though the pages, stopping periodically. He seems to know what he is looking for, thought Jude. If I do as he says, he will do nothing unreasonable. I'll be okay now.

Jude's mobile phone suddenly made a loud rattle as it vibrated on the coffee table surface. He looked at the man. He was watching him. Jude walked over and glanced at the phone's screen for the caller's ID. It was Spiro. Oh Lord, thought Jude. He lifted it slowly and pressed the green button to accept.

"Jude. *Je mirë?* Is everything okay with you?" he heard Spiro say.

"Yes. Of course it is! I'm relaxing with a cup of tea, like a true Englishman… *Mos ki merak,*" he said trying to add a light-hearted touch.

"Okay then…" said Spiro pausing. "I'll see you in the morning then." Spiro hung up and Jude put the phone back down on the coffee table.

He now waited silently holding his mug of tea, though he did not drink any, whilst the man looked at the computer screen for another thirty minutes. The man then folded the laptop closed.

"This is the version you propose to publish?" he said.

"Yes. It is finished now."

"You will take out this name on page 45... and insert a pseudonym. You will then have no difficulties with us." He produced a scrap of paper from his shirt pocket, wrote down something and placed it on the desk. He stood up briskly and walked towards the entrance hall.

"Who are you?" asked Jude gently. The man sauntered a step, turned and looked at him.

"Tell Mehmed... friends in Prishtina send their regards." Jude felt a little emboldened by the man's change of body language. He'd got what he'd come for.

"Were you at Edona's apartment... near the Bajram Curri Boulevard in Tirana?" He did not say anything. You were, thought Jude. "Were you... your people... on the *Qafë Krrabë* ridge road? Did you telephone me?"

"I know nothing of these things," he said. He then hesitated as if considering something. "The book... it is... interesting. Others may not take that view however."

"What others?" asked Jude. He looked at Jude with an expression of worldly knowing.

"Mehmed is a man with a long past."

"He also has a new future," said Jude.

"In this world?" he said with a cynical glazing passing over his eyes. "If others permit it..." Jude then heard men's voices rising up the stairwell. An officious knock was hammered on the door.

"Jude? *Ke ndonjë hall?* Is everything alright?" shouted Spiro. Jude stared into the entrance hall. His heart groaned, and his mind flashed through outcomes of this man's hand being forced. The man gave him a look of gunmetal coldness. It said: 'Don't move. Don't even swallow...'

Chapter 19

The coach's hydraulic brakes let out stuttering hisses to accompany the high beeps of its reversing alarm. Sheref watched the silver dome of the Macedonia Coach Terminal glint in the sun and slip away on his right behind him. The 'KTEL' ticket office there had informed him that the journey to Kastoria in northwest Greece would take around four hours. He knew that it would then be only a short taxi ride to the nearby Albanian border. He reflected momentarily on the morning. He had woken just after 7.00am, paid cash and collected his passport from the Hotel Persephone receptionist: she with the cherry lipstick, who had again maddeningly avoided eye contact with him. He had then waved down a dark blue Mercedes taxi on Monastiriou Street for the short drive to the terminal. He checked his watch: it read 9.06am, Sunday, August 24th. The coach was half full with passengers, all Greeks he thought, and he had taken a seat over the rear left wheel arch with no one immediately to his front or right for removal from close contact with them. The sun was already burning the left side of his head. He drew the pleated orange curtain halfway across the window for shade, and to psychologically fortify his private enclosure.

Sheref took out the road map and guidebook from his backpack and tossed them on the empty seat beside him. The coach began to accelerate past tall cranes angled in the city's port before the hazy blue Gulf of Thermi, and billboards for concerts with silver-moustached musicians, before filtering onto the Via Egnatia Motorway. He slunk a little lower in the seat and watched the oncoming flow of traffic to his left.

A stretch of water flashed by below the roadside fence and he checked his map. It was probably the River Axios, he thought. The coach shortly began to slow and he sat up to peer forwards. Lanes of traffic were queuing ahead into a wide row of booths. Above them was a line of blue signs, each with a white outline of a man wearing a flat-topped, peaked cap like a French gendarme. He felt his backpack pockets hastily to locate his passport. He hunched his shoulders around himself a little and pressed his fingers into the palms of his hands. As the traffic edged closer to the row of rising and falling barriers, he reassured himself that it was just a road toll station. As they passed through, on the right side there were parked lorries, and Kantina vans smoking from griddle meat with chairs set out on decks for customers. A Greek policeman slouched on the front wing of his white car drinking from a polystyrene cup. He rose and lifted his mobile phone to his ear closely watching the coach pass. When Sheref released his clench, rows of white dimples were imprinted on his palms.

He took a gulp of mineral water from a small, plastic bottle and splashed some over his face to ease the heat. He ran his finger and thumb around the edges of his top lip to clear off the sweat. He watched the bushes blooming with pink flowers in the lay-bys pass, and soon he was looking out across orchards of peach trees dotted with the pulsing sprays of water sprinklers. Away to the south, above lower slopes darkened by forest, a high ridge of jagged peaks rose up still tipped with snow. That, I think, must be Mount Olympus, he observed flicking through his guidebook: Greece's highest mountain, chosen by the ancients as the abode of their gods, Zeus, Poseidon and Hades. A pang of yearning seemed to escape from some cavern deep within him. His thoughts moved to Hanife and her submission to the religion of his land, but he? Who did he follow? Well, he had his path now with its own motion and trajectory. Where was that coffee shop hag's guide: remote with Zeus, or with him? "*Haydi!*" he whispered. She'd cheated him of two good lira and laughed at his back! He took out his camera, pointed it roughly at Olympus, and pressed the shutter button a few times. He circled it with a pen in the book. He glanced over the nearby entry for the Royal Tombs of Vergina, the first capital of Macedon, thought to house the remains of Alexander the Great's son, and where King Philip II was assassinated. He circled that too for good measure.

He noticed a road sign for the town of Veria pass on his right, and then the motorway began to climb. The coach's engine growled against the incline and they passed into the shade of a road tunnel and then another one. When they entered the third one he began keeping count. His eyes passed over the green lights and arrows above the lanes, the signs to turn on headlights, and those with the tunnels' length. Still they kept coming and he saw that the tenth one was 2.2km long. Here in the extended darkness he watched the wall lights, white on his left and red on his right, streaming past. Fans, like jet turbines, fastened to the roof, seemed to him to be propelling him forwards like a bullet down a barrel. Before the thirteenth tunnel, he saw a sign saying 'Call 1077 in an emergency'.

The coach rocked along past a row of unmanned tollbooths and the motorway began to descend gradually into a wide, flat valley. They passed under a line of pylons crossing the plain, their heads horned and arms hanging at the elbows clutching cables as they filed towards a distant power station. He stared ahead. There detachments of them converged to fetch and carry electricity. High red and white striped chimneys rose among them, and from a cooling tower a cloud of steam arched into the sky like a giant question mark.

A rocky outcrop with a pinnacle like some straying child below it passed by close to the motorway's edge, and soon it swept through a pass in a range of hills running left to right. As the driver drew off the slip road at Siatista, a squat factory chimney made of bricks caught his eye. He checked the time: it was just before mid-day. They now took a main road that wound through woods and open country with mountains, dry, brown and bare, to his right, and hills lower and undulating to his left. He thought he felt something like the brushing of silk pass over the skin of his right arm. He touched it. Road works and yellow earthmoving vehicles parked by a wide, empty stretch of pristine tarmac came into view. A strange new lightness of heart had come over him. It was a feeling of wellbeing, an inner warmth not sensed since childhood. He became aware that he had been feeling like this for perhaps ten minutes.

He turned to see a man sitting in the aisle seat on his right. His arms flinched slightly into his chest with the shock. How long had he been sitting there? How could it be that he had not seen nor heard him come? The man was staring straight ahead and did not look back at him. He wore a plain white T-shirt and light fawn trousers. His black hair flowed onto his shoulders thick and fragrant with a sweet aroma that Sheref now breathed in. He found himself staring at the man's face: a strong and shapely nose and eyes with a beauty that was almost feminine. His nationality was not apparent: Greek, Turk or Albanian, nor his age. Then he thought he heard the words: "Go back to your father." A feeling of cool air being blown onto his cheek made him touch it. He lifted his head to check the air-con valve but it was off. As he did so it was as if he rose outside of himself. Questions about what he was undertaking seemed suddenly to touch him. Where am I *going*? What *is* this I'm doing? Light, like the reflection of the sun flashing off a mirror or window, caught his eyes and dazzled him momentarily. He covered them with his hand and then removed it. He turned his head again to the man. He was no longer there. He yanked himself up by the seat in front to see if he was moving down the coach. There was no one in the aisle.

He saw a sign with 'Kastoria' written on it, and soon the road was skirting the shore of a lake on his right-hand side. A couple of smart hotels passed by and a warehouse with an illuminated sign above it where a model pressed a thick fur coat to her neck. Through gaps in the buildings he caught glimpses across greeny-blue water to a peninsular of land with white houses stacked up its steep sides. He scanned the guidebook entry for the town. *Kastori* was Greek for beaver, once central to the local fur trade. He took out a pen but somehow did not follow through in circling it.

The coach pulled up in a car park by a taxi rank and a row of quiet shops and cafés. He looked keenly for the man with the feminine eyes as he disembarked, but he did not see him. He bought some pastries from a baker's and ate them as he stared across a children's playground to the lake. A couple of swans skimmed over the water's surface as they landed by a patch of reeds. Wooden rowing boats bobbed at their moorings there, one striped with the blue and white colours of the Greek flag, with green fishing nets draped across them.

Sheref walked to a café and sat in the shade of its canopy on a low, leather sofa. The waiter set down a bottle of mineral water, cool with condensation, on the glass coffee table before him and he ordered an iced latte. His mind kept returning to the man on the bus. An odd, yet pleasant, bemusement lingered from the incident that he was trying to process. He took out his mobile phone and turned it on. He then fiddled with it a little; the back light was now flickering and the 7 button was functioning only intermittently. He shook it and tapped it. Why had he not fixed it? The latte was brought and he sipped it a little and drank a glass of water. His phone began to vibrate, rattling loudly on the coffee table glass. It was Hanife! He looked at it for a few seconds and then picked it up.

"Sheref! Where are you?" he heard her say anxiously. "Why was your phone off? I've been trying to call you!"

"I'm in Greece…" An answer came to him: "You know what roaming rates are like!"

"What are you doing?"

"I'm just drinking a coffee. There's a… nice lake here."

"Don't be angry with me… I told *baba* that you were going to Albania."

"Why did you do that?" he shouted curtly.

"He's here."

"What? No I don't want to…"

"Sheref?" The sound of his father's voice made him screw up his eyes tightly. He'd said his name softly, without accusation or reproach, for the first time in so long. Sheref lowered the phone to his chest for a moment. He swallowed. A tear welled up and it fell with a 'pat' onto his thigh. He could hear his father saying his name repeatedly, anxious they'd been cut off.

"Yes?"

"I have… this fine new samovar… at the Bazaar. It makes good tea… that is to say… when you have seen those *Arnavutlar*." Sheref understood what he was trying to say.

"Yes *baba*," he said. A few moments of silence passed and Sheref pressed the red button to end the call. He lowered his head and his shoulders shook as he sobbed. He brushed his cheeks quickly with his fingers, checked the receipt, and left his unfinished latte and three euros on the table.

He walked over a patch of dry grassy ground and then across a road to a pavement along the water's edge. He followed it thinking. The trees by the shore had been painted with skirts of whitewash. There were more cafés here with their tables arranged under the shade of canopies, mobiles tingling above them in the mild breeze. He passed a small boy with a face smeared with pink ice cream rocking happily on a child's ride. White, timbered mansions rose up the hillside on his left, and conifer trees clung to the rocky hillsides around. He sat down on a bench affected by the peace of the place. There he watched a man casting his rod and line out across the water and he thought of the Galata Bridge and the waters of the Golden Horn. The high, afternoon sun blazed off the surface, and a white sail turned slowly in the shimmering glare and moved back towards land. He had made a decision. He would stay here tonight. Tomorrow, yes, let it be so, he would return to Istanbul.

Chapter 20

When Jude awoke on Monday morning a little after 7am, the single bed sheet that covered him and Alex was twisted underneath him. He had not slept well for the second night in a row. Alex had perched herself on the furthest extremity of the bed from him. One bounce and he could have flipped her off and forced the issues open between them. He had thought about it. They had not been so with each other for over twenty-four hours before. He lay on his back in his shorts feeling hot and drained, thinking about what to do.

He rose and took a quick, cold shower. He dressed in a pair of light, khaki trousers and a white T-shirt and went through to the kitchen. He sliced open one of yesterday's bread rolls and spread on a little butter and a dollop of fig jam. He then opened the seal on the pack of *Lavazza* that Alex had bought him and thought about last night. He'd told her about the man bursting into their apartment, and the awful, eternal, fifteen final minutes of silence whilst he'd waited for Spiro and his friends outside to leave, and then the man's quick exit down into the darkness of the stairwell. Then had come her surprise revelation: that she, like Spiro, had noticed the man in recent days. He'd seen her eyes, keen with concern as they'd sat together and he'd told her all the details, and joyful at how Spiro had turned up after church with the book finished. Then she had lowered her face a little and her eyes had slid away.

He filled the cafetiere with coffee and hot water and left it standing. He located a screwdriver and after around fifteen minutes fiddling he had reattached the handle to the kitchen cabinet drawer. He took out a postcard he'd kept of a Nicaraguan peasant woman labouring on a coffee plantation and wrote on it:

'They sell the needy for a pair of sandals… and trample upon the heads of the poor as on the dust of the ground… Amos 2.

Sorry! Can we have dinner out tonight? Mr R.' He slotted it between the drawer and cabinet frame. He was pouring himself a coffee when he heard her come through to the living room behind him. She was wearing a baggy, oversized T-shirt with *'Coldplay. Parachutes.'* printed on it, and her hair had a flat patch above the left ear. Jude put a peppermint tea bag in a cup of hot water and handed it to her.

"Erm… Spiro will be here any minute now," he said. She took it, cast him an open glance, and returned to the bedroom.

Spiro shortly rapped his familiar knock on the door. Jude let him in and he stepped inside, smoothed his frond of hair and grinned.

"I was worried about you yesterday," he said affecting a fatherly expression. He placed a hand on Jude's shoulder and began to massage the muscles there. "I came here." Jude was not entirely comfortable with the new, instant bonhomie, but he had warmed a little to the man.

"I know," replied Jude. "He was inside… armed… whilst you were outside." Several expressions crossed Spiro's face whilst he processed the words.

"Pu, pu, pu... Dear God! Who was he?" he said after a few moments.

"I don't exactly know, but I don't think he'll be back," said Jude. "Come on now… come in. Let's get on with things." He sat down on the edge of the living room sofa, and Spiro sat opposite in an armchair still looking to Jude for a fuller account. Jude scrolled through the address book menu on his mobile phone and pressed dial.

"Hello Jetmira… this is Jude from *Shënomadh*," he said.

"Are your family well?" she said.

"Yes, my wife is very well… and your family?"

"Mirë, faleminderit… Good, good!"

"The book we discussed in your office… it's ready. I'm thinking about 1000 copies… A5 format… a colour cover. I have an agency photo for that… with the tile, 'The Shame of Honour Killing. The True Story of Mehmed Krasnichi.' Can you do them quickly?"

"Sigurisht! They can be printed and delivered to you in twenty-four hours."

"And the price please?"

"Një minutë… including transportation… that would be… 75,000 new *lekë*." Jude pushed his glasses up the ridge of his nose as he raised his eyebrows. It was well outside the price range she'd intimated

at when they'd met in Tirana. He mouthed the price to Spiro and watched him widen his eyes. Spiro beckoned with his hand for Jude to hand him the phone. He pressed the speaker mike so Jude could hear.

"*Hë me*! Hey woman… we are not all foreigners down here in *Shënomadh*. Come on, bring your price down!" he shouted.

"We are doing them for you quickly! If you want to wait a month or two, I can bring it down," she said.

"Are you… 'Speedy-Print'?" said Spiro. "Then why are you asking a premium for a service your business name says is standard? Don't discredit our people in the eyes of foreigners! Are you a patriot, or not?" He winked at Jude.

"Okay… we can do it for 60,000," she said. Jude nodded vigorously.

"That's better… *Ti je artiste, Jetmira!*" said Spiro. "*Po*? Yes?" She was saying something more that Jude couldn't quite catch, but it looked to him like Spiro was on it.

"*OK, ciao,*" said Spiro and ended the call. He handed Jude back his phone. "She'll begin printing it as soon as we email our files through to her. She says the bank transfer must be done today. When your bank calls her to confirm the payment has been initiated, she'll authorise transportation through the night… and you'll have the books in *Shënomadh* in the morning." Jude shook his head a little.

"Thanks again Spiro," he said. You might be old guard, he thought, but you're consummate at working your own kind! He stood up, smiled broadly at him, and punched the air in a sudden uncharacteristic gesture of triumph.

* * *

The mobile phone vibrated against the skin of Jude's thigh in his pocket later that morning. He drew it out and saw that Shpetim was calling. He walked out to the privacy of the balcony, and leant on the wall looking out at the sky before taking the call. Large, fluffy clouds tinged with grey hung motionless above him. A man sat on a nearby balcony in a cool spot between his air conditioning box and the family washing drying on a frame. It was hot again today, though the air felt closer and stickier than yesterday. His T-shirt felt uncomfortably tight across his chest.

"Are you feeling okay today Jude?" said Shpetim, his voice sounding tentative and subdued.

"Yes, I'm fine… Don't be worried for me on that count," said Jude. The fact that he'd had touches of tinnitus and some palpitations in the night was something that he had not yet shared with Alex, let alone think to open before Shpetim.

"I have to stay here in Tirana for a day or so… with this crisis, then I'll be back in *Shënomadh*, maybe Wednesday, okay?"

"Shpetim, it's finished now… the man's gone. And anyway Spiro's sworn a *besa* of protection over me. He's like that old woman with the semi-automatic… Not even your 'Special Forces' could get past him," said Jude trying to lighten his friend's mood.

"After you rang me last night, I made some calls… His name is Sam Prekazi. One of our local men had noticed him around May 5ᵀᴴ Street... He is ex-UÇK, later in the Kosovo Protection Corps... now a freelancer... with connections to some powerful people." Jude heard the sounds of something like a megaphone and shouting crowds in the background close to where Shpetim was. "I'll get a word to him. He'll have something personal with me if he..."

"Please Shpetim... don't. He did not mistreat me... Let it go. It'll be a weight off my mind..."

"I should have..."

"Don't say anything Shpetim," Jude interrupted. "It's not your job to watch out for *me*..."

"Job? Perhaps not. My *business* it *is*..."

"There's something else... When we were at the Blue Café yesterday after church, you said those things about that clandestine group in Turkey. What did you call them?"

"Ergenekon."

"It's just that Alex has had this strange dream."

"Tell me about it... quickly now, until I have to move."

* * *

After visiting the bank, Jude walked quickly up May 5ᵀᴴ Street. He passed by the entrance of an apartment block with a faded tangerine facade where an old woman in widow's black sat in the shade on a wooden stool. A pile of coarse cement powder was left on the pavement there with a shovel planted in it. A man came out of his doorway and hosed the drifting powder off his front step. The lines of water streaked the ground before him black.

In the downstairs room at the church building he set out chairs, arranged his photocopies neatly, and glanced over his lesson plan. He thought about his students, particularly Kristo and Blerta. Their participation was probably over now. It was not likely they would run the risk of meeting here with events in *Shënvogël* still being so incendiary between the two families. Yet it was a shame they had not seen the story of *A Tale of Two Cities* through to the end, he thought.

Fifteen minutes after 3pm, he decided to start with those that had arrived. It was a smaller class now; some other students had fallen away too.

"So… I hope you have finished the book by Charles Dickens. Did you like it?" he said. He looked around the students' faces. Some were smiling, others were indicating with little shakes of their head that they did. "You now know that the lawyer, Sydney Carton, made the aristocrat, Charles Darnay, exchange clothes with him in his prison cell." Jude lifted off his glasses as he prepared to open the discussion. "Disguised as Darnay, Carton was then driven through the streets of Paris in a wooden cart… and died on the guillotine there… so that Darnay could live out his life with his wife Lucie."

"It is really incredible what he did," said Flutura. "I cannot imagine how anyone could do that for someone else. Lucie was so beautiful…" She lifted a fallen strand of hair behind her ear. "And so lucky!"

"Well, my great-uncle died fighting the fascists here. He gave his life for his country!" said Bledi. "Don't you forget the family name… it's Shehu!"

"I could not do that for anyone," said Fredi.

"You wouldn't give your little finger for a noble cause!" said Bledi.

"*Ore!*" said Fredi to his friend. "Well, maybe for my mother... I could give her a vital organ, even if it shortened my life... to lengthen hers... This man Carton deserves a handsome statue in a park to honour his memory."

"So does my great uncle... and what's left now, a crumbling obelisk... with withered flowers left on May 5ᵀᴴ," said Bledi throwing up a hand in complaint.

"Why didn't Carton try to escape once he'd tricked the guards?" said Flutura.

"He had to see it through to the end... to really set them free," said Mira. "The zealots would have pursued Darnay otherwise."

"But how could he face such a thing without being terrified? I'd be hysterical!" said Flutura.

"Because he heard the words of Christ on the bridge in Paris,

I am the resurrection and the life.
He who believes in me, though he were dead,
yet shall he live.'

It says so on page 145," said Liridon. His finger was in the book and his big, bulging eyes moved anxiously around the other students. Jude felt his own emotions rising at this surprising little goatherd's answer.

"He faced death with a peaceful countenance. It says that too in the book," said Mira quietly. "He lay down his life... just as someone else did for us. He would be honoured before heaven, and live again forever."

To lighten the lesson now, Jude began an activity by miming lying in bed, tossing around, checking a wrist watch, and counting passing sheep.

"You couldn't sleep... you had things on your mind," said Bledi tapping the side of his head with a finger.

"Right," said Jude. "Now it's your turn to mime something that happened to you yesterday Bledi." The heavy-set man stood up and squatted in a sitting position that was a little unbecoming.

"You were driving your taxi," said Fredi.

"How did you know?" said Bledi irritatedly. "I didn't begin the mime yet!"

"I took a wild guess," said Fredi. Liridon began flapping his hand. It was technically not his turn, but Jude smiled and nodded to him. He stood up hovering a little uneasily before the other students, and ran his tongue along the tips of his bucked-teeth in preparation. He wiggled his fingers below his chin as he began to mime playing a piccolo or whistle. He then seemed to act out another character snatching the instrument from him, breaking it over his knee, and striking him. He drew himself up unswayed, wiggled his fingers and began to play the piccolo again, this time whistling an audible tune. He skipped from his left leg to his right, and then hopped back. He did it again. Fredi sat up grinning and lifted his hands above his head to click his fingers in accompaniment. Flutura joined in clicking her fingers. Bledi and Mira began to clap along. Liridon started to hop around the classroom. Jude clapped along with them. The students stood up and linked hands. Mira laughed out loud.

The classroom door swung open. A man with a squint and a feral nose stood there glowering.

"Get over here!" he shouted at Liridon. The young man froze and cowered away. "I said get here!" he shouted louder. He strode into the room and grabbed him by the shirt and yanked him. Jude figured that this was, incredibly, Shpat his 'owner'.

"Take it easy," said Bledi rising towards him. His presence seemed to stay Shpat's hand. Liridon looked around, almost defeated, except for something in his eyes. He then went before the man as they left the classroom. Jude sat down heavily. Silence had fallen over everyone. He heard a smack and a whine like that of some animal beaten outside and he flinched a little. Bledi exhaled heavily, slammed his fist down on the table, and left the classroom after them.

Jude took out the last item he had for the day's lesson, a Bible verse written in English on slips of paper, and handed them around the remaining students. It was *John 10:11.*

'I am the good shepherd. The good shepherd lays down his life for the sheep.'

"Do take time to think about it," he said. As he came to Mira she held on to two and looked at Jude.

"I'll make sure that Liridon gets one," she said.

Chapter 21

Alex skipped lightly up the orangey marble steps of Jaap and Odguda's apartment block. In the pocket of her embroidered, black, cowgirl shirt was the postcard of a Nicaraguan peasant woman she'd found in the kitchen. She tapped the top of it to press it further in. Odguda had invited her to come at 11am and she did not want to be late: the couple were particularly Northern-European in their timekeeping. She had only met Odguda socially together with Jaap and Jude, and had been pleased, yet a little surprised, when she had made a beeline for her alone after church yesterday.

"Hallo. Goedemorgen... come in," said Odguda as she opened the door. Uys popped his head out from behind her skirt folds like a little entertainer peeking at the audience from the wings. Whilst Alex's eyes were low she noticed Odguda's stout, brown leather shoes again. They walked through to the lounge. "Coffee?"

"Actually, would you have a fruit tea, peppermint, or something else?" said Alex.

"I think we have some *Rooibos*."

"Okay, thank you. That would be nice." Alex sat down on a low, teakwood-framed couch. Odguda came over from the kitchen shortly with a wooden tray of drinks. She put a plate on the couch between them and sat down. It had a type of apple tart criss-crossed with a grid of golden-brown pastry strips. Its aroma was wonderful. "Odguda... I hope you don't mind me asking... but don't your feet feel hot in those shoes?"

"*Nee*, I like to feel sure-footed... everyday," she said laughing. "That is a pretty shirt you are wearing!"

"Oh... I saw some Alt-Country music acts in London, and I liked what they were wearing. Do you like Alt-Country... or Country even?"

"I do like some of those Gospel Music groups, but listening to popular music was frowned upon where I grew up, dear," she said frowning.

"Well, I can understand that. Some of it is pretty unedifying," said Alex. Uys sidled up to the edge of the plate and rolled his head around his shoulders, fixing his eyes each time they passed on the apple tart. Alex stroked his cropped, blonde hair and his cheek with the backs of her fingers. He was such a beautiful child.

"Do you and Jude plan to have children?" Odguda said.

"Jude wants to wait a year or so," said Alex blinking and trying not to show the tinge of disappointment she felt.

"You are very blessed to be married to Jude. He seems so empathetic with people who are... I don't know, wounded or suffering. Jaap was so glad that Jude was with him in Istanbul."

"He has come through a lot... with his father, and with what happened to his mother."

"Jaap said something briefly about his mother, but I... if you didn't mind?"

"I think Jude would be fine about you knowing," said Alex. "His mother, Justine, was a secretary at a school. She was working in her office near to the headmaster's... an ex-pupil got into the building and began a violent assault on the headmaster in his office. When she and another teacher realised what was happening... they ran in to help him. The young man, Gary Bradshaw... he was from a troubled family, well-known locally... he lashed out at them to escape. He had a metal bar with him. He caught Justine on her head as he passed. It was a weak place on her skull... She went into a coma in hospital... she never came out of it. He was only fifteen when it happened."

"Oh, dear God. But he had the Lord with him, yes?"

"He had not given his heart to Him at that point. He had several troubled years... before that happened. It was only then that he was able, after some time, to forgive, and then grow... released, in a way, from what was such a terrible tragedy. Justine had previously worked with young offenders. Jude's dad told him that Gary was known to her... that she'd even tried to help him once."

"I see now," said Odguda quietly. As Alex looked at her it seemed that she was moved, and yet she realised it had touched her on a raw nerve. She took a sip of her *Rooibos* tea. Odguda cut the tart and lifted up the plate to offer her a slice. She took one and put it on a serviette.

"And you Alex... tell me how *you* came to the Lord?" Alex often felt a little intruded upon by this question. From the mouths of some people it felt like they were checking you actually had, and with Odguda, though it was not quite that, she thought she would be reassured to have a peripheral doubt or two quelled.

"Well, for me... it was through a dream," she said. Odguda turned her head slightly. "I was studying in south London at the time. One night, as I slept, I saw myself standing on the platform of a railway station, alone... as I often did to commute. A group of young men came up out of the underpass and scanned around themselves. They spotted me. They had these hungry, hard eyes... and I had a bad feeling about them. A train began to pull away in front of me, and a man leant out of the door and said, 'Are you getting on?' I hesitated... because I knew it wasn't stopping at my destination. Then I jumped up. As the train drew out, I saw a couple on a bench, lost in each other. The young men began to move towards them." Uys began to walk his fingers across the edge of the plate of tart. Odguda tapped them with hers and turned back keenly. "Three weeks later, I was at Clapham Junction. It was a mundane, rainy south London evening. I remember it clearly... the steel tracks gleaming over the oily, black sleepers and the signal lights blurry in the drizzle... It happened like the dream. The young men came up out of the underpass onto the platform. They saw me. The train in front of me began to pull away. A man leant out of the door and said, 'Are you getting on?'

I did. I saw the couple and the young men moving towards them. I banged on the window glass trying to get their attention… A couple of days later, a local newspaper, *The Wandsworth Guardian*, had a report of an attack on a couple at the station that night." Alex thought to take a small bite of her tart but she lowered it in her hand for a moment. "I got talking to the man who'd called to me from the train. He told me that he'd been praying and felt compelled to do it… and that he attended a church called the 'The Safe House'. The first day I walked in… they were singing a reworking of the old gospel song: *'This train is bound for glory, this train…'* I knew right there it was not freaky coincidence: it was Providence… and that's where I started my journey."

"That is such an interesting story," said Odguda. She smiled with her mouth but in her eyes she was troubled. Alex noticed the Van Halens' watercolour of windmills on the wall. It seemed to her like wheels were turning deep within Odguda.

* * *

It had begun in the night. Sheref had taken a room high up a steep alley in Kastoria that had a porthole-sized window facing away from the lake. It was clean but had no air-conditioning and was only fractionally bigger than the single bed slid into it. He had slept fitfully wiping the sweat off his face and neck with the bed sheet. He had heard again the sound of breath being exhaled close by that became a deep-throated snarl. He had felt something pressing down on him in the darkness and that he could not breathe. He'd thought he heard a voice. *Does a single gesture change your father's treatment of you? He thinks nothing of you! He spoke to you for love of Hanife! He has waited all his life for something… this… to be proud of you about!* He'd turned on his side and looked at the cell-like wall. *If you fail, you will be in debt to them: Omer, Kadir, Gazi… You will be a liability to them… they will kill you!*

He left the room just after 9am and bought bread rolls and a bottle of water in a mini-market by the lakeside. He ate and drank only a little. *Don't you love your country? Can't you do this one thing to protect her? Will you let them take it from your people?* He sat on a bench and looked at the lake. He stared for hours but it seemed he only saw the sun glaring on the water until when he turned away everything else was bleached of colour or covered with spots of white mist. *They treated you unfairly! They stole your education, your career… your life! Now you can show them what a foolish miscalculation that was!* He stood up and ran along the lakeside path to another bench. He pressed his eyes with the heels of his palms. His tongue felt thick and his mouth was dry. He filled it with water and spat it to the side. *You know better than most what these people are truly like! You have seen how they live! Phoneys! You know what this Jude Kilburn really is… You Sheref! You Sheref! You!* The voice seemed at times almost inaudible and then at others to be shouting at him: within him, close by his ear, or from some distant depth he could not tell. He turned his head sharply to see behind him but there was no one there.

By 2pm he felt that the earth had rotated 180 degrees at an axis point beneath his feet. He rose and turned towards the place where the coach had dropped him just over twenty-four hours earlier. He walked to a row of yellow taxis parked opposite the café where he had spoken to Hanife. He took out his mobile phone. Maybe she had texted him since yesterday? He tried to turn it on, but now it was malfunctioning completely. He took out his mirror lens sunglasses and covered his eyes.

A metre away from the open window of the first taxi in the rank, Sheref stood and looked inside. The driver was wearing a turquoise sun hat with the rim pulled down to the tops of his ears. He pulled out his white earphones and looked up.

"I want to go to the Albanian border," said Sheref.

"Oh... English. Okay. I'm your man," he said punching his fist forward and holding it there as if to touch another in greeting. He ducked his head left and right to some beat lingering there. Sheref opened the rear door and slid inside. The driver lifted his arm out of the left side window and held it forwards as they drove off in a parting gesture to locals he seemed to know.

The road wound upwards from the town centre, and as they turned a bend Sheref caught a glimpse down to the white buildings on the peninsular that stretched out into the greeny-blue waters of the lake. Then it was gone.

"The economy here... ffffeeew," said the driver blowing out a whistle and pointing downwards with his thumb. "The farmers have had enough! I tell you... they are going to get their tractors out and block the roads here before long!" He looked in the rear-view mirror at Sheref for a reaction twice and back at the road. "We taxi drivers will be right behind them. Well... a few hundred metres... don't want to get the paintwork scratched, eh!" Sheref could not be bothered with a response. He looked at a pile of business cards the driver had placed in a little, transparent tray by his gear-stick. Diamatos Arhontikis was, apparently, his name.

They accelerated along a country back road with little traffic and swung to the right before stopping at the entry of a highway.

"Look at that sign… 'Maniaki'. There are some crazy people down there!" said Diamantos. "Hey… do you get it?" Sheref closed his eyes in an attempt to block out the man. When he opened them, they were climbing a steep incline with a high bank of crumbling, copper-coloured earth on his left. A rocky gorge yawned down to his right. "What do you want with those Albanians?" He was grinning into the mirror. "They will shoot you or traffic you back to your country, my friend… No, no… My cousin married an Albanian girl in Thessaloniki… her fried zucchinis are better than any Greek woman's."

"Really," said Sheref unenthusiastically.

The road passed through a deep cutting of the same crumbling, coppery earth and onto a bridge that skirted down the left side of a valley wall. It then unravelled like a length of ribbon into the distance between the wooded mountain slopes either side.

"So where are you from then?" said Diamantos. Sheref did not answer for several seconds.

"I am from Turkey," he said looking away to the right at the passing trees.

"Oh… personally, Cyprus aside, I have nothing against your people. What's past is past, eh! We can be friends now!"

"Yes…" said Sheref neutrally.

"Cigarette?"

"Why not?" he whispered. Diamantos reached back with an open pack. One protruded higher than the rest and Sheref took it. Seconds later, Diamantos handed back an electric lighter that had popped from the dashboard. Sheref placed it to the tip and drew. He noticed a ladybird crawling down the window to his left. He wound it down an inch. He then pressed the glowing element to the beetle. There was a little hiss and a pungent odour rose into his nostrils. He tapped the lighter on the edge of the open window and glanced in the rear-view mirror. Diamantos looked away quickly. He handed the lighter forwards. He drew on the cigarette again, winced, and tossed it through the gap.

Sheref was relieved by the silence that followed. He stared through the window noticing things occasionally: Orthodox shrines like white, stone mailboxes burnt at the mouth, and smoke rising by a stream from humps like burial mounds. The taxi slowed as it turned left by a roundabout and Diamantos wound his window down. A blue hut marked with 'Border Police' by the roadside let out three men in ironed, military-green clothing and shiny black boots. Diamantos saluted, said something to them and braked. Sheref clenched his jaw tightly. The men looked at him and then waved them on. Sheref turned around. One was making a call on his mobile phone.

Fifteen minutes later, Sheref saw three radio masts on the hillside and the car drew to a slow halt at the rear of a vehicle queue.

"This is it," said Diamantos quietly. Sheref put forty euros on top of his business cards and got out without acknowledging him. Outside he was shocked. This was not the remote border point he had imagined. He walked past the long line of cars. Some still had their engines running; some were silent. Windows were wound down with elbows pointing out or an arm hanging limply down. A group of drivers stood outside together slouching on their hips and rolling their shoulders.

The border's offices crouched under a high, corrugated metal roof. A sign on the wall said 'Police and Customs of Krystallopigi'. Here men were huddled around an open cubicle window, and Sheref hovered behind them shuffling his feet a little. After fifteen slow minutes, he was at the front. Two men were pushing at his elbows, reaching around him to pass their passports through a gap in the glass. He glanced at the covers: a double-headed eagle in gold on dark maroon. The officer shouted something at them in Greek and they moved away. He looked at Sheref quickly. He opened the back cover of his passport and flicked back a page. He glanced again at him. He thumbed through a few pages until he found his visa and he examined it carefully. As he held it under a scanner, a glow of UV light crossed his face. He lifted up a telephone.

"*Einai edo,*" he said. Sheref waited. A man with a thick, grey moustache moved into an open door frame at the back of the room some minutes later. He looked at Sheref and then disappeared. The officer tossed his passport to him and flicked his hand away twice.

Sheref pulled his backpack higher up his shoulder and began to walk. He slackened his fingers in the palm his right hand and shook it to ease it.

After a hundred metres or so, he came to a decrepit sentry box at the side of the road and a rough ridge in the tarmac. He stepped past it with a quickening of adrenaline and a dark smile of satisfaction to himself. He had now crossed into the Albanian side of no man's land.

Chapter 22

Sheref fixed his eyes ahead on the offices of the Albanian border control. Signs above two cubicles in the middle of the road read *'Welcome to European Albania'* encircled by gold stars and *'Have nice stay'*. He stumbled in a trough in the tarmac and fell forwards several steps before he regained his footing. A man with dark, dusty feet selling bundles of a dried, green plant came towards him looking expectantly saying: *"Çaj mali?"* Sheref ignored him and walked along the line of cars to one of the cubicles. After a short wait, he handed the border policeman his passport through an open window. The badge on the arm of his blue shirt had a black eagle with a yellow tongue licking out. The man looked at him and lifted up a telephone receiver.

A young policeman with a serious expression touched his elbow moments later, and indicated the direction he would like him to move in. Sheref hesitated. The man in the cubicle handed the young officer Sheref's passport.

"*Hajde*," said the young man using the Turkish word for 'come'. He was led into a nearby room. He glanced around anxiously wondering if, possibly, he was being detained. It had a row of worn, wooden chairs along one wall and a desk opposite. A camp bed was set in a corner with a folded, grey blanket thrown on it. Whitewashed walls were scuffed and an exposed electric socket with two wires hanging out was set in one. It smelt of nicotine, dust and stale sweat. The young officer indicated he should remove his sunglasses and raise his arms. He began to pat underneath them and around his waist. He pointed and Sheref removed his body belt of euros. The officer opened it, looked inside and placed it on the desk. He emptied out the contents of his backpack and spread them out there then gestured for Sheref to take a seat.

Another man entered the room talking over his shoulder as he did so. Sheref saw him only from the side: thick, black stubble over heavy jowls, and a paunch straining the buttons of his blue shirt. The man made a cursory examination of Sheref's things and sat down behind the desk. He then turned his head and looked at him directly. He fixed his gaze on Sheref and held it. He kept on staring. He did not blink. His eyes seemed like steel ball bearings. His lips then drew back from his teeth with a grin that was humourless and knowing. He had three gold teeth in a row at the top and two more below them. Sheref felt the need to avert his eyes lest this man look right into his soul and read it. He opened his passport.

"Mr Sheref… *Dushman*," he said slowly and purposefully. "Interesting name… you are… Albanian?"

"My father's forefathers..." said Sheref just a little louder than a whisper.

"Speak up please. And what... you were doing in Greece?"

"Travelling." The man lifted his camera, turned it on and scrolled through his photos. He opened the Greek guidebook and flicked through the pages. He pushed the postcards apart on the desk and looked at them. He lifted up the one of the 'White Tower' in Thessaloniki.

"And how did you like this place?"

"I bought it with a plan to go, but I did not make it there," said Sheref involuntarily touching his own nose.

"I see," he said. "And how were the... 'Royal Tombs of Vergina'?"

"Again, I had the intention... but they were closed on the day I was in the area," he said realising how it looked. "But Kastoria was a beautiful location, the mansions, the lake... shame about the beavers..." The man looked at him with his constant penetrating stare and grin.

"What is... purpose of your visit in Albania?"

"Tourism..."

"For example?" he said flicking through the pages of Sheref's *Guide to Albania*. Sheref realised he had marked up nothing in it. His feet shuffled a little on the floor.

"There is a museum of Iconography in... one of the southern towns," he said.

"Really?" said the man, a note of something new in his tone. "You are interested in such things?"

"Yes."

"And how long you plan to stay?"

"A week… two maximum."

"You are carrying a lot of money? There are some criminals and opportunists in our country, Mr Dushman. You might… become detached from it." Sheref wiped the edges of his upper lip with his thumb and forefinger as if he were smoothing down his imaginary moustache.

"I was not sure how easy it would be to find cash machines," he said. The man paused, thinking, staring metallically.

"And your health?" Sheref was unclear what he meant. He just looked at him. "There are some… technicalities… that must be observed. Please wait here. You can pack up your things." The man stood up. "*O, oficer Bujari!*' he shouted through the open door. "Bring our Turkish friend some mountain tea… *çaj mali*… to drink whilst he waits. He looks sick." He left the room with Sheref's money belt of euros tucked under his arm tapping his passport on the tips of his fingers.

Sheref hunched his shoulders around himself as he rested his elbows on his knees. He pressed his fingers into the palm of his hand as he thought. Why had they drawn him out of the flow like this? Were they making further checks now? What could they find on him? Nothing. Did they think this crude 'leave him to sweat' technique would make him suddenly reveal something? What did the man mean 'technicalities'? Could those be cleared up with, perhaps, some euros? He sat and he waited. The darkness fell outside but was prohibited from entry by a sterile white lighting. No one came in to see him. No tea was brought. He looked at his watch; it was after midnight. He had been sitting here for almost five hours. He took out his keyring and looked at its blue disk and black pupil. He rubbed his thumb softly across it and stared at the wall as if he might see though it, and into what was coming.

* * *

In the stone courtyard of the *Darka e Qengjit* restaurant Jude crossed with Alex a pace apart from him. She was wearing a watercolour print tunic over her jeans and looked brighter. A fountain spraying from a steel tube into a small, blue pool trickled softly in the centre. The three-quarter moon shone a pale sheen onto the edges of a low cloud and down over the surrounding buildings. Jude drew out a black iron chair from a table for Alex to sit on and then one for himself before sitting down on its firm, cream cushion. He glanced quickly at the varnished wooden beams of the porch and a pair of bellows hung on one. Albania was changing; *Shënomadh* was catching up.

The waiter quickly brought two thick, leather-bound menus and set them on the white linen table-cloth before them.

"Shall I order some things for us Alex?" said Jude. He knew what she liked. She smiled moderately. "Could we have the spit-roast lamb… a three-cabbage salad and a bottle of T'ga Za Jug… and the Greek yoghurt with honey after, please." He handed the waiter the menus and he left. A few seconds of silence followed as Jude looked down at his jacket sleeve. "Alex, I'm… sorry," he said looking up. "Let's go soon together… to gather some more pine cones below the rock pinnacle, okay? I'll be your donkey for the day. You can put a wooden frame on me, load me up and sit sidesaddle swinging your legs on the way back down. What do you say?"

"Okay. Just don't go all Balaam's Ass on me!" she said arching an eyebrow in amusement.

"I shouldn't have said what I did about Spiro," he said. "Anyway, he came through! I was so focussed on my own goal. I had dust on my glasses… I had… a compassion deficiency with him… Can you, perhaps, sub me a little?" He gave her a broad smile now.

"I'll think about it," she said, her eyes softening. "Anyway, I said some things about your practical skills… with spanners and such that I'd like to retract." Jude laughed.

The waiter returned with the wine and glasses. He uncorked the bottle and folded a white linen napkin around it. He left and came again with the salad: finely chopped red and green cabbages with grated carrot. He placed the red wine vinegar and olive oil bottles neatly beside it. The man had a bald head, a thick neck and a granite expression. He left.

"He reminds me of someone!" whispered Jude taking off his crushed velvet jacket and hanging it over the chair back.

"'Oddjob'… or to you *Mr Powers*, 'Random Task'" she whispered back with a mischievous smile. The man returned with a covered metal dish of lamb and a basket of bread.

"Could you bring us a candle for the table? Would you mind?" said Jude.

"Don't worry sir, we've got a generator," he said and left. Alex covered her mouth.

Jude breathed a sigh of release. He felt a sudden surge of boyish energy and glanced around. On a nearby trolley was an artfully arranged bowl of fruit with a honeydew melon on top. He jumped across and returned holding the melon upright in his hand. He set his glasses on it.

"My name… is Michael Caine," he said affecting a South London accent and wiggling it like a ventriloquist. "And I am going to show *you*… how to cook a proper omelette with champignon mushrooms." He dropped the impersonation. "The Albanians got him you know… in *The Ipcress File*. Have you seen that?"

"Stop it you clown!" she whispered. Jude set it back in the fruit bowl. He waited for Alex to serve herself some lamb and salad then followed suit.

"Do you remember when we met at 'The Safe House'?" said Alex.

"I took you later… to the Jongleurs Comedy Club in Clapham to see Milton Jones."

"What was that one about half-way though his set?"

"Oh… I went fell walking in the Lake District. Well… that's not true. I fell walking in the Lake District…" he said.

"You almost needed a nebuliser to recover your breath!" She had cocked her head to one side, and was playing with one of her *Liquorice Allsorts* ear rings. Her skin-pink lipstick had smudged a little, and Jude had the urge to lean across and wipe it off for her.

"How did you get me down here Alex?" he said shaking his head a little. "You with your 'Zlata's Diary' stuffed in your cowgirl shirt pocket! You and the suffering peoples of the former Yugoslavia! I only came down here that first time so I could ride in the cabin of the Volvo truck… next to you all the way to Tirana. Five years after that, we were living here…"

"The doors kept opening Jude. He led the way. It was meant to be."

"Now, don't go all Calvinist on me!" Alex smiled and gave him a look that said 'touché'. "Do you remember when we came into the country… that guy at the border?"

"He was scary!" she said.

"'Flori' they called him. He was like 'Jaws' from the Bond movies… with gold teeth. He could have bitten his way through barriers to get to Greece if he'd had a mind to."

"A lot of corruption paid for those molars… I bet his dentist has a second home down in Halkidiki now." Jude laughed again.

Alex picked up a flat cake of freshly-baked bread dusted with flour and broke a piece off. A feeling suddenly pricked Jude. It was something like a fear of separation from her. He lifted the wine bottle and poured some into Alex's glass a little too hastily. A small amount flowed over the rim onto the tablecloth and spread like a deep purplish-red slash there. Alex dabbed it with her napkin.

"Since that man stepped out of the shadows and into our apartment yesterday afternoon, I've been thinking… about some of those believers in Turkey," he said. "Paul was sprung from jail and Stephen was stoned… there is divine protection and there is martyrdom, Alex. It's not given to us to know which it is to be, is it?" A high-pitched note rose in volume in his ears. He shook his head to one side to try to clear it. Alex threaded her hand through the plates and glasses to take his.

"I should have told you I'd seen him by the *Don Café*," she said. "It might have helped… you'd have been ready. I was visiting, sulking stupidly, when I could have been by you…"

"He'd have come anyway."

"May we have the strength to face all things by the power Christ gives us," she said leaning forwards earnestly. She squeezed his hand tighter. Jude remembered how Mehmed had given Marko a T-shirt with that verse on. Her chair grated on the stone floor as she pushed it backwards. She came to Jude's side, took off his glasses and kissed him. Jude wiped the lipstick smudge on her lip with his thumb and held her chin softly.

"Alex. In your dream… the blue glass charm. You said Alexandroupoli, Xanthi… It was only in Greece?" He searched her eyes and he read something more. "It was here in Albania too?" She nodded.

Chapter 23

The same sterile white border lighting shone on the tarmac road as Sheref walked along it. It was warmer outside in the night air than in the Border Police office, and the moon was giving pale outline to the odd low cloud and the steep, rocky hills on either side. It smelt different here; the rough bark of some dog sounded different; the people, plenty of them despite the hour, stood and watched him differently. He checked his watch: 2.37am, Tuesday, August 26th. The officer with the steely eyes had kept them on him as he'd tossed him back his passport and money belt and told him he could leave. He had checked the euros. There were fifty missing. He had quickly decided it was expedient to go without challenging him.

Ahead of him was a row of parked cars, some topped with a white '*Taksi*' sign, others visible by their glowing red rear lights. Several men came towards him.

"*Ku do shkosh?*" one man shouted. He walked past them; he did not like to be hustled. He stopped at the third car in the line. It was an old, brown Mercedes Benz 240d with ageing classic lines. He felt drawn to it. They had been a much more frequent sight on the roads of Turkey when he'd been a boy, but were less so now. The driver opened his door and lifted out his heavy-set frame. Sheref tried a few words of Turkish. The driver looked back at him and shrugged.

"I want to go to *Shënomadh*," Sheref said in English. The driver straightened up and tapped his chest.

"I am going there," he said.

Sheref opened a rear door and climbed inside. The seat sank into the worn springs and the smell was old: the vinyl upholstery, the metal. The driver climbed in and started the engine and it jumped into a clattering rhythm. He swung the wheel to the left and they accelerated out beyond the lights of the border buildings and onto an unlit road. They had been driving for around fifteen minutes when the car pulled off onto the gravelly earth of what looked like an old petrol station. A lamp glowed dim orange behind the dirty windowpane of a whitewashed stone hut. There was one old pump on the forecourt with mechanical dials on its face. The driver rattled the nozzle in the petrol cap and the pump whirred for a minute. He banged on the hut window and it opened. He handed something through.

"*Natën e mirë!*" a voice like an old man's called out from the interior. The stones crunched under the car tyres as they drew away.

As they continued down a gradual descent there was little to see but blackness outside pricked only by the odd, little group of white and neon lights.

He rested his head backwards and listened to the droning tick of the diesel engine. He closed his eyes. It seemed like seconds later that he awoke as the engine began to cough. It lurched and spluttered as they pulled into the roadside. The driver muttered something and thumped the steering wheel.

"Please… wait here," he said and got out. He unlocked the boot and slammed it down then walked past the window with a petrol can in his hand. The darkness swallowed his outline. Sheref breathed out a long sigh. He waited.

It was perhaps thirty minutes later that the driver returned. There was a rattle as the petrol cap was removed again. He climbed back in. He turned over the starter-motor and the engine coughed and ran still spluttering a little.

"*Më falni,*" he said putting his hand on his chest. "Old Leo has been putting raki in his diesel again." He drove to a turquoise sign that read 'Alpet'. It rose above a gleaming steel and glass petrol station lit from all directions like an airport terminal. He filled up there and drove on again.

Sheref's head began to droop forwards in the dark tedium of the drive, and then he would jolt it upright. He caught sight of road signs occasionally: *Bilisht, Maliq, Grabovicë…* As he dozed he saw a white football scarf and eyes full of venom before him, and then he felt a fist smash into his cheek. His chin bounced down onto his chest as the whole car rattled after striking some deep pothole. He was wide-awake again. Soon there was a juddering sensation coming up through the car's body.

"*O, zot i madh!*" the driver shouted. He drew it over to the roadside and got out. He walked to the rear left wheel by Sheref and kicked it. "*Oh, u shfry!* It's flat.*"* He pointed down in an animated way. Sheref had figured that much. Not again, he thought. He got out and stood watching at the side of the road. A truck with a single headlight thundered past with its horn on like a locomotive, rocking the Mercedes in the draught. The driver lifted the boot hood and dragged out the spare wheel and a Bilstein jack. He had the change done in fifteen minutes, and breathing heavily he lifted a bottle from the boot and washed his hands. "Water?" he said offering it. Sheref opened the rear door and got in.

They drove on and the road hair-pinned left and right as they slowly descended a hillside. Soon, they passed through a small town where the metal shutters of stores were still padlocked to the ground. The road then drew parallel to a lake, and away on the far shore he saw lights reflecting like spikes across the black surface. They began to slow again. They passed a crowd of men huddling in the darkness. He saw a row of police cars with their blue lights pulsing. Placards were stacked against a wall. They drew up to the red, rear lights of another car and stopped. The driver got out and Sheref wound down the window and craned his head out to see. A forklift tractor was lowering a boulder into the road about fifty metres away, and beyond it a car was blazing ferociously right across the centre of the road. He heard shouting and it seemed a scuffle had broken out there. The driver shortly climbed back inside.

"There is a protest… against the government… we must wait. Maybe after an hour we can pass," he said letting out a sigh. Sheref then heard the driver say almost under his breath, "Always cheating with the ballot boxes... someone here." Sheref ran his palm over the surface of his clenched fist. He wanted to strike at something: the seat, the door, anything. He pushed the urge down into his intestines. It seemed like ever since he'd left Greece that he was trying to move forward against a headwind!

The first patches of lighter sky rose to the east across the lake. He watched them turn a slate grey and then pale blue, and the stars faded. A pink and yellow aura rose over a ridge of mountains and then the sun came and the land was bathed in a red light. The driver turned his music player on low. A clarinet held a long note, and then fell lilting and melancholy, before a steady, pounding brass rhythm joined it. The car began to move forwards. It was light when they wove slowly past three stone boulders cleared to the roadside and a blackened car shell. The road wound along the edge of the lake he had read on the Internet was called *Ohridsko*. He knew he was close now. He saw a road sign for *Lin* and soon they were climbing, the full expanse of the lake, perhaps 30km, stretching out behind him. They crested a pass and the road began a long, zigzagging descent into a new valley, flat in the bottom with a patchwork of green and brown fields.

A sign read '*Shënomadh 12km*'. When they entered shortly, the first impressions of an Albanian town in daylight slid past Sheref's eyes. He saw bare red-bricked apartment buildings hung with washing; a monument in the form of a big, concrete fist clasping the end of a rifle barrel, sprayed with graffiti; a horse and cart loaded high with plastic bowls and buckets turning a corner; expensive cars.

"Take me to a hotel," said Sheref. The driver pulled up under the shade of a row of horse chestnut trees and pointed down a narrow side street.

"Fifty euros," he said. Sheref passed him three twenty notes. The driver leant across to the glove compartment and opened it. He took out a bag of peanuts, a book and then a wallet and put them on the seat. Sheref noticed the author's name, 'Charles Dickens'. The driver took a ten euro note from the wallet and passed it back.

"*Rrofsh!* Enjoy your stay in *Shënomadh*," he said.

* * *

Jude opened his eyes and blinked to clear his vision. Something, like a flash of sunlight from a car mirror or a neighbour's window, he thought, had disturbed his sleep. He checked his mobile phone: 5.34am. He ran his hand back through his hair and exhaled. He turned a little to see Alex. She had slept close by him and her arm was still thrown over the centre of his chest. He could feel her warm breath on his shoulder. He could smell her perfume, a sweet, woody scent with a note of berries, and her hair that had last-night's restaurant in it. He had slept so much better for the restoration of all lines of communication with her again.

He lifted off her arm slowly and slid his legs down to the floor. He washed and took out a fresh, baggy shirt and a pair of light brown cotton trousers with a tie-cord. He took them to the living room and dressed quietly there. He filled the kettle and switched it on and prepared the cafetiere with two heaped spoons of *Lavazza*. As he pressed the plunger down he stood well back. How many shirts had he splattered through absent-mindedness? When his coffee was ready he took a *Pocket New Testament and Psalms* off the coffee table and with the same hand unlocked the balcony door and stepped outside. The nearby mountains were red with the rising sun. The air was fresh and cool on his bare feet but he didn't mind. He watched a horse and cart laden high with plastic bowls and buckets clatter past below on its way to the bazaar. Pigeons were cooing on the roof of the neighbouring apartment block. The sparrows were squabbling on a TV aerial. A canary was singing in its cage on a balcony below. They all seemed to be raising a racket about something this morning, he thought.

He sat down on a plastic chair, sipped his coffee, and set the cup on a sloping window ledge. He closed his eyes and rolled his neck around his shoulders. He let his *New Testament* rest in the palm of his hand and it fell open with the pages dividing either way. He fingered the edges to the left until he came to the book of *1 Peter*, which he had started to dip into. He read the beginning again.

'To God's elect, strangers in the world, scattered throughout Pontus, Galatia, Cappadocia…'

He read on pausing to think occasionally until he came to words in chapter five near the end.

'Be self-controlled and alert. Your enemy the Devil prowls around like a roaring lion looking for someone to devour. Resist him, standing firm in the faith, because you know that your brothers throughout the world are undergoing the same kinds of sufferings.'

At first the words passed unobtrusively before him. Then they seemed to arch out of the page in his mind's eye as if a magnifying glass were passed over them. He tried to read on, rationalising and playing it down. It was a known general truth, for sure, he thought. Then he heard the words within him their volume increasing.

The birds seemed to quieten down around him; the very air seemed charged with something; the hairs on his forearms rose. It's for me, now, he thought. He began to breathe heavily. The beating of his heart accelerated. He felt the blood draining from his face. His cup slid off the ledge, bounced and splintered, spraying his shirt with coffee.

Chapter 24

Jude stood in the living room brushing the coffee from his shirt with his hand. Alex came through from the bedroom fastening her dressing gown.

"What is it Jude? I heard a noise... what's happened?" she said searching his face.

"I was careless... where I put my cup. It slid off," he said distractedly. He took a couple of steps towards the kitchen and then turned around suspended mid-action. He could not think quite what to do next. He sat on the arm of the sofa at an odd angle and took off his glasses. "I was reading *1 Peter*. It was like it came out of the page at me... as a warning... that there is something coming." He stared at their house telephone. Alex did not respond for several seconds.

"If that is so, it is a confirmation," she said. "We've been put on notice. We are ready. We can be vigilant... and watch and pray together. Two are better than one!" Jude turned his head towards her, focussed his eyes on her and smiled. She was his jewel: she was so positive. "Give me your shirt... and go get another one." Jude did as he'd been told.

When he returned she was opening cupboard doors in the kitchen and clattering about.

"First things first… a good breakfast," she said handing him a tray loaded with side plates, cutlery and a jar of fig jam. Jude carried them through to the balcony. He set out a second plastic chair and their wooden, fold-down table and he laid out the items he'd brought there. When he returned his Mr Rochester's Mug was filled with hot water and a teabag. Bacon was sizzling in the frying pan and eggs were rattling in boiling water. Soon, some of yesterday's bread rolls, still soft, and fizzy apple juice were added. They sat down together on the balcony.

"Alex, thank you," he said as he slowly made himself a second bacon roll. He gulped down several mouthfuls of tea. He drew in a deep draught of the morning air and let it out.

"Your colour has returned," she said smiling.

Jude felt a sudden urge. He stood up and looked down onto the dirt ground below them. Who was there? A youth in a pink T-shirt with sunglasses balanced on the top of his head brought out a tray of coffees to a table by the *Don* Café. A man with sailor's arms had set out his bathroom scales on the pavement hoping to earn a few *lekë* weighing passers by. An old woman with a big grass brush bound to a knobbly stick like a witch's broom was raising it to swipe at a little street dog. He sat back down feeling a little better that the coast seemed clear from first watch. What had he expected to see? Another Sam Prekazi step back into the shadows? He didn't know. It was silly. Alex was following his moves with her eyes. There was concern there, he knew.

His mobile phone began to ring and vibrate on the living-room coffee table. He stood up again, walked through the doorway, and picked it up.

"Oh, it's Jetmira?" he said turning around to catch Alex's eye as she came in after him. He answered and held it tucked into his neck supporting it on his shoulder as he listened. As Jetmira talked, though, he straightened up his head and held it firmly to his ear. Alex took a call on the house phone briefly at the same time and lowered the receiver quietly. Jude looked at Alex as he nodded and said into his phone, "*Po, kuptoj.* Yes. I understand." He felt his eyes glazing-over as he stood there. He pressed the 'End Call' button and sat down on the sofa. He ran his hand back through his hair as he stared at the floor. "Jetmira said the truck with my books on left Speedy-Print late… this morning before 4.00am," he began looking up at Alex. "The driver had a drop to make in Elbasan… before he came on to *Shëno-madh*. When he didn't make that, she got concerned and called him. Well, his phone was ringing and no one was answering… then suddenly it was. She could hear all kinds of noise and shouting in the background. A man said he was at the scene of an accident… that he'd come from a nearby village to help. From him she worked out what had happened…" Alex came and sat opposite him in an armchair and leant forwards feeling her own fingers. "It seems that the driver was crossing the *Qafë Krrabë* ridge road in the darkness. Some anti-government protesters had blocked the road with rocks. He swerved to avoid them and went over the edge. His truck was smashed to pieces down the mountainside… He was thrown clear, but severely injured… poor man… The assumption is the books will be ruined… it's a long way down there."

"Oh Lord," said Alex covering her mouth. "And what else did she say?"

"That I need to seek recompense from the driver. He's his own separate business… like a sub-contractor. It was his responsibility. She did her part and cannot refund the money I transferred yesterday. That… she is sorry." He lowered his head and closed his eyes momentarily. "He's probably a one-man-band, Alex… his own life wrecked. It's a non-option, isn't it?" He paused though not waiting for an answer. "She offered to print it again, if I want. She'll give me a thirty-percent reduction if we leave out official documentation… Maybe Alex… just this once… I could do it that way. We might be able to get that much together, if we juggled and scrimped, don't you think?" He looked up at her grasping after a line of hope he'd dismissed in his heart as he'd spoken the words.

"You wouldn't be happy with that later, Jude. You know what she's proposing."

"You're right Alex. It's just… I can't believe it. The whole endeavour is sunk… for the foreseeable future anyway."

"We'll pray Jude. We don't know what might happen." Alex stood up and walked out on to the balcony. She returned with his 'Mr Rochester's Mug' and handed it to him. He drank a little tea and stared into it. "There is something else you should know," she said closing her eyes and opening them, her eyelids fluttering a little as if she was shrinking from saying it. "That was Odguda on the phone…

She and Jaap are leaving Albania... the day after tomorrow."

"What?" said Jude. "I knew they were thinking about it... but why so suddenly? Why this moment? Did she say?"

"She didn't. But I think, maybe, I have a notion why."

* * *

With his cheek pressed into the crumpled sheets Jude lay face down on the bed. He had been here for some hours. He could not bring himself to check how long: it seemed of little importance. Alex had let him have his own space. He had locked the bedroom door. He drank another mouthful of cold tea and set his mug back on the bedside cabinet.

He thought about Jaap and remembered the comic incongruity of this sober Dutchman doing a little air guitar. He recalled the Istanbul planning sessions at Jaap's house and his 'light aircraft fuel' coffee. He remembered lifting him up from the ground into a sitting position by the ferry piers on the Golden Horn, and unscrewing the top of a bottle of water for him as bystanders gathered around. Jaap had made a choice that was his right. The break would do him good, he thought, if that was what it was. It was warm in the bedroom, but he shivered a little. He felt he wanted to seek out the company of friends, or even lively strangers, in the human warmth of some café.

He turned his head to rest his other cheek on the sheet. He imagined the scene up by the *Qafë Krrabë* road: the truck arching through the air, the books strewn down a steep, gravely slope like rubbish on a dump. His shoulders and his neck muscles ached and he felt like the jackboot of some big, stone monument was on his back pressing his outline indelibly into the mattress. Maybe he could still take Jetmira up on her offer... maybe. Then it wouldn't all be lost. It might yet be ready for the biennial conference! No, he told himself again. He heard the words from somewhere: *It's finished now, over. There's nothing you can do!* He lifted up his fist and thumped the pillow. He struck out sideways at his Mr Rochester's Mug. It flew against the wall and broke. He stared at a section of the broken figure's face and his own rash act compounded his feelings. He sat up and collected pieces from the floor into the palm of his hand.

He strode back into the living room. Alex was sitting on a chair near to the balcony door and she looked up from her Bible opening her eyes.

"I..." he said holding out his hand limply. She nodded. She must have heard it, he thought. He went to the refrigerator and took out the block of Macedonian white cheese and the jar of pickled green chilli-peppers. He tore open the plastic bag with the remaining bread rolls, cut them roughly, and filled them all with slices and pieces. He stood there munching determinedly until they were all gone. As he wiped his mouth he saw his own reflection in a chrome surface; the skin under his eyes had blackened. He felt trapped in this box-like apartment: he had to get out.

"I'm just going for some fresh air Alex, okay? I'll be fine," he said. She stood up and stepped towards him. He grabbed his bag and pulled the strap over his shoulder. It had the materials for his English classes in, and he had a vague idea that he had a class to teach this afternoon. He strode directly to the door and closed it behind him.

In the dimly lit stairwell he descended the stairs a little faster than was safe, stumbled and jumped the last four steps to keep from falling. He walked across the dirt ground below their apartment block and on to May 5TH Street. He turned left past the row of taxi vans to join the main road right towards the centre of *Shënomadh*. He walked past cafés filled with men conferring intimately, each of which he felt drawn to enter. He came to a wooden bench beneath a row of horse chestnut trees and sat down. In the nearby shade two men had drawn chairs up to an upturned plastic crate where they had placed their Backgammon board. The dice rattled on the wood as they cast them out. Another man stood over them slowly fingering a string of amber worry beads behind his back.

A breeze disturbed the thick canopy of leaves above him. He turned around and looked back over his shoulder. There was no one there. A narrow side street with 'Hotel' signs painted roughly in blue on white, wooden boards stretched back. A cluster of chestnuts thudded to the ground nearby still in their shells like lime green maces. For a moment, he thought of the early Christians and the persecutions they had faced. He imagined some Roman instrument of torture being brought down on his flesh, tearing it off. Was he ever likely to face such an ordeal here? Of course he wasn't.

He slid to the left of the bench. He stood up and sat back down. He slid across to the right and turned around. A high-pitched note rose again in his ears and then it diminished. He felt his heart begin to gallop, banging at his rib cage; it fell to a canter and then it charged away again. A feeling like an electrical charge rose up his spinal cord and it thrashed around sending sparks down to his nerve ends. He saw white stars circling before his eyes. He took off his glasses. He brought his hands up across his face and felt the cold sweat on his forehead. He rocked forwards, drew his hands away and looked at them.

He could leave Albania. Yes, that's what he could do! He would go home and pull out their suitcases. He would convince Alex that it was the right thing to do. They would throw in the essentials, grab their passports, lock the place up and get in a taxi. They could be at Mother Teresa Airport near Tirana in two hours and get on any flight out of here. Yes! He got up and he began to walk back towards their apartment. Then he broke into a run.

Chapter 25

On the edge of a black vinyl sofa bed Sheref sat and rubbed his eyes. Mosquitoes had bitten the backs of his hands and he scratched his skin agitatedly. He looked around his hotel room in the morning light. On one of the soiled walls was a calendar girl holding a bottle of *Coca Cola*. Facing it was a faded family photo of a group of stern faces. The dusty net curtains were all tied up in knots. It was cheap at ten euros a night and he was not complaining. He remembered how he been startled in the early hours at the sound of a rifle shot and some howling dog until he had realised what was happening.

He turned on the portable TV whilst he washed quickly. He opened the wardrobe and checked the items he'd placed there. He took out his stone-washed jeans, white trainers and a loose, orange T-shirt. He had seen how the town's young men dressed last night, and with little effort it was easy to blend in. The reception on the TV was fuzzy, and some cold-faced woman wearing her hair in a black bun was reading the morning news bulletin with a shimmering globe behind her. He picked out the occasional Turkish word and the channel name, *TV Shënomadh*. The news ticker read '*Wednesday, August 27th… 9.04 am. 87 degrees Farenheit. Anti-government protests set to continue…*' in English along the bottom of the screen. He reflected as he watched. After the taxi-ride through the night from the border, he had slept for most of the previous day. He had ventured outside in the evening, though, and felt strangely more at ease here than he'd imagined. These *Arnavutlar* had been part of the Ottoman Empire for five hundred years, that much he knew, and there was a familiar taste in the air. He had kept to the shadows, watching and listening, avoiding the pools of white streetlight on the pavements. Families had been promenading to and fro. Girls wearing their best clothes, all made up and hair primped, linked arms together as they walked. Dark-skinned men had squatted at the roadside toasting cornhusks, fanning their coals with squares of card to an intense orange glow. He had bought one and eaten it in precise rows as he'd searched.

He put his backpack over his shoulder. He turned off the TV and locked the room behind him. He paused at the glass-fronted reception cubicle to get his passport back, but the woman was outside slumped on a chair in the street. She wore a white caretaker's jacket and her dyed purple-black hair was tied tightly behind her head. He noticed her eye him shrewdly as she drew his passport from her pocket. He put on his mirror lens sunglasses and walked out of the side street onto the long avenue of horse chestnut trees. He turned left into the high street and stopped at a currency exchange shop to buy 200 euros' worth of Albanian money. He fingered the green 1000 *lekë* notes curiously. He moved along to a camera shop selling postcards. There was not much of a choice, and he settled on one of the monument of a big fist clasping the barrel of a rifle he'd seen at the town's entrance. Next to it, the *Restorant Ali Pasha* had its menu board standing on the pavement, and he lingered as he read dishes he knew: *Tasqebab, Bamje, Pilaf, Çorbë...* He could eat here later.

He walked on past flowerbeds until he came to a café with a paved forecourt set out with tables. He went inside and looked around at the clean stone walls. There were tubes of white glass lit with blue bulbs mounted on them, and the tables had a single flower placed in a glass of blue liquid. He sat down on a low sofa by the window. He took out his *Guide to Albania* and flicked though it circling a few places of interest: Berat, Gjirokaster. What was there in *Shënomadh*? Some gun-bunker they were trying to market to the foreign tourists as a site of historical interest? Nothing.

He began to focus his thoughts. How would he locate Jude Kilburn? It was a small town where foreigners would be known. He could ask around saying he was an old friend from England dropping in on a surprise visit. Someone would know sooner or later. Language was the problem, but he could try out his English. The waiter came over: a slim, young man with neatly-creased, black trousers.

"Latte," said Sheref pointing to the table menu.

"Yes sir," he replied in English with a jocular grin. Sheref waited for him to bring his coffee watching him. The young man placed it down in a cup set off-centre in the saucer. It had a blue serviette with 'Blue Café' printed in script lettering on the edge. No, he had decided. It could arouse suspicions, draw unpredictable sources of attention to him. It was too risky. He stirred in a sachet of sugar. He would simply hang around the town's central zone cafés like this, the better supermarkets, the bazaar – Kilburn would need his provisions. The chances were he would catch sight of him before too long.

He sipped at his latte and looked through the café window watching the passers-by closely. He focussed his eyes momentarily onto the glass and caught his reflection. He lifted a finger to touch the small scar on his forehead above his right eyebrow. It was late one evening in Leeds. He was sitting with Gul at one of the Formica-covered tables at the Taksim Takeaway. His mind's eye was back there again. He heard the men laughing before they entered. Maybe eight of them strutted in, some wearing white, blue and yellow football scarves. They squirted chilli sauce on to the mirrors. They kicked in the glass counter. They lifted out the chopped cabbage salad and forced it into Hakan's mouth before beating him. Sheref stood up and told them to stop.

"Get out! You have no right to do this… I'll call the police!" he said. One of them came over and pressed his face up close to Sheref's.

"Oh yeah?" he said. "And your lot… had no right… to do what you did to our boys in Istanbul!" The punch on his cheek knocked him to the floor. He struck his forehead on the metal base of the table. The men all bundled out as quickly as they'd entered. There was a shattering of glass as the front window collapsed. Hakan sat there bloodied and sobbing.

Sheref knew what had happened at the UEFA semi-final, when those two Englishmen were killed in pre-match violence. Everyone in Istanbul knew, but that was years before he'd come to Leeds. Why us, he thought? Why did they pick on me? I wasn't even a Galatasaray supporter! I'm Fenerbahçe! He inhaled sharply through his nose as his face contorted into a snarl. He clenched his jaw tightly, and ran his hand over the surface of his whitened knuckles. He looked back through the window glass to the high street. Well now, he thought, this will be the hand that will execute a little further justice in pursuit of a glorious cause.

* * *

Alex was sticking labels on the bottom of four finished pine cone baskets as Jude sat on the living room sofa watching her.

"I like that one. It looks like a ship built by the Elves," he said.

"That one is Mirela's. Well... it's some of the way towards meeting Mr Zanati's order," she said.

"Seeds... of social change," he said. She smiled and gave him a quick look that said, 'I appreciate you saying that'.

Jude now felt that he had been brought back onto firmer ground. He reflected on yesterday. He re-entered their apartment stairwell still running. As he climbed, his pace slowed. He stopped on the top step of the flight below their floor and sat down in the semi-darkness. Different verses of scripture came into his mind.

> *'Dear friends, do not be surprised at the painful*
> *trial you are suffering, as though something*
> *strange were happening to you...' 'Let us then*

approach the throne of grace with confidence so that we may receive mercy and find grace to help us in our time of need.'

He did what he should have done earlier in the day. He took several deep breaths and prayed. His heartbeat steadily slowed. The high-pitched note in his ears eased. The electrical charge of anxiety diminished in power. He felt as though the Spirit wrapped around him there like some gossamer cloak. He then prayed for the truck driver, ashamed of his own self-absorption. He and Alex could not leave Albania like this.

He drank another mouthful of his coffee. He felt drained, and way down in the root tips of his nerves the jangling had not completely ceased. Alex came and sat opposite him and began leafing through a receipt book. She seemed quite self-possessed, he thought, and yet? He picked up his mobile phone. He'd used most of his credit that morning, and he needed to call Mehmed and let him know what had happened to the books. He still felt crushed on that score, and he had not yet mentioned Sam Prekazi to him either, though he thought somehow that might not be a huge surprise. He had already called Spiro and the man had insisted he would come over to console with him. Jude didn't really want him sitting around looking long-faced. As long as he didn't call him 'son' and massage his neck muscles, it would probably be bearable.

"*Mos ki merak.* God will find a way!" he'd said. Maybe old Spiro was right. He had called Mira and Fredi and apologised for yesterday. They were ringing round the others for a replacement English class later in the afternoon. The call to Jaap to wish him a good rest had been harder. There had been some silence. Jaap had said he would email, but had seemed to want get on.

He put his phone back on the coffee table and decided that a good way to divert his mind for a while would be to watch some TV - better still, something light and comical. He slotted a Norman Wisdom film *On The Beat* into the DVD player, and was soon laughing lightly to himself as the little policeman ran away from a chasing horde of London bobbies, jumping over back-garden fences as they all fell and stumbled into fishponds.

It was time to cook lunch for Alex and himself he decided. Omelettes, why not? He took out the frying pan, beat the eggs and milk, sliced bacon and Florina peppers, and soon it was all sizzling. He sprinkled on the last crumbs of white cheese and ground over some black pepper. The aromas rose and he felt much better. No champignon mushrooms necessary! He laughed again to himself as he thought about the Norman Wisdom film, and he wondered if, in fact, yesterday he might not have overreacted ridiculously.

* * *

Shpetim Gurbardhi unfastened the top two buttons of his shirt and put his feet up on another table chair. He sat with Luan in the yard of the family house watching a portable television balanced on a low wall with the use of an extension cable. It was late on Wednesday evening, and he had been back in *Shënomadh* for just over an hour. He closed his eyes and rolled his shoulders to loosen the muscles a little. He set his phone on silent: he was tired of hearing Lionel Richie sing without ceasing since the anti-government protests had escalated. Certain elements were suspected of planning to whip things up into something that might aim to topple the government by force, or so he'd been briefed. Monitoring operations in which he was involved had been stepped up. After supper, he thought to crash out and catch up on much sleep he had lost over the last forty-eight hours.

A dog in a neighbouring yard was barking lazily at something out in the darkness. Below a distant ridgeline a single light twinkled like a fallen star as a thin line of fire crept below it. His mother shuffled down the stone steps with bowls of calf-meat broth, yoghurt and slices of bread. He ate quickly, thumped Luan high on his arm in the absence of conversation, and watched a late news bulletin on '*TV Shënomadh*'. His eyelids were beginning to grow heavy when an item on the death of British soldier in Afghanistan drew him out of sleep that would have taken him completely before he'd put his body anywhere comfortable. He thought about Jude, and guilt, like a little mouse, crept out of its hole in a low corner and stood looking at him. Jude had told him about the phone call threat, and this Sam Prekazi had just barged into his friend's home before he'd even thought to check the radar. And now there was this dream of Alex's. Well grandma had lived by her dreams and coffee-cup readings, bound up by their so-called meanings! What was to be made of this one?

He picked up his mobile phone and balanced it on its end. He ran his fingers down either side, and then flipped it over as he fixed his eye on a crack running from the edge of the bread bowl to its centre. He dialled a number and lifted it to his ear.

"*Alo!*" shouted a voice roughly.

"Tell Flori Moshohori… that Shpetim Gurbardhi wants to speak to him," he said. The man grunted and there were the sounds of footsteps and a door creaking on its hinges.

"*O, Shpetimka!*" said Flori shortly. "Is the President hiding in his bunker? You haven't lost him have you?" He could hear other voices laughing nearby.

"Well… if you bandits kept your own kind outside the borders… we'd have a few less distractions, wouldn't we?" He heard Flori exhale a little air through his nose, which he knew was about as close to laughing as the man came. "Have you had many Turkish citizens through recently?"

"*Po, sigurisht!* We've had a few."

"Anyone interesting?"

"Well now… we did have this one through on Monday evening," said Flori. "Deputy Commandant Georgiadis at Krystallopigi saw fit to call me over him… after they'd let him through their side. He'd had a call from their Border Police at the hut down the valley. A taxi driver had said something about his passenger as he'd passed them. Well… Georgiadis had taken a look at him. They'd run a few quick checks… nothing on any black lists… let him through… But he thought I might want to look him over. He must be after a favour!" The sound went lower momentarily as if Flori had covered the mouthpiece and a muffled command was shouted. "So… I had him brought in when he arrived. We searched through his things… nothing… just a lot of euros in a money belt. A hunched up little man…

heavy eyes... looked sick to me... said he was a tourist. Odd itinerary... not keeping to it either... and with an interest in Orthodox Iconography? Doubtful. So we held him for a few hours. Nothing. We let him pass."

"You didn't 'tax' him, did you?"

"What me? Never!"

"Oh Flori, Flori... Where was he going?"

"Apart from that museum? Who knows?"

"Could you send one of your men out to talk to the taxi drivers? See if anyone knows where he went?" said Shpetim. He scratched his nose and glanced at Luan as he waited. Fifteen minutes later, his phone vibrated in the chest pocket of his shirt.

"A taxi driver called Bledi Shehu picked him up," said Flori. "You'll like this... he's a *Shënomadh* man."

Chapter 26

At a window in the *Restorant* Ali Pasha Sheref sat overlooking the high street. He had finished his breakfast of rice and soup, and he wiped down the edges of his lips with his finger and thumb. He kept his eyes on all those who were passing by and quickly checked his watch: it was 9.25am. The proprietor had mounted a large, blue glass 'evil eye' charm on the wall above the cash register. As he caught sight of it he tipped generously into a glass and told himself that this would be the day.

He put on his sunglasses, stepped down onto the street, and set off walking. He turned right along the avenue of horse chestnut trees past the side street where his hotel was. Old men wearing *Republika* hats were huddling around games of dominoes in the shade, and the leaves rustled above their heads as a fresher breeze caught them today. At the avenue's end he turned around and back to the high street and then right. He stopped at the Supermarket Katerini and he entered though its sliding doors. It was air conditioned with a long aisle of refrigerated products, and another where he saw filter coffees and breakfast cereals. He ambled around it glancing at the customers and took a small bottle of *Vikos* mineral water to the checkout. He lingered outside for a while watching, left and right, sweeping his eyes across faces - faces. He turned back and crossed over to the opposite side of the street. Tables were set outside an open-fronted café with mirrors and a red and white themed plastic interior. A boy passed by hawking carrier bags of hazelnuts to indifferent customers. He read 'Elita Café' on a menu and he stepped inside to look around. A waiter came towards him but he spun around and left. He was not there. He walked on further and crossed back over the street to check inside the Blue Café. He continued walking now for some distance beyond the shops towards the monument of a fist clutching a rifle barrel. An old woman there dressed in black was rummaging through a smoking wheelie-bin with an iron bar hooked at the end. After some minutes, she shuffled on bent and empty-handed clutching her bar. What if Kilburn had left town? He could wait. What if he was back in England on a break? It was too early to entertain that thought. Sheref returned the way he'd come revisiting places and ambling into new ones.

By mid afternoon, his eyes were sore from observing constantly in the sun's glare. He pushed his fingers underneath his lenses to rub them, and then scratched the mosquito bites on his hands vigorously. He walked down the cobbled entrance road to *Shënomadh* bazaar for the second time. A dark-skinned woman with spiky, matted hair held out her hand and stared at him imploringly. He walked past her through a cloud of smoke from a stall charcoal-grilling rows of *qofte* sausages, and others piled with hills of boots and shoes. He turned left into an arcade covered with canopies and stopped by a shop selling vases and ceramic ornaments. Next to it he saw a stall with knives and he took off his sunglasses. He walked closer and looked over the glinting rows of kitchen knives, flick-knives and fisherman's knives. He pointed and handed the seller a 1000 *lekë* note. She handed him back a package bound in thin, white wrapping paper and a few coins change. It was then that he heard a single spoken word behind him.

* * *

Mr Zanati's smile was framed with a line of disappointment on his forehead. He looked at Alex's four finished pine cone baskets on the floor of his shop.

"I can have some more ready for you very soon," said Alex buoyantly. "My husband and I are planning to go gathering cones... he's organised a mule for me!" She stifled a smile at her last remark. Mr Zanati's forehead line softened and he shook his head placated. He wrote out a receipt and handed it to her.

"I am waiting," he said in a business-like manner, though she could see in his eyes he was smiling.

"*Faleminderit*," she said as she made for the door of the shop, "bye."

She stepped out into the arcade and lifted the strap of her bag higher up her shoulder. A young man standing a metre away was looking at her. She paused briefly, noticing it. There was something about him that was not Albanian - a tourist perhaps with his backpack, she thought. His face looked drawn and his skin pallid. Large, round, brown eyes were heavy-lidded. She saw his pupils contract to pin pricks. He covered them with mirror lens sunglasses and began to walk away. What had she discerned there in his expression? It was as if he had recognised her: she was sure of it. He took short, quick steps as he moved past her. Her eye caught a small, blue merchandising logo on the side pocket of his backpack, *Turkcell*. She began to walk up the arcade. She turned around to watch him as he moved quickly round the corner. Then she remembered a detail: the formless, faceless figure in her dream had been wearing the colour orange. The full realisation swept over her in a wave. She felt a knotting sensation at the base of her sternum. Her breathing quickened. She was going to confront him, challenge him... tell him to go back! She ran down the arcade to the bottom and looked left and right. She could not see him. She ran around another corner and looked about her. He was not there.

She walked briskly up the cobbled road out of the bazaar. A woman thrust two packs of children's socks into her face and she pushed them away flustered. She passed over the end of the avenue of horse chestnut trees and peered along it. She heard a skidding noise behind her. She flinched. A man on a black bicycle brushed past closely with one leg dragging on the ground holding his mobile phone to his ear. She crossed to the main road out of the town centre. She broke into a run for twenty or so paces and then back into a striding walk. Her sandals were cutting her toes. The pavement was lined with café tables shaded by fluttering parasols and she was forced into the road to pass them. A car horn blasted and tyres screeched. She ran on ignoring it. She came to a narrow back road that cut through the buildings towards May 5TH Street and slowed into it. As she turned a corner she saw it had been blocked by a mound of firewood logs still being tossed off the back of a truck. She turned around. Did she see someone step back out of sight? A cat bolted from a doorway hissing. She now felt trapped. Her mouth felt dry. Her head was banging as the blood pumped around it. Their apartment was just a block away. She must get back to tell Jude!

* * *

Shpetim bounded down the steps of *Shënomadh* County Police Directorate with a folded print out in his hand. Flori had done all Shpetim had asked him to since last night. He'd got Deputy Commandant Georgiadis to send him the digital photo and data scanned by the Krystallopigi passport reader, and then emailed the file to him. He was a bandit but a capable one, he reflected.

"*O, Shpetim?* Where are you going?" shouted a uniformed officer with a gold-braided cap. Shpetim saluted him with his finger as he jogged past and kept his own counsel. He was going to find out what exactly this Sheref Dushman was doing here.

His brother Luan, bringing a little family help, was sitting in uncle Burim's silver Mercedes with the engine running. Shpetim threw his light grey suit jacket through the open window and got in. Luan swung the wheel sharply and they U-turned causing a youth passing on a moped to kerb it. There was another man he wanted to find, and he had been calling his mother's friend Greta at the Director-ate of Road Transport Services, waiting to see what address Bledi Shehu's taxi was registered to. She had been away from her desk, though, for an hour and a half. He jiggled his right leg on the ball of his foot as they sped down the high street past the Blue Café towards the Unknown Solder's Monument. He was now going down to the Directorate in person. His phone rang. He checked its face: it was 12.15pm. He took the call.

"*O, Greta! Ku ishe futur?* Where have you been? Did you finish your coffee break?"

"I don't work for *you* Shpetim Gurbardhi! But for your mother's sake… I'll help you," she said brusquely. "Wait… here it is. There's no phone number but he lives on Veterans' Street… 293. Greetings to Alma." She hung up. He repeated the address to Luan. Once again Luan drew into the edge of the road, swung the car around in a U-turn, and accelerated back towards the high street.

As they drove along the avenue of horse chestnut trees they flashed past two to a second as he counted, and he watched with the photo ID in his mind's eye. He felt an urge to pray and he closed his eyes briefly. They turned left past a sign saying '*Gomisteri*' as an oily man emerged from behind a barricade of black tyres, and then along a long cobbled avenue.

"This is the place… I think," said Luan braking. Shpetim jumped out and walked up to a wide, metal gate in the wall of a stone house. He pushed it and looked inside the yard. A man in a baggy string vest was watering tomato and pepper plants with a hose.

"*O, xhaxhi?* Is Bledi Shehu here?"

"Oh no," he said. "He used to live here… this is his parents' house. They moved to Tirana. We rent it… and a tidy sum we pay for it too! Bledi lives with his grandmother in an apartment block over in

District 6. He's still a bachelor… at his age! Who are you anyway? What's he done?" Shpetim was back at the door of the car. He climbed in.

"Quickly Luan," he said. He rubbed the side of his nose and jiggled his leg on the ball of his foot a little faster.

Luan now sped along a newly-tarmaced stretch of road and then turned off a steep drop onto dirt ground scraping the undercarriage.

"Don't say a word to Burim," said Luan. Shpetim grinned. They drew alongside a squat, bare-bricked apartment block on ground that was strewn with rocks and glass fragments. Shpetim jumped out and jogged up to a circle of children sitting on a car bonnet playing cards.

"Who knows Bledi the taxi driver?" he said. One of them pointed up a stairwell. He jogged into it and up one flight. He knocked on a door.

"Who is it?" said a wavering voice.

"I'm looking for Bledi Shehu?" The door opened partially on a chain and a shaking head eyed his chest.

"What did you say?"

"Bledi… I need to speak to him."

"Well he's just gone… to the border."

"Can you give me his number?"

"Eh? Oh… wait a minute," she said. She undid the chain and the door swung open. She shuffled back towards him in lop-sided slippers. "Well… you can call him yourself. This is his phone." She held up an old *Nokia*. Shpetim let his head drop and rubbed his temples with his thumb and middle finger.

"Ask him to call me when he gets in… it doesn't matter how late," he said writing his number on a piece of paper. *"Më dëgjon nënë?* Did you hear me?"

* * *

Sheref took short, slow steps along the pavement of May 5TH Street ready to jump back out of Alex Kilburn's line of view. He lifted the peak of the baseball cap he had exchanged for his sunglasses. He edged up to the corner of an apartment block and peered around. She was running across a patch of dirt ground towards another apartment block entrance. He watched and he waited there for some time. Then he saw her pass by a window on the fourth floor, left hand side of the stairwell. A sly smile of accomplishment passed over his lips.

He turned to see a tough-looking man nearby on the pavement staring at him by some bathroom weighing scales. Sheref averted his eyes and hurried back down the street and onto the main road towards the centre of *Shënomadh*. As he walked quickly past the rows of café tables and then onto the avenue of horse chestnut trees he was thinking. Why had she been in such a hurry after he had seen her in the bazaar? Was it him? What could she possibly know? Now, in some ways, he would prefer to assemble a little device and leave it to perform its task at a distance: a mobile phone and a few other items would suffice. It would be a simple task in Istanbul with supplies, but it was impractical here. No, he had chosen his method. In the avenue near his hotel he walked past two boys wrestling on the grass in a ring of friends. One screamed in pain as their horse-play turned aggressive.

He turned the corner of the side street. A teenager came out of his hotel ahead of him wearing a dirty, red tracksuit with 'Albania' on the back, and then ran in the opposite direction past a billiard hall. The caretaker was not outside as usual slumped in her chair. He walked in past the empty, reception cubicle. His door was slightly ajar. He pushed it open gradually. There was a new odour in the room. Coins, euros and *lekë,* he'd left balanced in neat little piles on a shelf above the sink were gone, and so was his Fenerbahçe lighter. He darted quickly to the wardrobe. He reached his hand inside its top compartment. His camera was gone! He felt deeper inside left and right.

"No!" he shouted. He ran back into the side street and up to the billiard hall looking. He could not see the teenager. He began to inhale in short snorts through his nose. He walked back into his room. He slammed the wardrobe door and as it swung back out he lashed at it tearing the skin off his knuckles. He'd made a stupid, rudimentary error! Now, his passport was gone. He sat down on the black vinyl sofa bed. He rocked over sideways and shrivelled into a ball. What was he going to do now? Go to the police? It was as if a huge stone door had been rolled across his exit.

Chapter 27

Jude slipped quietly out of his apartment into the stairwell with his rucksack slung over his shoulder. He turned around to see Alex's face in the gap of the closing door.

"Lock it," he said softly. "Keep it so… and don't answer the door to anyone." His boots clumped heavily down the flights of steps, and he walked across the dirt ground onto May 5TH Street. As he passed a cobbler sitting on a stool, slowly hammering nails into the sole of a customer's black shoe, on the face of his mobile phone it read 8.04 am, Friday, August 29th. He was heading for the mountains behind *Shënomadh*. He wanted to find solitude and seek Him. No one would follow him there.

He strode up the dirt track towards the first ridge of hills praying and thinking over yesterday's events. He was clear that Alex's description of the man in the bazaar was like one individual he had chatted with by the ferry piers in Istanbul. He and Alex had talked about what they should do for much of the evening. How willing would the local police be to commit its resources to act on their fears before anything had happened? How effective would they be now even if they did? He had decided finally this morning, just before he left, that he would call Shpetim.

"I'm glad you've told me this Jude," he'd said. "I'll do all I can now." Jude had breathed out deeply as he'd lowered the phone from his ear and looked at Alex.

He took the track that forked up the pass jumping across rocks and brushing through the oak scrub until he came to the fording point. He remembered how the policeman with the chestnut mule had shot the snake behind him here. He remembered too how he had given that day to God to speak to him. Had he been speaking through that incident? He had not considered it before. At the top of the pass the dry, grey stony valley opened out before him. He scrambled down the path sending loose stones and dirt tumbling. Where it divided in the valley floor he kept right, climbing towards the high cross further along the same ridge as the rock pinnacle and pine trees.

As he climbed towards the towering concrete structure it seemed to him that his senses became more acute. He noticed tiny yellow, white and purple flower heads; a jet trail across the sky fraying away to the horizon; columns of smoke rising from the fields where stubble was being burnt. He heard the buzz of flies and the distant boom of dynamite in a quarry. He could smell the dry grass and dust. He drew nearer and a prayer came to him. He spoke it out loud: "If you can Lord, let this day pass safely... but let it be as you would have it."

He did not wish to linger on the summit and returned the way he had come. By the time he was back on the track descending towards the edge of the town, it was approaching mid-day. The wind had risen and was whipping up the dust around him in squalls. Smoke from the fields had drifted over the grid of apartment blocks below and lingered there like a wispy serpent. May 5TH Street seemed darker, veiled from the light above, as he came down it. He crossed the dirt ground before his apartment block, and he noticed Spiro enter his stairwell ahead of him. He paused to look up to the fourth floor, and then he looked back over his shoulder.

* * *

Shpetim fastened the buttons of his white shirt, took his mobile phone and a slate grey suit jacket, and left the house immediately after Jude's phone call. It was now urgent, he felt, to find and confront this Sheref Dushman. In a town of 30,000 people, he knew he could locate him given time, maybe not too much, unless he chanced upon him quickly. He decided he would check out the three main hotels, though he knew there were dozens more and some that didn't even sign in their guests. He made some calls to local contacts. Then he walked repeatedly between *Shënomadh* County Police Directorate and the high street watching.

At 10.55am he took a phone call from his SHISH director ordering him to return to operations monitoring the civil disturbances. He rubbed his temples lightly with his thumb and middle finger. The consequences for him if he delayed would be very serious. He walked out into the centre of the high street and looked both ways searching. His phone vibrated in his hand. He took the call.

"*Alo,*" a man shouted. "*Bledi Shehu jam.* You came yesterday? My grandmother just told me. She's not as she was... her legs, her ears, her head... you know."

"Bledi... police. You brought a Turkish citizen up from the border on Tuesday morning. Where did you drop him?"

"*Po.* By the hotels on *Rruga* e *Gështenjave*... what's wrong with that?"

"Nothing. I'll be in touch." Shpetim hung up. He looked down the high street to the top of the avenue of horse chestnut trees around 200 metres away. He began to jog towards it.

He turned the corner and ran on until he came to the side street. A woman in a white cleaner's jacket sat on a chair outside the first hotel. He took out the folded print out with an enlarged, grainy passport photo of Sheref on it and showed it to her.

"I'm looking for this man. Have you seen him?" he said authoritatively.

"Yes... he checked out about two hours ago."

"How did he seem to you?"

"He paid his bill... what can I say?" she shrugged. She smoothed back her tight, purple-black hair considering something. "He had strange eyes, though... when he took his sunglasses off... cold, cloudy... huh, like a fish left too long out of the water." Shpetim stood thinking as he stared at her. She began to shuffle uneasily. Maybe he had just moved on to another town, he thought. Or maybe this is his final day?

He spun on the ball of his foot and walked back onto the avenue. He began to walk quickly past the trees as a wind started to churn their leaves. A shower of chestnuts drummed down onto the tarmac scattering as he crossed over. He jogged past the sliding doors of *Banka Alpha* where an LCD clock read 11.30am. He lifted his phone to his ear and pressed a speed-dial option.

"Luan, can you get over to May 5TH Street, Jude's block," he said. "Yes… I know Burim's got the Mercedes!" He slung his jacket over his shoulder and the holstered pistol wrapped inside it thudded into his back as he moved. He jogged along the pavement of the main road clipping a café chair with his hip knocking it over. He stopped and ran back to pick it up apologising to an angry waiter. He jogged quicker now breaking into a run along the edge of the road. A man with a bundle of firewood sticks hoisted on his shoulder turned in front of him. He ran out into the centre of the road through the oncoming traffic, and then swung left into a back street shortcut through to Jude's block. As he turned a bend it was blocked with a mound of firewood logs. A man lifted an axe high above his head and brought it down splitting one open and cutting through to the stone with a sharp clank. Shpetim ran up the mound and down the other side stumbling as his training shoes caught one. He slowed his pace as he came to the edge of May 5TH Street above the *Don* Café. He was breathing quickly but he was not short of breath. He looked around the base of Jude's block carefully as he walked across the dirt ground towards it.

* * *

By a wall at the side of the *Don* Café on May 5TH Street Sheref stood shifting his weight from leg to leg. He glanced down to the main road where a green Mercedes taxi with a white top was parked waiting for him. He had paid the man a 100 euro retainer for the day. He had mustered his resolve and he thought back through his plan. It would be harder now but still possible to get out of Albania. He would tell the driver to take him to the border. Just before it, he would point south to the village of *Miras* on his map and indicate that he should go. There he would wait for nightfall and cross through the Pindus Mountains into Greece. He would then make for the coast and freighters or private yachts across the Aegean islands. His backpack was ready in the taxi boot.

He had been waiting for almost two hours, scratching the backs of his now festering hands. He kept his eyes on the fourth floor apartment window for any activity inside, but until now he had seen none. Just one man had entered the block in the last fifteen minutes. Then, in an instant, all the lights in the windows went out. A generator whirred into action outside the café. He checked his watch: 11.45am. A cold wind picked up sending dust and a sheet of newspaper gyrating madly past. He rubbed the flesh on his forearms where goose bumps had spread.

It was then that he saw him. He watched Jude's long stride swinging down the pavement on the opposite side of the road towards his block. As he drew closer he was transfixed to see the man who'd been the focus of his thoughts for over a month. He was not quite as he'd remembered him down by the

Golden Horn. There was something familiar about him, or if not him, people he'd met in his city, like his landlady's son, what was his name… Terry? It was something he'd liked: a warmth, a ready-friendliness… He hesitated. Then he struck the feeling down.

He took off his baseball cap and sunglasses. The muscles in his jaw drew as tight as piano wire. He clenched his fist around the knife handle in his right-hand trouser pocket. He began to walk after him as he crossed the dirt ground before his apartment block. Jude Kilburn entered the stairwell around 100 metres ahead of him. Sheref broke into a jog and then bounded up into the blackness of the first flight of steps like a wolf.

* * *

Jude trod slowly up the steps of his apartment stairwell. His legs were heavy from the walk, and the electric lighting was out so he was feeling his way around corners in the darkness. The sound of feet scraping the grit up steps behind startled him. He felt for his mobile phone to use the lit screen as a torch but he fumbled and it clattered down. He dropped to his haunches and felt the floor with his fingertips. He found two sections and clipped them together. It shone a dim glow about two metres ahead of him. Someone was coming up rapidly. He quickened his pace striding up three steps at a time. He heard a baby crying and the sound of an old, romantic film score on a TV set as he passed a door. The sounds faded but the footsteps grew louder echoing all around him. He was suddenly yanked back and his rucksack pulled off his shoulder. He spun around. It had caught on the handrail. He shook it free. He heard knocking on a door higher up. He ran past the light of a small window before entering the darkness of the flight up to the fourth floor. He felt the hair rising on his forearms and a high-pitched note began to pierce his ears. It was as if some shadow was almost on top of him. A bar of light broke down the stairwell from an open door. The footsteps stopped. Julieta the neighbour slid out a rubbish bag and closed her door. Jude kept climbing. A full column of light now spread across the landing as another door was opened.

"Hello Spiro. Jude is out I'm afraid," he heard Alex say. He saw their two forms silhouetted in the doorway. A third figure stepped down by them from the next flight of steps up.

"Put it down. *Ulu poshtë!* Get down... on the floor!" the figure shouted.

Something like a bird's shadow flashed past the corner of Jude's vision. The deafening explosive blasts of three rounds fired from a pistol echoed up and down the stairwell like thunder claps. Jude clasped his hand to his left eye as plaster fragments struck it stinging painfully. He saw the form of a man just below him tumble down into the darkness. He lurched after him. Jude fell striking his shoulder against the wall scraping his cheek as he slid down the steps to a halt. He could hear the shuffle of the man's footsteps below him on the stairs. He rose up but the man was now well ahead. He stopped at the small window, yanked it open and peered down, cleaning the flow of water from his eye. Seconds later, a young man broke out of the entrance onto the dirt ground staggering and clutching a shoulder over his bloodied orange T-shirt.

"Stop him! Stop him! *Kapeni atë!*" Jude shouted down. The young man looked back up at him and Jude saw who he was. The man with sailor's arms now jumped over his bathroom scales and advanced towards the young Turkish man with the stance of a wrestler. The young man picked up a rock and hurled it at the scales man. It stuck him on the forehead and he dropped to his knees and fell sideways. A crowd of men at a *Don* Café table rose shouting and began to move towards the Turkish man. He ran out onto May 5TH Street and down past the taxi vans. Suddenly, a van door was opened in his path. He smashed into it like a wall and was knocked backwards onto the tarmac. A man stepped down from it wearing circular, blue sunglasses… Defrim. A crowd gathered around to beat him. An old woman with a grass brush on a knobbly wooden stick was lifting it high in the crowd and bringing it down. Jude turned around into the darkness and climbed back up the steps to the fourth floor to see Alex. His heart was pounding as he rose onto the landing, but he felt the blood drain from his face at what he saw.

* * *

Shpetim looked into Alex's face. He could see her wide eyes filling with tears. She had kind eyes: he had always thought so. She had placed her hand on his forehead. It felt warm. The throbbing pain in the side of his neck had not eased since he'd drawn the knife out by the haft. The skin down his left-hand side had felt warm and wet. Now, he felt a frost rising through him, a cold prickling that was turning slowly to numbness. He saw Jude kneel down next to him and close his eyes, and Shpetim felt better. Soon, he heard Luan shouting repeatedly into his mobile phone: "*O, Zot. Shpejtoni, ju lutem!* Quickly… please!" He saw Spiro, and he saw Aleko the local SHISH man arrive and turn his face away. He saw another man whom he did not know whose face seemed to glow luminous momentarily with a faint blue-white light. This guy had feminine eyes and long flowing hair. He smelt its sweet fragrance. And then it was getting harder to see anyone: a dark mist closed around his eyes like an aperture.

Chapter 28

Jude stood at his living room window. His left eye was swollen but he could still see through the grey haze of rain to where a ridgeline of mountains looked like a graph charting decline. Deep rumbles of thunder sounded as though the earth was cracking open. Below him on May 5TH Street a man sprinted for cover; three others pressed their backs into the wall by the *Don* Café as grey water rushed along the gutter. In *Shënomadh* autumn always came in a day.

He straightened the collar of his black crushed velvet jacket. He could scarcely process what had happened: there had not been enough time. Shpetim had lost too much blood in the stairwell; the ambulance had taken too long to arrive; the hospital had bungled the blood transfusion. He lifted up his shirt collar and tied a knot in his black tie inattentively. He turned and took Alex's arm, and together they closed the apartment door behind them.

The cobbled streets shone in the grey light as they walked under Alex's umbrella. He stopped near the Gurbardhi house to take a single white geranium from a crack in a wall and slipped it wet into his pocket. Parked cars blocked the nearby streets at odd angles, and a large crowd of people had gathered around the gate in the stone wall. In Albania, he knew, the extended family and many in the neighbourhood all made a point of attending. An old, black Mercedes hearse was parked outside with the rear door raised wide open. They waited.

The coffin was brought out on the shoulders of a shuffling huddle of men. Alma and Skender came after it held upright by the arms of others. Jude had stood some distance back, but Skender's eyes found him. Jude saw the broken heart through them. He took a couple of steps towards Jude.

"*Zhduku anglez!* Get out of here!" he shouted. "If you'd not come here... bringing your foreign conflicts..." Supporting arms restrained him from advancing more. Luan looked at Jude and shook his head as he helped to pull Skender away. He felt Alex hold his arm tighter. The eyes of many people lingered coldly on Jude. He kept to his place in the road, though he felt the words pierce him. It was okay, he told himself, he understood.

In the rear of the hearse wreaths of flowers buried Shpetim's coffin. The crowd began to break up and move towards their cars. Bledi was waiting with Fredi in his taxi on the high street for them as he'd arranged. Jude sat in the rear with Alex and the rain drummed on the metal roof and slithered in eels down the windscreen. Cars in the funeral cortege filed into position ahead of them behind the flashing blue lights of Shpetim's police escort to the cemetery. Rainwater came through a broken seal in the sunroof of Bledi's old Mercedes and ran down his cheek.

"Shpetim came to *my* house... I called him yesterday morning," said Bledi, exhaling a long breath through his nose and slamming his palm onto his steering wheel. "I brought his killer here... *Obobo... O, Zot!*" It gave Jude a strange sensation as he looked around the old car's interior.

"You were doing your job... you were not to know!" said Jude reaching forwards and putting a hand on Bledi's shoulder. The engine clattered rhythmically and Bledi edged them into the long line of cars and old, turquoise coaches that were stopping all other traffic in *Shënomadh*.

Under the dripping cemetery trees he and Alex joined the mourners with their umbrellas forming a patchwork canopy like a miserable circus tent. The gravestones, high and ostentatious and shattered and crumbling in light-grey marble, huddled in around them. Glistening bunches of plastic flowers were dotted here and there. Hundreds of people were present, some from church but many faces he didn't know, though he had seen Spiro and even Kristo had come. There were uniformed officers with their gold-braided caps, and stern looking persons with them, their umbrellas held by subordinates. Ahmeti from church, his black shirt hanging on him again like a sail, spoke for a while and read from *1 Corinthians 15*. Jude lowered his gaze as he listened.

> *"If only for this life we have hope in Christ, we are to be pitied more than all men. But Christ has indeed been raised from the dead, the first fruits of those who have fallen asleep."*

Raindrops fell into a puddle at his feet sending out intersecting concentric circles. He looked up as a man with a prominent, Gurbardhi nose, perhaps Burim, invited the men to drink raki in a café after. It was nothing Jude felt like participating in.

The hole where Shpetim had been placed yawned black. Three attendants began to shovel in the earth in a workman-like manner as the water washed in the rest. Others tossed in a handful of muddy soil. Shpetim's mother Alma arched her body back in grief and others caught her. As a mound of earth rose there, wreaths of woven, green-leafed branches were laid across blanketing it fully. Jude walked in turn to the graveside and placed the geranium from his pocket there. A stone cherub sat on the post of an adjacent grave looking in his direction.

At their apartment Jude sat down heavily in an armchair facing Alex on the sofa, and tossed the door keys onto the coffee table. It was mid-day Saturday, just twenty-four hours after events in the stairwell, he thought. He took off his glasses and covered his eyes with a hand.

"Can I make you some tea?" she said. Jude shook his head. He went to their bedroom and closed the door behind him. He lay face down on the sheets. He stayed there and he wept.

* * *

The bed of a brook trickled as Jude jumped over it and scrambled up a steep bank of earth past some sloe berry bushes. From the top of the rise he could see down across the tops of the pine trees to the stony valley floor. The shadow of a rain cloud lingered across it. His eye now followed the broken line of the footpath down the facing valley wall and up to the concrete cross away to his left along the ridge. It was just three days since he'd last walked it.

He could see Alex around two hundred metres away stooped over picking up pine cones and dropping them into her sack. The donkey he'd hired for the day was tethered to a nearby silver birch tree, chewing the undergrowth at the full length of its rope. It had turned out to be a placid and obedient creature, a better choice than the larger frisky, brown mule the villager had also offered him. It brayed plaintively and it echoed in the valley.

"Hey Alex... keep an eye on him!" he called down gesturing like he was lifting a hangman's noose around his own neck. "I'm just going up a little." She waved back.

The pine branches were wet with the morning shower and fingers of sunlight splayed through them. A single thin plume of white smoke rose through the trees maybe a kilometre away, and the hollow drumming of a woodpecker seemed to come from close by it. He walked into a small clearing to the stump of a pine tree that had been freshly felled. The cut through the trunk was wet, neat and raw three-quarters of the way through, and splintered and torn away for the remainder. He sat on the flat part like it was a chair drawn up for him.

He touched his left eye. The swelling from the plaster fragments had gone down now, though it was still sore. Pieces of Friday and Saturday fell again around him: the scrape of grit as footsteps quickened in the stairwell behind him; the young man looking back at him from the dirt yard below clasping his bloodied shoulder; Shpetim slumped outside his apartment door as Alex touched his forehead. Then the wreaths of green-leafed branches covering the mound of dark, wet earth over him. He could not yet make the pieces fit a form. He could not see a pattern in the design. The distant sound of a chainsaw searing onto wood rose up the valley. He felt a wave of guilt rise in him. *Why did you allow Shpetim to be taken now? Why was it that I lived?* He said the words quietly to the trees, and he could think of nothing more in answer than: *"Now I know in part; then I shall know fully."*

He remembered Shpetim greeting him in the Sky Tower restaurant: "Are you well? In good health? Your father? And everyone in your house?" He saw him lift Luan up by the leg and tumble into the bush in the Gurbardhi yard. He watched him criss-crossing his pizza with tomato ketchup at the Blue Café. He remembered a conversation when they'd first met.

"Jude. Do you know *Gëzim*? *He* lives in Leeds."

"A lot of people live in Leeds!" Jude had laughed. He saw him admiring the Union Jack cover of his mobile phone. He slid a hand into his front pocket and drew out his wallet. He opened it and took out the piece of torn playing card with the Ouse Bridge in York on it.

"We'll make the match, my friend, one day… face to face," he whispered. He swallowed hard and brushed his jacket sleeve across his eyes. From the carpet of needles by his feet he picked up two green pine cones that must have come from the felled tree. He pressed them to his nose. They were sweet with their fragrance and the resin sticky on his fingers. He tossed them into his quarter-filled sack and continued about the clearing where many more were strewn.

He wandered on a way and returned towards Alex, sliding down the slope past the sloe berry bushes and dragging his now full sack behind him. She was sitting on her bulging sack eating an apple. She seemed pensive as he approached but she turned and smiled as he arrived. He walked across to the donkey and caught an apple that Alex threw over. He held it flat on his palm and the animal snaffled it with a single chomp. He untied the rope from the silver birch tree and gave it to Alex. He tied another rope around the neck of each sack, heaved one over its wooden frame, and it slithered down a little dragging the other one up as a counterweight.

"You could make a fleet of Elven ships with this lot," he said smiling at Alex. "They can all sail for the 'Undying Lands'." She ruffled the donkey's mane and patted its neck. "Get on then! Not me... 'Firefoot' here."

Chapter 29

A soft tap came on the front door of the apartment as Jude sat on his living room sofa sipping a cup of coffee. He checked the time on his mobile phone, 11.07am, and looked at Alex, who was doing some baking in the kitchen. She shrugged with her eyes. He got up and stepped around a sheet of newspaper and pine cones into the entrance hall, cleaning some silver spray paint off his fingers with a tissue.

He opened the door and Liridon from his English class was standing there. Jude waited a few seconds to see if he might open with a word or two, but he stood grinning and rubbing one foot with his other, a fresh, purple bruise on his forehead.

"Well... come in Liridon," said Jude. "It's really nice to see you!" The youth shuffled inside nodding his head gratefully. Jude tossed him some slippers and he kicked off his cracked, dung-soiled training shoes. On the back of his coarse, orange jumper, which had a large hole in the right elbow, Jude noticed a couple of strands of straw. He picked them off for him. For a moment, he had to turn away and hold his breath from the pungent odour of animal shed that had entered with him. "You came just at the right time for…?" He looked over at Alex as they came into the living room.

"Sultana and walnut flapjacks," she said.

"There you go Liridon. Have a seat," he said gesturing. The smell of cooked oats and treacle filled the room as Alex drew the tray from the oven. She brought a plateful and two glasses of fizzy apple juice and set them on the coffee table. Liridon pushed a flapjack whole into his mouth before finishing the glass of juice in several gulps. He wiped his mouth on his sleeve and ate a couple more flapjacks whilst Jude looked on and chewed on his. Alex took Liridon's glass and refilled it with juice. He drank it quickly again. "Hey… I was just thinking of having an early lunch today. Could you eat some with me?" said Jude rising from his chair and walking towards the kitchen. Liridon replied with a grin only. Jude took out some bread, white cheese, tomatoes and a cucumber and brought them to the coffee table. Liridon was staring around their living room with his big, bulging eyes.

"It is a nice house. You have nice things… nice pictures," said Liridon.

"Alex makes it nice," said Jude. "I don't always keep it in order as I should." Jude ate a little whilst Liridon lowered his head to his plate and bit at several items in quick succession to load his mouth. Alex brought him a tall glass of tap water and he drank most of it. Jude smiled at him waiting. Liridon belched.

"*O, më fal*," he said putting his palm on his chest. He glanced at Alex as she was closing the bedroom door behind her. He looked back at Jude.

"I really liked the book we studied, *A Tale of Two Cities*," he said.

"I'm pleased about that," said Jude.

"I like Bledi and Fredi… but I don't like Flutura and Kristo." Jude smiled at his frankness.

"Well, Kristo has a great difficulty in his family right now," said Jude.

"Oh. I did not know… and… I'm very sorry… about what happened to your friend." Jude nodded.

"Those verses from the Bible you gave to us in class… about sheep and shepherds… I liked them too. I'm a goatherd for Shpat," he said.

"Mira has told me so," said Jude, his brow furrowing a little.

"Can I know God like you Mr Kilburn?"

"Yes… and better."

"When?"

"Would you like me to pray with you now?" Liridon grinned and jigged his head to the side to indicate that he did. Jude led him in a short prayer and he repeated the words.

"I want to leave Shpat!" said Liridon.

"You have a new owner now… you must talk to *Him* and ask him what he wants you to do," said Jude. Liridon was quiet for some moments, as if he might be continuing to pray. He was looking at his hands. He reached into his trouser pocket, took out a silver pen with a black eagle emblem, and put it on the coffee table with a tap. Jude recognised it as the one Alex had given him. Liridon did not look up. "Thank you," said Jude. The sound of Alex's voice in the bedroom rose a little as she sang, '*As I went down in the river to pray, studying about that good old way, and who shall wear the robe and crown... Oh sisters, let's go down...*' Liridon's ears seemed to prick up. "Oh," said Jude noticing. "I have something you might like." He got up, walked to the side desk, and pulled out a small drawer. He felt around underneath some papers. He took out an old *Hohner* mouth organ and buffed the chrome sides on his trousers a little until it shone. "It's a G major. I have no use for it. Here... keep it. You can learn to play something new!" Liridon put it to his lips and blew a high note and an easy low chord.

"I have to go now," he said. "*Kam punë.* Work!"

"Okay," said Jude and followed him to the entrance hall. He handed him his training shoes gingerly. "Come again on Friday afternoon if you can... bring a tune!" Jude closed the apartment door and leant back on it. A smile rose slowly and began to spread across his face. There was a soft knock behind him. He turned and reopened the door. Liridon held out his arm towards him.

"I took these too," he said. "I don't know what to do with them now." He dropped a cigarette lighter and a passport into Jude's palm, and skipped off down the stairwell. A couple of harmonic 'toots' rose in his wake.

Jude closed the door, took the items into the living room, and sat down in an armchair to examine them. The lighter had what looked like an acorn leaf on it. The passport was dark blue with a crescent moon and a star in the centre. He turned to the photo page and looked at it. It was *him*! He read the name: *Mr Dushman... Sheref, Okan...* He lifted up his glasses and pinched the inside corners of his eyes with his thumb and forefinger. He then scrutinised the face in the photo. What drove you to come all this way, he thought? What wrong were you hoping to right? Lali Lafazani had reported on *'TV Shënomadh'* on Monday evening that *Sheref* had now been transferred from the town hospital to the County Police Directorate. That these things should come into *my* hands? He lowered them to the coffee table. He ran his hand back through his hair.

* * *

Squares of warm sunlight were patterning the bed sheets again when Alex awoke. Summer had returned briefly to collect some forgotten possession just when she'd thought it had left for the southern border. Jude's head was face-down in his pillow buried under his caramel-coloured hair. She slid her legs out and dressed quietly in a white T-shirt and blue cotton chemise. On the living room sofa she turned her Bible reading plan to the verses for Wednesday, September 3rd. It was from *Romans 8:17*

> *... we are God's children, heirs and co-heirs with Christ, if indeed we share in his sufferings in order that we may also share in his glory.'*

She sat for a while in silence thinking about it and praying. She checked her email account on Jude's laptop. After reading the first new message she clapped her hands and then lifted them above her head to wave them in the style of an Albanian dance. The time on the desktop was 7.36am. Now she was going to do something a little special for breakfast.

As she unfolded the wooden table and set two plastic chairs next to it on the balcony she looked down into May 5ᵀᴴ Street. A young mother with her baby wrapped up like a ball in a jumble of bright clothing walked by and she watched her patting its back. The woman with matted, black hair and a floral cotton dress worn over her trousers wandered by on her way to the bazaar. She must talk to her. A man with circular blue sunglasses jumped down from a taxi van and waved up at her. This time she waved back.

In the kitchen she began toasting some sliced white bread. She would cut it into triangles and mount it on the little steel rack just as she used to do for the northern holiday makers at her parents' bed and breakfast house. Jude would like that: he was a 'grockle' too! How could it be that she had married one? She smiled to herself. It was time to open the 'Full English Breakfast in a Tin'. She worked the can-opener around the edge and shook it into a saucepan. She began to sing as it simmered, *'Great is thy faithfulness, oh God my father, morning by morning, new mercies I see. All I have needed thy hand has provided…'*

She heard the mattress creak and Jude cough as he rose. She felt such grief for the Gurbardhi family, for their loss of Shpetim, but also for Jude. Shpetim was his closest Albanian friend. He would miss him badly and he was separated from his old friends back in England too. He did not have many new ones here… and Jaap was gone now. She had wondered if the strain of events might not overwhelm him, but no. She had seen something temper and strengthen inside of him. She was sure of it.

He came through scratching his head wearing another baggy, white shirt and faded cargo pants rolled up onto his shins. His cheek was still grazed from when he fell down the stairwell. He wrapped his arms around her shoulders from behind and kissed her on the top of her head. She touched the graze and kissed him there.

"Mr Rochester sir, would it please you… to take your morning victuals on the balcony?" she said.

"It would so my Jane. You may serve it yonder." She noticed he had repaired the corner of his glasses with a sticking plaster. "They just broke… they took a bashing when I fell, you know!"

"You… librarian!"

"That…" he smiled, "is no insult."

She filled a tray with breakfast items and he carried them outside. She took down his Mr Rochester's Mug, which was now a crazy-paving reconstruction with high quality super-glue. She made the tea inside it, took it out steaming into the morning air, and placed it down in front of him. He lifted it and looked at the nobleman's face, rotating it to view from different angles.

"It holds the tea differently," he said, "but, I think it much improved… seasoned even." She sat down with him and began to butter a triangle of toast.

"You know," he said, "I still haven't told anyone in England about all this. Not dad… or Jack… or anyone at 'The Safe House'."

"There'll be a time for that." She looked across at him as she nibbled off a crust and he caught her trying to stifle a smile.

"What?" he said.

"We've had mail," she said trying to keep her face from revealing too much.

"Not another half-eaten chocolate bar? Please... don't tell me it was a *Curly Wurly*?"

"Email actually... I read it this morning. We've had an additional gift to our regular support for September... £400. That would work out at about 60,000 *lekë*, wouldn't it?" Jude inclined his head towards her slightly. "You can do it now... reprint the book," she said. "You can still make it happen. You didn't cut the corner. God's honoured you Jude!" She watched him as he took in the news. A smile rose slowly on his face and spread broadly across it.

Epilogue

18 months later

From the side door of the Scutari Restaurant a man stepped out into the cold night breeze of central London. He had what he'd been waiting for. He walked a few paces and looked left and right along Greek Street, and then passed under a flashing, red neon sign before crossing Soho Square. He did not like these people or what they did with Albanian girls, but meeting them had been necessary, and they had helped him. He walked unhurriedly now onto Oxford Street and turned into the flow of people. His contact inside, Kushtrim, had shown him how to handle it. It was a *Tokarev TT 33*, used by the Albanian police, he'd reminded him, a semi-automatic with eight rounds in the magazine already inserted into the grip of the pistol. After drawing back and releasing the slide mechanism once, it would fire each time the trigger was pulled ejecting the casings from the side. It was accurate and reliable. Was he clear? He was not in the mood to go directly back to the tower block behind Waterloo Station and the room he had been sharing with other Albanians. He kept walking, past Oxford Circus, past the lit shop windows, reading the names: HMV, Carphone Warehouse, Tie Rack, House of Fraser... He was thinking.

He descended onto the southbound platform of the Jubilee Line at Bond Street. He heard the track metal sing and felt the air move before the train broke out of the tunnel at the far end. He sat in the corner of a carriage and watched the advertising posters slide away. He thought back over his journey to England, most of it hidden in a stuffy, secret compartment behind the cabin of a freight lorry. Three weeks here and he had found the man he had come for. It was '*gjakmarrje*', blood for blood. The man had it coming, and he was in Hounslow. Kushtrim, however, also had a book. He'd said he knew the man in it well: they went back a long way. He had taken it and read it to help pass the days in the tower block other than watching the trains come and go. It had happened gradually: questions, the erosion of his resolve, a yearning even for an alternative way. Then a sickness at being bound through the years by the black cords of family honour had risen in him. An inner warmth had also crept though him that was inexplicable. He drew the book from his inside jacket pocket again and glanced at the dedication: *To Shpetim Gurbardhi. John 15:13.* The name was familiar, but where had he seen it? Yes, on the Albanian TV news - was it last year?

He got off one stop early at Westminster. As he climbed the tube station steps and out into the night, the Houses of Parliament rose up, lit spectacularly, sandy white, like he had once seen in a school text book. He kept to the north-facing walkway of Westminster Bridge as he crossed it, and he stopped midway to lean on the railings by a metal post lit with three bright lamps. Kushtrim had said other things about the man in the book: that if Mehmed Krasnichi had used Kushtrim's name, he'd have left for Albania immediately, but as he hadn't, he'd wait until he was back next time. Then he was going find this 'rat who had run into the church' and his 'propagandist collaborators' and 'punish... silence them'. He looked down onto the black, flowing waters of the River Thames, lit with green lighting from beneath the arches of the bridge. He had made up his mind what he was now going to do. There was one more thing he could do as well: find this Mehmed and warn him.

There were CCTV cameras everywhere in this city, he'd learnt, so he would not unwrap it from the cloth. He took the *Tokarev* and dropped it. It made little more than a faint 'plop' as it hit the water, but the ripples spread out widely. He watched as they were carried on the current towards the shimmering, white reflection of the London Eye to dissipate completely.

The Characters

In Jude's family

Alexandria (Alex) Kilburn – Jude's wife
Bernard Kilburn – Jude's father
Justine Kilburn – Jude's mother

Jack – An old friend in Leeds

In Alexandria's life

Julieta – The neighbour
Mr Zanati – The market trader
Mirela and Diellza – From her women's group

Jude's students

Mira – Has a daughter called Lule
Fredi – The waiter
Bledi Shehu – The taxi driver
Liridon – The goatherd (and his relative Shpat)
Kristo – The young English teacher
Flutura – The beautician
Blerta Malikuqi – In student politics

In Tirana

Edona Mollasi – The student who wrote the manuscript

Jetmira – The director of 'Speedy-Print'

At the Blue Café

Mehmed Krasnichi – The subject of Jude's book

Marko – Mehmed's companion

At Shpetim Gurbardhi's house

Shpetim – A friend of Jude's in the Secret Police

Luan – His brother

Skender – His father

Alma – His mother

Petrit – His grandad

Burim – His uncle with a Mercedes

In the village of Shënvogël

Veli and Fatmira Fitore – Kristo's relatives

Valon and his daughter Kela Malikuqi – Blerta's relatives

In Istanbul

Hanife Dushman – Sheref's sister

Omer – The waiter

Kadir – 'The driver'

Gazi – The man in the café

Yagmur – The coffee cup reader

Osman – Turkish owner of mobile phone shop where Sheref works.

At the church

Jaap van Halen – The missions' pastor
Odguda van Halen, Jaap's wife and Uys their son
Spiro Krenallari – An English teacher

At the border

Flori Moshohori – Albanian Border Police
Deputy Commandant Georgiadis – Greek Border Police

Others

Defrim – The taxi van driver with gizmos
Diamantos Arhontikis – The tax driver from Kastoria
Sam Prekazi – The intruder

In London

An unnamed young man come "for blood"
Kushtrim – Albanian mobster

* * *

Some Albanian words used in the book

The town of Shënomadh: (Pronounced 'Sheno-ma-the' – all together)

bejkon dhe kërpudhë – bacon and mushroom

besa – a binding promise

budalla – stupid

çaj mali – mountain tea

Ç' kemi? Mirë? – How are you? Good?

çobani – shepherd (sometimes derogatory)

Ç'thua, more! – What are you saying!

'Darka e Qengjit' – The Lamb's dinner

Faleminderit – Thank you

Gëzuar! – Cheers!

gjakmarrje – blood feud/ revenge

Gomisteri – Tyre repair shop

Jam i lirë – I'm free

Jo – No

Kam punë – I have work

Kapeni atë! – Catch him you people!

Ku do shkosh? – Where are you going?

Ku je, tani? – Where are you now?

kukurec – tripe

Po, kuptoj – Yes, I understand

lekë – Albanian currency

May 5TH – Martyrs' Day in Albania

mezet – appetisers

më falni – pardon me

Mirëdita – Good day

Mos ki merak – Don't worry

Natën e mirë – Good night

Obobo! – Oh, dear!

Ore! – Hey!

pa diskutim – without discussion

Po – Yes

qofte – minced meat sausage or kebab

qullac – mummy's boy

Rrofsh! – Thanks!

rruga – road

shoferi – driver

Shqipëria – Albania

shumë mirë – very good

Sigurisht! – Certainly!

Xhaxhi – a respectful term like mister

zonja angleze – English Mrs.

zotëri – mister

Zot i madh! – Great God!

At the 'Ali Pasha' restaurant

tasqebab – meat stew

bamje – okra

pilaf – rice

çorbë – stew/soup

Some Turkish words

Arnavutlar – Albanians

Baba – father

Ben iyiyim – I'm fine

Ergenekon – A clandestine ultra-nationalist group with links to Turkish security forces, which acts in what it deems to be the country's national interest. Readers might like to know that it is widely believed to exist and that its name refers to an ancient Turkish myth.

Iyi şanslar – Good luck

back cover

It's a thug's life

Here is the story of the turn-around
in the life of a convicted football
hooligan. Shocking, captivating
and inspiring, its publication saw
massive media interest with
features in *The Mirror, The
Sun* and *The Daily Mail*, as
well as appearances on
*Channel 4's Football
Fight Club*, BBC's
Songs of Praise,
plus an HTV
documentary

Dave is drawn
into the dodgy
world of 'firm
life'. Till one day
he is fleeing
through the
Stockholm subway
after a sickening
incident at the European
Championships and the
improbable presence of
a passer-by points to his
coming salvation. He
was soon to have an
encounter with Jesus
Christ that would
transform his life.

Heart of a Hooligan   biography   160pp   RRP £4.99   978-1897913 52 9

Heart of
a Hooligan

The story of Dave Jeal

Muthena Paul Alkazraji